ILLUSIONS OF TRUST

ILLUSIONS OF TRUST

JEFFREY S. STEPHENS

A POST HILL PRESS BOOK
ISBN: 979-8-89565-336-4
ISBN (eBook): 979-8-89565-337-1

Illusions of Trust

Cover design by Cody Corcoran

Post Hill Press
New York • Nashville
posthillpress.com

Published in the United States of America
1 2 3 4 5 6 7 8 9 10

For Brian Kenny, who taught me everything worth knowing about how to practice law with integrity

PROLOGUE

It was just after midnight, and Vernon Platt was seated in a large easy chair in the bedroom of his penthouse apartment, wrapped in the soft comfort of a white terrycloth bathrobe, feeling as relaxed as he allowed himself to feel lately. His hair was still damp from the hot shower he had just taken, and he used the collar of his terrycloth robe to wipe at the moisture that trickled down the back of his neck. Then he picked up the book on the table beside him and, while his guest was dressing in the bathroom, tried to read.

Despite the effort to enjoy this quiet moment, his thoughts about the pending congressional investigation soon intruded, and he was forced to once again confront the impossibility of his situation.

All his influence, all the political favor he had courted over the years, all the prestige he had coveted like a miser accumulating a bag of sovereigns—suddenly it all counted for nothing. Platt was realistic enough not to be surprised, but human enough to be disappointed. How could they do this to him?

He had been served with a subpoena that compelled him to appear before congress. If he refused to answer their questions, word on Capitol Hill was that the committee would give him immunity. That would strip him of his constitutional right not to incriminate himself, obliging him to reveal everything they wanted to know.

My God, he thought, *how about immunity from the destruction of my reputation? More significant*, he thought, *who is going to protect me from the people my testimony will incriminate?*

An old friend who served as counsel on the minority panel gave him a preview of the transactions they were investigating. There were various deals Platt had brokered over the years, involving large federal and municipal contracts awarded to vendors of questionable character, but he was confident he could navigate his way through most of that. The main problem related to work he had recently done for a pharmaceutical company seeking FDA approvals.

"I have an attorney-client relationship to protect," Platt had told his contact, intending to hide behind the veil of professional secrecy.

But his friend cautioned him not to count on that. "Majority counsel has documents proving you were acting as a lobbyist, not as a lawyer." In addition, Platt was told, there was paperwork showing he received substantial fees from both sides for negotiating the arrangement. That meant there was no way he could claim he legally represented either party. To make that even clearer, Congress had evidence each of the parties had used their own attorneys.

Platt was the classic power broker in the middle.

He had privately assigned two associates in his firm to research the issue, and they came to the same conclusion. Even though he was a lawyer, he had been acting as a dealmaker, and there was no confidential privilege that would shield him from testifying.

What a disaster, he told himself yet again.

It was clear what the subcommittee wanted from him. Platt knew what had been done, who was involved on the business end, and the identity of the politicians who participated. Once he was given immunity, he would have to answer their questions or face charges for contempt of Congress.

"Goddamnit," he said aloud. *How in the hell could they force me to choose between a life-threatening betrayal and a career-ending jail term?*

Just then he heard the hair dryer go on in the bathroom and found himself wondering why, with everything he was facing, he had wasted the evening with this vulgar pretender.

They had known each other for a few years, but Platt regarded some minimal emotion as a required element for anything he would describe as a relationship. Earlier tonight they had a few drinks, a few laughs, shared his bed and then a shower. It was superficial at best but, Platt would have to admit, an enjoyable diversion.

Platt was an extremely cautious man, a trait he hoped would be his salvation in Washington next week. He understood that discretion was the price one paid for becoming a public figure, especially when indulging in a personal life that was, as some would describe it, not exactly mainstream.

Now, seated in his favorite armchair, he gazed at the doors that led to a terrace providing a generous view of New York City's incandescent summer skyline. For an instant he lost himself in the image of the expansive city out there. His city. He became absorbed in thoughts of who he had worked so hard to become, and the utter injustice of what he would face at the hands of these hypocritical bureaucrats.

Feeling the anger rise inside him again, he did not hear his guest quietly enter the room and come up behind him.

PART ONE
MARRIAGE

CHAPTER ONE

Early the following morning, attorney Russell Palmer was in his office, about to meet with Christina Franco. One of his former clients had introduced him to Christina when they ran into each other a few nights before at one of his favorite restaurants. Palmer was not so sure the encounter was accidental after she asked if Palmer would take some time to discuss Christina's marital problems. Yet, despite the clumsy staging, and although he rarely handled divorces, he agreed.

To begin with, Palmer knew Christina Franco's husband was a prominent businessman. He was also aware her father was a United States congressman and her mother the heir to a large family fortune. Added to that, the Francos were members of New York's elite social circles. The result caused him to wonder why a woman with so much going for her was having trouble in her marriage—all the while reminding himself that curiosity can be a costly instinct.

At the appointed time, Christina arrived and was shown into Palmer's office. She removed her dark Chanel sunglasses extended her hand, and said, "It's good of you to see me."

"My pleasure," he told her. "Can Maureen get you something? Water, coffee?"

"I'm fine," Christina said, then insinuated herself into one of the upholstered armchairs facing his desk.

Palmer nodded to Maureen, who responded by raising one eyebrow as only she could, then turned and closed the door behind her, leaving the two of them alone.

In her late thirties, Christina had smooth skin that was slightly tanned, long blonde hair brushed neatly in place, a mouth and nose that were nearly perfect, and shining green eyes that were even more so. She was tall and shapely, and he judged her a fair study in what you get when you combine good genes, regular exercise, and the right estheticians.

Taking a seat in the black leather chair behind his oak desk, he said, "If it's all right, I'm going to have my colleague join us."

"That's fine. Beryl spoke highly of him too."

Palmer nodded, hit the intercom, and moments later Robbie Whyte walked in.

Palmer stood again and made the introductions. "Since Mr. Whyte is an investigator and not an attorney, I cannot technically call him my partner but, for all practical purposes, he is."

She stood, putting the entire package on display as she took Whyte's hand. "As I told Mr. Palmer, I've heard a lot about you and your firm."

Whyte turned to Palmer. "You and I have a firm?"

Palmer did not bother to reply. "The important point," he told Christina, "is that Robbie works with me and his presence therefore does not invalidate the confidential nature of this discussion."

They all took their seats, Whyte and Christina facing Palmer.

"As I mentioned when we met with Beryl—" Palmer began.

But she stopped him. "I know. You're not actually a divorce lawyer."

"That's correct, I'm not."

"But Beryl told me you have a reputation for handling—how shall I say this—uncommon problems. When we ran into you at Cellini's, it just seemed, I don't know, fate? Because my situation is definitely unusual."

"It was kind of her to introduce us," Palmer said, offering up a polite smile. "But with all respect, Mrs. Franco, almost everyone believes their problems are unusual."

She was wearing a gray skirt and a cream-colored blouse wide open at the neck. She took a moment to cross her long legs, and Palmer could not help noticing she did nothing to adjust her skirt as it rode slightly up her silky thigh. Then she said, "I suppose that's true," sounding as if there might be more to the thought.

Palmer waited, but when it appeared she was done, he said, "I think you also know that the matter I handled for Beryl was not a divorce."

"But it was a *difficult* situation. She's told me all about it." Then she added with a killer smile, "And she said you were brilliant. Both of you," she added with a glance at Whyte.

"I appreciate the compliment," Palmer replied, "but—"

"All I ask is that you hear me out before making a decision."

"I told you I would, and I will."

She sat up a little straighter. "To begin with, I assume you know who my parents are."

"I do," he said.

"You're probably also aware that my husband is extremely successful."

"I am."

"Our assets are not only considerable, they're also rather complicated." She paused, and Palmer watched as she had a slow look around. They were on the ground floor of the three-story Manhattan brownstone where he lived and worked, his office decorated in the style of a cozy den rather than a sterile workplace. It had a wood-burning fireplace that was currently on vacation for the summer season; a colorful Persian rug on the floor; and framed, signed lithographs that hung on the gray, grass-cloth covered walls—no diplomas or awards or photos of the famous people he might want you to know he had represented. When she was done with her survey of the room, she turned back to him. "I suppose many of your clients are people of means."

"Some of my favorite clients are poorer than you can imagine."

She nodded, her expression suggesting this might be useful information. "Beryl told me you're not about the money. That you even take cases where your clients can't afford your fees."

Palmer responded with a brief nod. "Getting back to your situation, if we—"

"Yes, my situation." She paused before saying, "I have a very comfortable existence."

"I know something about your husband, as I've said. Describing your life as very comfortable is quite an understatement."

"Then you understand I wouldn't be here if there were not serious problems."

"Such as?"

"He's been unfaithful. Repeatedly."

"When you say repeatedly—"

"Different women. Some affairs longer than others. And an impressive string of one-night stands, or so I'm told."

"Told by whom?"

"Friends."

Palmer bit at his lower lip, a lousy habit he couldn't shake. "Friends," he repeated.

Treating him to a lower voltage smile this time, she said, "I take it you don't believe real friends would tell me such things."

"I'm not here to judge, at least not yet. I'm still in the listening phase of this exchange."

"I appreciate that."

"How long has your husband been unfaithful?"

"That I know of?" She took a moment before saying, "We've been together almost fifteen years, and I would say throughout most of our marriage."

"What's taken you so long? To consider divorce, I mean."

"Honestly?" she asked, but did not wait for an answer. "In the end, life is all about compromises, isn't it?"

"Is it?"

"I thought you weren't going to judge."

"I'm not judging, I'm asking. You've been putting up with this for years, why ask for a divorce now?"

Christina pressed her lips together, looking as if she needed a moment to consider the question. "I suppose I could say enough is enough, but it's more than that. He's become increasingly arrogant, as if he doesn't care what I know or how I feel about it."

"How have you, uh, reacted to his infidelity up to now?"

"You mean, have I also had lovers?"

"We can start there if you like."

She stared at Palmer, and he felt her intense gaze appraising him, like a painting at an auction. "Is this discussion truly confidential? Even if you don't take my case?"

"Same as if you were in the confessional."

"Then yes, once I realized what he was doing, I haven't been perfect either."

"You make that sound rather casual. What I'm really asking is—"

"Whether I've had another *relationship*," she interrupted again, making that last word sound as if it were some awful concept she didn't want to deal with.

"Have you?"

"No."

"Then this is about two people engaging in sex outside their marriage, until one of them decided it isn't fun anymore. Do I have that right?"

"That sounds nasty."

Palmer began laughing, which he did frequently and often at the wrong time. But her attitude toward cheating had pushed a button, and humor helped him get past the lousy feeling. "Sorry," he said, "but you think *I* make infidelity sound nasty? You're from a distinguished family, married to a very rich man, living in luxury—all of which you admit. Yet despite these advantages, you and your husband seem to have some rather peculiar ideas about marriage."

She took some time to look him over again. He was just over six feet tall, trimly built with handsome features, dark wavy hair kept short without a part, and light brown eyes, all of which somehow worked to make him appear a bit younger than his thirty-eight years.

When she continued to gaze at him without speaking, he said, "We're in the business of helping people in trouble, not people who create their own problems. Especially issues which they can easily resolve themselves. If you think there's any chance you can save your marriage, see a therapist. If not, skip the therapy and get yourself a good matrimonial attorney. It'll be easy to find someone to help you take as much of Mr. Franco's money as possible, and you can go on living your very comfortable existence."

For the first time, he saw a fleeting hint of vulnerability in her eyes. "That's rather harsh, don't you think."

"I'm sorry, I don't intend to be harsh *or* nasty, but I am inclined to say what I think. I told you that when you asked for this consultation."

"Yes," she admitted, "you did."

"It's clear you have to make some serious life decisions ahead, but I'm not the person to get you there. Have you spoken with other lawyers?"

"I have. All highly recommended, all very expensive, and all the same. They look at my situation and see dollar signs. As I've said, Beryl told me that's not your style."

Palmer's interest in the matter was waning, and he felt the urge to get out of his chair and bid her a good day. But he could see that Mrs. Franco was not going anywhere. Not yet.

"You asked why I haven't filed for divorce before now," she said.

"I did, and you answered."

"There's another reason." She paused. "If I do, he'll have me murdered."

"Mrs. Franco—"

When she cut him off again, this time with a raised hand, Palmer marveled at how comfortable she seemed with this maddening pattern of sudden interruptions and silent pauses.

"I know what you're going to say," she told him. "That it's not the first time you've heard that sort of intimidation from an angry spouse, but in my case it's literally true." Then she added, "If he even knew I was here today…" but did not finish the thought, allowing her voice to trail off as if the remainder of what she would say was obvious.

Whyte finally spoke up. "Your husband is a very successful man. Why in the world would he say something so absurd? Why not just make a financial arrangement and send you on your way?"

Before he could finish the question, Christina Franco was already shaking her head. "You may be familiar with Edward's public image," she said, "but you don't know who he really is, how abusive he can be. You don't know the people he associates with. Dangerous people." They watched as she reached into an alligator-skin Hermes purse Palmer knew had cost as much as a small car. She pulled out her cell phone, punched in the access code, and placed it on his desk. "Edward obviously has no idea I recorded this," she told them, then hit the arrow that began a video.

The images were dark, and the angle of the shot was not very good but, as the two men leaned forward, they could make out the image of her husband pacing back and forth in what appeared to be a large bedroom. As he moved in and out of the frame, the audio remained clear, his voice as cold as a cemetery breeze. It began as an argument that ended suddenly when Edward Franco stated exactly what would happen if she tried to leave him. Then, at the end of his threat, he leaned forward and—with a look of sheer malice they could make out even in the dim lighting—he whispered a name in Christina's ear that was clear enough to be heard on the recording.

Peter Frost.

Palmer and Whyte looked at each other. It was a name they knew only too well, and they could see from the concern in her eyes, Christina did too.

CHAPTER TWO

Palmer sat back and slowly swiveled his chair as they watched her turn off the phone. He took a few seconds before saying, "I admit your husband sounds serious."

"Believe me, he is. And the man he mentioned," she added uneasily, "he's *very* serious. I've heard Edward talk about him."

Palmer took a deep breath. "Even so, you should find an attorney—"

"You mean a matrimonial barracuda trolling for rich women? I told you, I've already spoken with more than one."

He nodded. "Have you shared this recording with any of them?"

"There was no point; they wouldn't know how to handle it. I need a lawyer who'll fight for me *and* protect me. Someone who won't back down. You have a different skill set. Different experience." She hesitated again before adding, "For instance, just now, I could tell you both recognized that name."

Palmer shook his head very slowly. It was another of his habits, this one usually reserved for moments when he realized he was about to make a bad decision, even as he tried to talk himself out of it. But she was right. When Palmer heard her husband whisper Frost's name, he felt his stomach tighten and his protective impulses kick in.

Christina went on. "I hope the two of you remember, contrary to what you said before, I did not create this problem. And you admitted, when you take on a client, it shouldn't matter whether they're rich or poor."

"Did I say that?" Palmer asked.

"More or less. Trouble is trouble, right?"

"It's an argument."

"Any other lawyer would love to represent me," she said. "The money, my family, the headlines." Then she sat back and had another good look at him. "I realize you choose your cases carefully."

"I do."

"That's a luxury most attorneys don't have."

"I'm very fortunate in that regard."

How Palmer came to be that fortunate was not something he was about to share with Christina Franco. Instead, he asked if Whyte had any questions.

"I'll start with two," the detective said. "How many times has your husband resorted to this sort of conduct, and how many times has he followed through?"

"Followed through?" she repeated with a dismissive wave of her well-manicured hand.

"Yes. I want to know how often he threatens you and whether he actually engages in violent acts."

"Edward has a bad temper; and mostly it's just talk. But there have been a few incidents. He shoved me against the bathroom door last year, bruised my arm. Another time he knocked me to the floor." She treated Whyte to one of her theatrical pauses. "Once he slapped me across the face. I told him if he ever did that again I would kill him."

Whyte glanced at Palmer, but neither man said anything.

When she showed Whyte one of her smiles, this one was filled with melancholy. *She must have a thousand varieties*, Palmer thought.

"I know what you're thinking," she told Whyte. "You're thinking that we're rich, spoiled, irresponsible people who throw around death threats like they're party favors."

"It crossed my mind," the detective admitted.

"Well, I'm not that way, I'm really not," Christina insisted. "But when someone slaps you across the face…" She hesitated. "It's so demeaning."

"Can't argue with that," Whyte replied. "Have you ever made a report to the authorities about these attacks?"

She showed them one of her sadder smiles. "And be smeared all over the news? I don't think so."

"All right," Whyte said. "Tell me about the other day, when you had this confrontation in your bedroom."

She nodded. "It was different."

"Why?"

"That morning, when I told him I was going to leave, he knew this time I was serious. The children were at school, and the argument got loud. When he made his threat, I knew *he* was serious."

"How is it that you happened to record him?"

"The fight started in the kitchen. He became so abusive that I walked out and went into our bedroom. I sat on a chair and began texting a girlfriend. When he came in, I could tell he was still furious. I managed to hit 'Record' before I set the phone down next to me."

"He didn't notice?"

Christina sighed. "He was in a rage, as you've seen from the video. When Edward gets that way, he can't see straight."

Whyte sat back and ran his hand through his silver hair. "Please try to understand my natural skepticism. People having marital trouble say a lot of things they don't literally mean."

"Maybe so, but that morning was bad. I told him I wasn't going to put up with his cheating anymore. We went back and forth until I stood up, told him we were finished, and as I explained, headed into the bedroom."

"That leads me to an obvious question," Whyte said. "If he's serious about this threat, what do you know that worries him so much?"

She blinked. "I'm not sure what you're asking."

"I think you know exactly what I'm asking." Whyte had turned to his right, looking directly at her as he engaged in this interrogation. "If he wants to keep you as his wife, threatening your life doesn't seem an effective way to do that. It certainly isn't going to endear you to him, am I right?"

Christina frowned. "I would have to agree."

"That means he's threatening you for another reason. Maybe a divorce would expose something that won't look so great in the light of day. Or maybe you know something you might use against him."

Palmer had remained quiet as he observed their exchange but, when Christina took one of her breaks to think things over, he decided to change course. "You told us he's been engaged in adulterous conduct for a long time," he said. "When did you first start talking about splitting up."

She sighed again, as if they had pivoted to a tiresome issue. "I knew I'd made a mistake marrying him early on, but it's hard to admit that to yourself. It was easier to get caught up in the life we lead. The travel, the glamor, the people, I plead guilty to all of that. Especially as he became more successful. I organized his social events, hosted parties, went everywhere he asked me to go, hoping things would improve. But at some point, I had to be honest with myself. He was all about appearances and possessions. I was just another part of the picture. Arm candy. A congressman's daughter. Someone filling a role in the movie that's always about him."

"That doesn't answer my question," Palmer said.

She nodded. "A couple of years ago, maybe more. That's when I finally told him things had to change or I wanted out."

Palmer looked at Whyte, who turned back to her. "That's a long time. Did the two of you work on your problems?" the detective asked.

"Of course," Christina said as if the answer was obvious. "We saw a counselor, talked about our relationship, all of the things couples in a failed marriage do. None of it made a difference."

Palmer was not convinced her regret sounded all that sincere. "You think his resistance to a divorce is part of that movie, as you call it? That it might damage his image, something like that?"

She shook her head. "Most of our friends are on second or third marriages by now. So no, if that was the issue, he would just blame the divorce on me. Paint me as a selfish bitch and move on."

"For someone so unhappy, you've hung in there a long time," Whyte said.

Christina did not disagree. "I enjoy a wonderful lifestyle. Then, of course, there are the children."

"Where is he about that?" Palmer asked.

She responded with a disdainful smirk. "He thinks he's the father of the year, of course. But he couldn't tell you the name of a single teacher our son or daughter has ever had. He doesn't let those details get in his way."

Whyte nodded. "You could have left years ago and still had a wonderful life with your children," Whyte said.

"That's why hindsight is so clear, isn't it? As I said, I was trying to make it work."

"And now that you told him you're leaving—" Palmer began.

"He responded by threatening me," she said, finishing the thought.

"Let's get back to your finances and how that factors in. You ever argue about his money?" Whyte asked. "He ever say anything about not letting you take his assets, any of that?"

"Not really," she told them. "Let's face it, I don't need anywhere near half of what he has. My mother controls my trust, so he can't make any claim against that, and in a few years the principal becomes mine."

"Does he ever mention that trust?" Palmer asked.

"Never."

"You think he's trying to postpone a divorce until you receive all the funds in the trust?" Whyte asked.

"No. He does quite well on his own, as I think you know."

"Then I'm back to the same question," Whyte said. "What do you know that scares him enough to threaten murder?"

Christina tilted her head slightly as she said, "I may be missing something, but I have no idea." Then she asked, "If I figure it out, wouldn't he be at risk whether I leave him or not?"

"Not necessarily," Palmer told her. "If it's serious enough to threaten his assets, as long as you're married, you're less likely to want to tear down that Jenga tower."

"Jenga?" Whyte said with a puzzled look.

"A children's game," Christina told him with an indulgent smile. "You add or pull out a block at a time, trying not to make the pile collapse."

"Can you think of anything," Palmer asked, "a transaction he wouldn't want exposed?"

"For instance?"

"Just as a hypothetical, maybe he had you sign documents or tax returns that implicate the two of you in something improper. If you're married, under the law you can't be compelled to testify against him," Palmer explained. "That means there is less risk to him as long as you stay together, as compared to an adversarial divorce."

Christina looked even more puzzled than Whyte had at the Jenga reference. "That seems too fantastic to me. We're discussing this as if Edward's done something terrible. I realize he's a tough man, but if he's doing something wrong, I'm not aware of it."

"That may be," Palmer said, "but if this firm is going to become involved, we're going to have dig through everything you know about his business, past and present, and where you think he might be vulnerable."

When she did not reply, Whyte said, "That name your husband dropped, at the end of your argument."

"Peter Frost," Christina responded with a nod.

"Have you ever met him?"

"Not that I recall, but I know who he is. And I know enough to be afraid of him."

"You said your husband knows some dangerous people—"

"And from what I understand," she interrupted, "Peter Frost would top the list."

"We're going to need details," Palmer told her. "Anything you've ever heard about Frost, what he has to do with your husband's business."

She nodded.

"I have no idea how serious your husband was," Palmer said. "To be candid, I certainly have my doubts. But you're going to have to trust someone."

"That's why I'm here." she said.

Whyte turned to Palmer with a look that made it clear the detective still had more questions than answers about Christina's story. He also knew Palmer was ready to jump in with both feet, as usual, without checking to see how deep the water was or what might be lurking below the surface.

In this case, they would soon learn the pond was deep and infested with sharks.

Meanwhile, Christina's phone had buzzed a couple of times, but she ignored the intrusion. Now they heard a different ringtone. "My mother," she explained, "I'll only be a moment." Then, as she listened to the call, Christina rose to her feet, a look of shock on her face. She finally replied, "I'm on my way," and the discussion ended.

"You all right?" Palmer asked.

"Vernon Platt," she said in a dull tone.

"The lawyer?" Palmer asked.

"He was my mother's best friend."

"Was?"

Christina looked down at Palmer. "He's dead," she told them.

CHAPTER THREE

After Christina took a moment to compose herself, Palmer accompanied her to the front door of the brownstone and showed her out. Returning to his office, he pulled back the curtain on the window facing 64th Street, watching her climb into the rear of a chauffeur-driven Bentley. As he was about to turn away, he noticed another car. It had been parked just a few spots behind Christina's sedan, and now quickly pulled out and proceeded after her.

Coincidence? he wondered.

Palmer hated coincidences.

"Did you see that?" he asked as he turned to Whyte, who was still seated in the armchair facing him.

"See what? You're the peeping Tom."

Palmer described what happened after Christina left the office.

"Let me get this straight," the detective said. "You're suspicious about two cars traveling east on Sixty-Fourth Street in Manhattan in the middle of the morning? I mean, you have heard of *traffic*, am I right?"

Palmer responded with a frown.

Whyte was almost twenty years older than Palmer, half a dozen inches shorter and several pounds heavier—his thick build and spreading middle leading Palmer to suggest a few hundred daily sit-ups, to no avail. Whyte had a jowly face, a mouth that was almost always expressing something between suspicion and cynicism, an uneven nose, and steely eyes that could look right through you if he had a reason to do so. All of that was topped by a thick mane of silver hair that made him appear older than he was.

He was a devoted friend to Palmer and an invaluable mentor.

Maureen came in and Palmer asked what she had learned about Vernon Platt.

"Seems he either committed suicide or had a terrible accident," she told them as she took the chair where Christina had been sitting beside Whyte. "At least according to the early reports."

"How?" Whyte asked.

"Fell or jumped off the balcony of his apartment," Maureen told them.

"Suicide?" Whyte said. "Not what I would have expected, given that guy's reputation."

"Agreed," Palmer told him.

"How was your interview with Mrs. Franco?" Maureen asked.

"Depends which of us you want to hear from," Whyte said.

"She really is quite the looker in person."

"No argument there," Whyte admitted.

"You know who she is?" Palmer asked.

"Of course I do," she told him. "You may be shocked to know this, but when I'm not slaving away in this office, I actually find time to watch television and read the occasional magazine."

"Good to keep yourself informed," Whyte replied with a smile.

"In an effort to keep the two of *you* informed, I pulled together some background on her and her husband," Maureen told them. "Kind of mind-boggling." She stood and went to Palmer's computer, which sat on the credenza in back of his desk. Turning the monitor so they could all see, she began to bring up a series of images.

The hits seemed endless, stories featuring Christina and Edward, both together and individually. As to the latter, there were articles from major financial periodicals cataloguing Mr. Franco's triumphs in the venture capital world. A founding partner at Breakfinch Capital, he had investments everywhere from tech start-ups in Silicon Valley to independent motion pictures in Hollywood to microchip factories.

There was another stream of reports, chronicling his wife's ubiquitous presence at fashion shows, charity events, and exclusive resorts around the world. Photos displayed her in an array of gowns, bathing suits, and stylish lounging attire.

As to the Francos' life as a couple, there were items covering international appearances at various A-List events such as the Grand Prix in Monaco, the Cannes Film Festival, fashion shows in Paris, as well as glamorous festivities at home, including the Oscars and the annual Gala at the Metropolitan Museum.

"I'm exhausted just reading this," Maureen said.

Palmer bit his lower lip as he stared at the screen. "She did say her life is very comfortable."

Maureen turned from the monitor and stared at him. "You think?"

After Maureen scrolled through another collection of photos, Palmer said, "He can obviously afford to pay her off if she wants out. Why make stupid threats?"

"Threats?"

"Saying he'd have her killed if she tried to leave him," Whyte explained.

"Sounds like nonsense from an angry husband," Maureen said.

"That's my take," the detective said. "But then he mentioned our old friend Peter Frost."

Now they had her attention.

Maureen O'Brien was approaching fifty, a petite, raven-haired, dark-eyed ball of energy. She was tough, smart, fair, loyal, and capable of providing perspective whenever Palmer or Whyte lost theirs—for instance, when their desire to uncover the truth in things took them far beyond their obligation to simply represent their clients.

"Peter Frost?" she repeated. "Look for the pony in the picture, RP."

Palmer smiled. It was one of Maureen's favorite expressions and, if it never quite made sense, he always got the point. "This was obviously not the first time the Francos have argued, which she admits. But she claims this was different, and whether her husband meant his threat or not, I would have to say *she* believes him."

"Does she?" Maureen asked Whyte.

"Seems to," he conceded.

"Which means she's in need of our representation," Palmer said.

"Don't you mean *worthy* of your representation?" Maureen asked with a wry smile.

"Funny," Palmer said.

"Then we're taking the case?" she asked.

"That's the question," Whyte said.

"There's going to be a very large fee," Palmer told them.

"We don't need the money," Maureen pointed out.

"And we don't need to be tangling with Peter Frost," Whyte said.

Palmer drew back slightly, as if requiring a better look at the two of them. "Are you guys a tag team?"

"Maybe we should be," Whyte said.

"Especially since you cannot resist a damsel in distress," Maureen added.

"I admit that may be true, from time to time."

"And, when it comes to women, you almost always make the wrong decision," Whyte said, regretting it as soon as he uttered the words.

Palmer did not immediately reply, taking a moment to reflect on his latest failure, where the young woman he was seeing turned out to regard fidelity in a relationship an outdated notion.

Seeing the look on his young friend's face, Whyte said, "Sorry, I didn't mean it that way."

"Sure you did," Palmer replied, "and you aren't wrong."

After another brief silence, Maureen said, "How about we get back to Mrs. Franco. I assume it doesn't hurt that she's stunning as well as rich."

"Come on," Palmer said. "You know very well I never cross that line with clients."

"But she won't be a client for long. Soon she'll be divorced, but she'll continue to be beautiful and rich."

Palmer turned to Whyte. "Remind me again why she works here."

"She's the conscience of the place."

"Ah, right, I remember now."

"What would a man like Edward Franco have to do with Peter Frost?" Maureen asked.

"Good question," Whyte said.

Palmer said, "We don't know, not yet, but Franco used Frost's name when he threatened his wife. And we know that, just as Frost gets involved in all kinds of deals, Franco's company has its fingers in a lot of pies."

"Companies don't have fingers," Maureen said.

"Forgive the mixed metaphor, *el Exigente*. The point is, Frost works his way into all sorts of situations. Maybe he became involved in some of Franco's transactions, one way or another."

"Frost is a ruthless sociopath," Whyte reminded them. "Whatever he's up to, Mrs. Franco should get herself a high-end divorce lawyer and a bodyguard. Move out of their house. File for an order of protection. Finished business. This is not what we do."

"You never scare off that easily," Palmer said.

Whyte shook his head. "I do when there's reason. Even Christina had the sense to be frightened just hearing his name."

"That's interesting," Maureen said. "She knows who he is?"

"Yes," Whyte told her. "But on the other hand, she claims to have no information about her husband's business or what Frost might have to do with it. How do you square those things?"

Before Palmer could respond, the phone rang. He turned to Maureen. "Excuse me, Jiminy Cricket, you mind getting that?"

Maureen took the call at Palmer's desk. After listening for a moment, she said, "One second please," then put the call on hold. "Some jerk is on the line," she said. "Third time he's called today and won't give his name. Should I tell him you've left the country?"

"He say what it's about?"

"Not a clue. When he called this morning you were tied up with our newest client."

"All right," Palmer said, and picked up the phone. "Hello?"

"Russell Palmer?"

"That's right."

"I'm calling for an old client of yours. He's about to get himself in a jam."

"What friend might that be?"

"Marvin Taub. I hear that you're the loyal type, especially for a lawyer. That's why I'm calling."

"Who are you?"

"Me, you don't know. But our friend, you should take care of him." Then the man hung up.

"I tell you," Palmer said as he replaced the phone in its cradle. "The beauties you meet in this business…"

"What was that about?" Whyte asked.

"Not sure." After repeating what the caller had said, he turned to Maureen. "See if you can trace the call, then find me a phone number for Marvin Taub."

She nodded.

"I'm not done discussing this Franco case," Whyte told them.

"We're listening," Palmer said.

"What about her reaction to the news that Vernon Platt died?"

"She said he was her mother's best friend."

"Yet another complication," Whyte said.

"I'm listening."

"The whole thing feels a bit off," Whyte told them. "She comes here to discuss a divorce, which we don't generally handle. She plays a video where her husband is threatening her, and Peter Frost's name is tossed around. Next, she gets a call about Vernon Platt dying."

"From her mother."

"I don't care if it came from the Pope." Whyte treated them to one of the well-practiced scowls they had come to know all too well. "You're the one who hates coincidences."

"Duly noted."

"I'm serious."

"I can see that."

"But you're determined to protect this woman from whatever she's up against."

"Not sure yet."

Whyte took a deep breath and exhaled slowly. "I know you've made up your mind," he said. "Just remember, I'm not always right about these things, but I'm never wrong."

"As you've mentioned more than once."

"Then what do you see as our first move?"

"I'm glad you asked," Palmer said. "I've already got an idea."

"I can hardly wait," Whyte groaned. "Is it incredibly clever?"

Palmer smiled. "If we're dealing with Peter Frost, is there another way to go?"

CHAPTER FOUR

Early that afternoon, after spending the past few hours with two junior officers inspecting Vernon Platt's penthouse, Detective Lieutenant Hugh Lawson decided to take a break. He was nothing if not thorough and by now these surroundings were becoming as familiar to him as his own living room in Woodlawn. Maybe more familiar, since his wife was fond of moving things around their modest Bronx apartment.

As the lead police officer on the scene, he had gone over every inch of the place, then went over it again. Now, easing himself into the upholstered armchair in the bedroom for a short break, he had no reason to guess it was the spot where Platt had been sitting last night just before he fell to his death from the balcony of his twenty-second floor apartment.

Lawson was African American, fifty-two years old, standing just under six feet tall, solidly built with short hair, dark skin, and blunt features. Robbie Whyte had long ago judged him the most talented homicide detective he ever worked with, one of the few active NYPD officers with whom Whyte remained in regular contact since retiring from the force. He was convinced Lawson should be a squad commander by now, figuring he would already have been promoted if the captain above him wasn't a jealous, racist piece of shit.

But Lawson never complained. He knew he was a good detective, had spent years doing what he loved, and was proud of his record for uncovering the truth in matters of life and death. He also knew there were some things he could not control—such as bigotry—and did his best to take the high road. Most of the time.

"It doesn't figure," he said aloud to no one in particular. The two men from his unit were with him in the bedroom, searching for clues they had come to believe did not exist. Both turned to him as Lawson repeated himself. "It just doesn't figure."

"Sir?" Officer Nally asked.

"Look around you," Lawson said. "We know Vernon Platt was successful, just look at this place. And he had a great reputation. Why would a man like that commit suicide?"

Nally shrugged. "People kill themselves for all kinds of reasons."

Other detectives from Lawson's precinct had spent the morning speaking with people in Platt's law firm. There was no indication he had been depressed, or even in bad spirits. On the contrary, Platt had lunch with a couple of his partners the previous afternoon, and they described him as being in a confident frame of mind. It was well known that Platt had been summoned to appear before Congress but, according to his colleagues, he viewed his upcoming visit to DC as just another day at the office.

Lawson received that information in a call from one of the detectives, but he was extremely hands-on and would be sure to follow up with his own interviews. For now, all Lawson knew for certain was that Platt was a lawyer and wasn't likely to kill himself over a subpoena.

It just didn't figure.

His gut told him that Platt had been murdered. It was the only logical conclusion, and murder was Lawson's business. Complain to your accountant that you're suffering from a headache, he'll tell you it's being caused by your pending tax audit. Talk to a podiatrist and tell her you've got a backache and she'll say you need to have your bunion treated. Lawson understood that everyone's point of view was informed by their unique perspective. He was in the grisly business of solving homicides, and he believed he could smell a murder from a borough away.

However, the apartment bore no evidence of a struggle. If Platt *was* murdered, how did someone just toss him off the terrace without some evidence of a fight?

Maybe the killer did a great job of cleaning up afterward, but that did not seem likely. If Platt had been shoved over the railing, whoever did it would split the scene as soon as possible.

Maybe someone had broken into the apartment and taken him by surprise, but there was no sign of forced entry at the front door.

Which told Lawson that if Platt had been pushed off the balcony it had to be by someone he knew. Presumably someone he knew very well, since Platt was wearing nothing but a bathrobe when he hit the pavement.

And yet no fingerprints were found, not even on the doors to the terrace.

Not even Platt's, Lawson noted.

The doorman who was on duty did not recall Platt having any visitors last night, but he also did not even remember Platt arriving home. He explained that Platt could have driven his car into the underground garage, using the automatic door opener, then taken the elevator up from there. There were closed-circuit monitors, but the man admitted he could have been doing something else and simply missed the arrival by Platt.

And any possible guest.

Lawson shook his head. Some doormen keep an eye on everything; others make lousy witnesses—especially the ones working overnight, who often doze off during their shift.

Meanwhile, there was something that especially bothered Lawson—there was no suicide note. Would a man like Platt take a flying leap off his balcony without telling the world why?

Lawson stood up from the velvet armchair and walked toward the terrace. After a few minutes looking around, he called out to his men, who were making another cursory run through the living room. "Beckwith. Nally. Get out here."

They were hopeful he was about to call the detail to an end. They were tired of combing through the place and finding absolutely nothing, stumbling into one another, bored with the futility of their effort.

When they walked out to the balcony they found Lawson outside, on his hands and knees.

Getting to his feet, he said, "The doorman told you Platt had a housekeeper."

"Yes Lieutenant," Nally replied. They had already discussed the housekeeper three times.

"When you get ahold of her, I want to know the last time she cleaned this place. Forensics found no fingerprints in the bedroom except for Platt's. And none at all in the bathroom. How the hell is *that* possible? The man was in a bathrobe. You telling me he wasn't in the bathroom the entire night?"

The two detectives, who were not telling him anything, looked at one another. "Yeah," Beckwith conceded. "You'd think at least *his* prints would be there."

"No kidding," Lawson replied with a quick nod. "I think someone wiped this place down, but good. And that book," he said, pointing into the room at the open volume on the table beside the armchair. "You were careful about leaving it open to the same page, after forensics dusted it?"

"Sure," Nally said.

Lawson led them back into the bedroom, leaned over the table, and using two pencils to balance the book, carefully turned it face up.

"You don't think he was reading that before he offed himself," Beckwith said, guessing at the lieutenant's thoughts.

Lawson glanced at the book, a history of Soviet imperialism. "It looks like something that might put you to sleep," he said with a weary smile, "but I doubt it would drive him to suicide. But it *is* possible he was reading it before someone dragged him outside and shoved him off the terrace. I want this book dusted for prints, five pages before here," he said, indicating the place it was opened to, "and five pages after. Check the corners, see if they were turned. And speak to his secretary again. See if he brought the book to his office this week."

Beckwith nodded.

"Excuse me, sir, but I don't get it," Nally said, a new member of Lawson's team. "There's no evidence of anything here but a jumper."

"That's your story," Lawson said.

The two officers looked at each other, before Nally asked, "You actually found something, Lieutenant?"

Pointing toward the open doors leading to the balcony, Lawson said, "I believe I have."

CHAPTER FIVE

Late that afternoon, after spending time in federal court arguing an evidentiary motion in a pending lawsuit, Palmer and Whyte returned to the 64th Street townhouse. Palmer dropped wearily into the black leather chair behind his desk and took the message book Maureen handed him. Without looking at it, he asked, "What's up?"

"Not you, apparently."

Palmer stared at her without responding.

"Things didn't go well?" she asked.

Whyte entered the room. "Couldn't be worse if the judge was on the other side's payroll," he said, then took his usual seat opposite Palmer. "He's made it clear he hates our client, Palmer, and our case."

Palmer nodded. "We spent the entire time spinning wheels." He blew out an invisible cloud of frustration. "Do me a favor, let's talk about anything else right now."

"Fine," Maureen said as she sat in the chair beside Whyte. "As requested, I attempted to trace that anonymous call about Marvin Taub."

"And?"

"Dead end."

Whyte nodded. "Probably a burner phone that's now sitting at the bottom of a trash can."

"You reach Taub?" Palmer asked.

"Called his cell, left a voice mail."

"Well, if there's anything to it," Palmer said as he loosened his tie, "Marvin will call back."

They fell into an unhappy silence, until Maureen said, "Horrible news about Vernon Platt. I remember him from that matter you handled with him a few years ago."

"Awful," Palmer agreed.

"A decent guy," Whyte added.

Palmer nodded his head in agreement.

"I hear Hugh Lawson is handling the investigation of his suicide," Whyte told them.

"Your old pal," Palmer said.

Lawson and Whyte had worked together years ago with the NYPD. "Good man, great detective."

"That could be helpful," Palmer said.

"Meaning what?"

"Christina Franco said Platt was her mother's best friend."

"I heard her."

"You should see what Lawson has to say," Palmer suggested. "After all, you admitted the timing of Platt's death is rather interesting."

Whyte turned to Maureen. "Did I say that?"

"Words to that effect," she replied with a smile.

"Hugh is a real pro," Whyte said. "I'll need to figure out how to approach him."

"As in, how you explain your interest in Platt?"

"I assume you don't want me to mention the Francos."

Palmer leaned back in his chair. "I don't think our client would be happy about that."

"She's not technically our client," Whyte reminded him. "Not yet."

Palmer frowned. "Can't you just ask what he's found so far?"

Whyte shook his head. "He's going to want to know why I'm asking."

"True," Palmer said, then bit at his lower lip as he thought it over. "We don't want to get into the whole Franco thing. Especially since, as you say, we haven't taken the case yet."

"And thanks for that," Whyte said. "But I'll touch base with him, see what he's willing to share."

Maureen, who had left them to answer the phone at her desk, came back in and said, "You have a call from a Mr. Carrigan. Says he wants to speak with you about the Franco case."

Palmer looked to Whyte, who said, "What the hell?"

Maureen shrugged. "What do you want me to tell him?"

"I'll take it," Palmer said. He picked up the phone and gave his name.

"Mr. Palmer, I'm Henry Carrigan."

The voice was all business, so Palmer waited.

"I understand Christina Franco has asked you to represent her."

"Sorry Mr. Carrigan, I can't—"

"I'm calling because I'm concerned about Edward."

"You're concerned about Mr. Franco?"

"I am."

"What's your relationship with Mr. Franco?" Palmer asked.

"That's not relevant."

"It is to me, if you're calling on his behalf."

"It's not on his behalf, not exactly. He has no idea I'm speaking with you."

"Then why exactly are you calling?" Palmer asked. "You must know I can't divulge anything to you about a client. In fact, I'm sitting with an associate who will confirm, if necessary, that I have not even said whether I'm representing Mrs. Franco."

Mr. Carrigan was not easily deterred. "I have no idea what Christina's told you, but you need to know that she's an extremely dangerous woman."

"Dangerous?"

"Extremely."

"And to whom does she pose this danger?"

"Edward."

"Mr. Carrigan—"

"I'm not asking you to respond, I just want you to listen. Christina is not who she appears to be or, I should say, who she *pretends* to be."

Palmer waited, but when it seemed the man was done, he said, "Thank you for the call," and hung up.

Whyte nodded. "I got the gist. What do you make of that?"

"Her husband obviously put him up to it."

Whyte fixed him with one of his classic stares. "Maybe so, but that does not answer the underlying question."

"How would either of them know she came to see me?"

"As you would say, *precisely*."

"Maybe her husband is having her followed," Palmer suggested. "Remember the other car? When you ridiculed me about—"

"Get over that," Whyte interrupted. "As for your *maybes*, what if *she* told this guy she came to see you, and *she's* the one who put him up to making the call?"

Palmer smiled. "That's quite an Orwellian doublethink, even for you."

"I'll take that as high praise," Whyte said. "But before we wade any deeper into this cesspool, we ought to find out who the hell Henry Carrigan is and what he has to do with the Francos."

"I'll leave that to you," Palmer said. "Which means you're going to be busy."

"Is it not obvious to you that this Franco situation is becoming strangely complicated, and we haven't even agreed to take the case?"

"Yes," Palmer admitted, "which means you may be right about taking a pass." Then he added, "Let's at least figure out what's going on here before we decide."

CHAPTER SIX

The following day, Whyte invited Lt. Hugh Lawson to a late lunch. Lawson selected JG Melon on Third Avenue, safely outside his precinct and a favorite spot for both men. They arrived at the same time, Whyte asked for a spot in the rear of the dining room, and they were shown to a table covered with one of the restaurant's iconic red-and-white checkered cloths where they promptly ordered burgers and beers.

"Let me guess the reason for this delightful invitation," Lawson said.

"No need to guess."

"Damn, I wanted to show how clever I am," he said with a smile.

"I already know you're clever, but have at it," Whyte said.

"Vernon Platt is dead. Just a week before he's supposed to testify in DC. Reports say the investigation has to do with some shady dealings, and the rumor mill has it that Edward Franco is involved. Which means Franco's father-in-law, Congressman Scott, might be dragged into this. Not good for a liberal Democrat to be mixed up in that sort of trouble. Then there are stories that Scott's daughter, Christina, and her husband Edward are having marital problems. Tell me when I'm getting warm."

Whyte waited.

"The part I haven't worked out yet is, how do you and your comrade-in-arms fit into this picture? You working for Edward Franco? The congressman? Neither of those is likely, they're both big firm guys." Sitting back, Lawson asked, "Perhaps the lovely Mrs. Franco has caught your partner's eye?"

Whyte smiled. "Does it matter?"

"Might. You want to indulge me?"

"Not yet, since I'm not sure of the answer."

Lawson ran the palm of his hand across his short, dark hair and stared at his old friend. "That the truth?"

"How about I tell you there's no way we're representing Congressman Scott or Edward Franco, and I'm not sure yet about Franco's wife. Can we leave it there for now?"

Lawson chuckled. "That only makes me a little less uncomfortable sharing information with you."

"Then tell me what you can."

Lawson waited as their beers were served, then had a taste of his draft. "You knew Platt back when he worked as a federal prosecutor in the Southern District."

"We met a few times."

"You couldn't find a more honest guy in that office, and they have some good people down there."

"As opposed to the DA's office," Whyte said with a frown.

"I'm still on the job, so I'll keep those opinions to myself. You're free to say whatever you like."

Whyte nodded. "Yeah, I think Platt was a decent man." Then he added, "He certainly was back in those days."

Lawson took a moment before saying, "I'm guessing you're here because you want to know if I think he killed himself, but I'm still trying to figure why you'd care."

"Let's say I'm trying to connect some dots, and I heard you've been assigned to the case."

"Who else was that fool going to send?"

Whyte laughed. "I thought you were going to be careful about tossing your opinions around. Since you're still on the job."

"Not when it comes to Captain Shithead."

"No argument from me, Hugh. That racist sonofabitch should be shining your shoes."

"And kissing my black ass," Lawson said with a short laugh, "don't leave that part out." He paused. "You were the only guy in that precinct to have my back when he came at me."

Whyte shook it off. "I did what was right."

"But not what was easy," Lawson said. "What do they call it now? Systemic racism? What a load of horse manure. I call it ignorance, plain and simple, one bigot at a time."

Whyte knew better than to debate the point. He waited until Lawson said, "Let's get back to Platt."

"That's why I'm here."

"I think it's a homicide."

"Anything to back that up yet?"

"There are some things don't make sense."

"For instance?"

Lawson hesitated. "No suicide note."

"That *is* odd."

"Yes it is, and keep it to yourself. Not public information yet."

"Never heard it," Whyte assured him.

"Good."

"What else?"

Lawson grinned again. "Once you're ready to tell me why you and your eccentric partner are so interested—like if you're representing Christina Franco—then we can have another discussion."

"You think Palmer is eccentric?" Whyte responded with a feigned look of surprise.

"More quirks than I can name."

"Name two."

"Only two? First, he thinks he's Crusader Rabbit, running around trying to slay the evildoers of the world, as if that's his personal mission from on high. Second, he has a bizarre sense of humor. He'll laugh at anything and at the most inappropriate times. That young man is liable to start telling jokes at a funeral."

Whyte did not argue the point. "Some people think he's a wiseass, but he's not. Humor is a coping skill for him." He smiled. "And the two things you named aren't the worst qualities to have, you agree?"

"I didn't say bad, I just said eccentric. I'll even throw in a third. He's a germophobic hypochondriac."

"That's actually a third and a fourth. And I thought those were secrets."

"Not if you've ever spent ten minutes with him and his little bottle of Purell."

"I'll let him know you were thinking of him."

"Please do."

"Getting back to the subject at hand," Whyte said, "can you tell me if you know anything about a man named Henry Carrigan?"

"Not that I recall. He a player here?"

"Maybe. I intend to find out, and I'll let you know if I do." Then Whyte played his hole card. "How about Peter Frost?"

Lawson did nothing to disguise his interest. "How does he figure in this?"

"Not sure. You know anything about a relationship between Frost and Edward Franco?"

"Not a word, but it would certainly make for an unholy alliance. What have you got?"

"Let's say Franco feels comfortable using Frost's name to create leverage."

"Details?"

"To be provided later, but that's a fair start, right?"

"Could be."

"What about Frost and Platt?"

This time, Lawson shook his head. "I can't see that connection at all."

"Neither can I," Whyte admitted, leaving both men to wonder at how these players all fit together.

* * *

While Lawson and Whyte were having lunch on the Upper East Side, Peter Frost was seated at a corner table at Roberto's. Located on Crescent Avenue, just off Arthur Avenue in the Belmont section of the Bronx, it was one of the best Italian restaurants in a city with more great Italian eateries than anyplace outside Italy.

Frost was in his late forties, tall, tan, and muscular. His hair was prematurely white and cut military short, his features chiseled, his eyes arctic blue. He was dressed in a tailored suit of black gabardine and a white polo shirt. His voice was raspy, as if he were perpetually hoarse, and he almost always spoke in a whisper.

Across from him was an emissary sent by Congressman Eugene Scott who, after more than fifteen minutes of back and forth, was doing an unsatisfactory job of providing the information Frost wanted.

"I still don't understand what you're saying about timing," Frost told him for a second time.

This envoy, whom Frost had never met before, looked to be a few years past fifty. He was short, balding, and had the paunchy shape one earns from life as a second-string functionary. His pale, nondescript face was further evidence of the same, as were his off-the-rack gray suit, blue oxford shirt, and red tie.

"It's difficult to say exactly," the man replied, "but it's in the pipeline."

"The pipeline," Frost repeated with a smile that bore not a hint of amusement. "*You're* supposed to be the pipeline. That's why we're sitting here."

"Of course. I just don't want to be making promises we can't keep."

"That's too bad," Frost told him, "because that's exactly what I want. A promise. A commitment."

"We're working on the—"

"I've heard enough about what you're trying to do. We want results."

The man felt himself blinking as Frost fixed him with his lethal gaze. "It's been difficult to push the issue recently, with this hearing coming up. The level of scrutiny—"

"It seems fate has resolved part of your problem," Frost interrupted him again. "Platt isn't around to testify, so now it's time for the congressman to deliver. Am I clear?"

"Yes," the man said. "Very clear."

Frost sat back, signaling that the meeting was at an end. With no little sense of relief, the messenger stood, bid Frost a good day, and left.

Moments later, a swarthy, thickly built man in a dark polo sweater, who had been standing at the bar near the entrance to the restaurant, strolled into the dining room and joined Frost at his table.

Leaning forward, Frost asked, "You get all that?"

The man plucked a small device from his ear, held it up for Frost to see, then shoved it into his pants pocket. "Got it."

"What about tonight? Is our boy clear on what needs to be done?"

The man responded with a scowl. "Even a fruitcake like Joey can follow a script that simple."

"Maybe so, we just want to be sure he doesn't improvise."

"If he knows what's good for him—" the man started, but Frost cut him off.

"What about our friend's wife?"

"According to plan."

Frost nodded thoughtfully as he lifted his martini glass. "It had better be," he said, enjoyed a taste of the vodka, and added, "Or maybe she needs to be reminded."

His companion nodded.

"What about my young friend?"

"You mean Palmer?"

"Yes," Frost replied with undisguised annoyance.

"Don't worry, we've got him right where we want him."

Frost stared at him for a moment before saying, "If you think so, you don't know Russell Palmer."

CHAPTER SEVEN

The following morning, Palmer was sitting on the leather sectional sofa in the second floor living room of his three-story brownstone, having his morning coffee as he scanned various channels for the latest reports on Vernon Platt's life, career, and death. When Palmer's cell phone rang, he saw the call was from his newest potential client.

"Mrs. Franco," he said.

"Christina, please." Before he could respond, she said, "I'm sorry to be calling so early. I wanted to apologize for leaving so abruptly the other day."

"That's all right, on both counts," Palmer said.

"Have you been looking at the news? About Vernon?"

"I'm watching now," he said. After a pause he added, "You said he was your mother's best friend."

"Yes. He was close with all of us," Christina told him. Then, after her own hesitation, she said, "And he did some work with Edward."

"When you say 'did some work...'"

"Vernon helped with some of Edward's deals, but I don't know which ones or any of the details. Over the years he became what I think they call a power broker. He helped facilitate all sorts of transactions."

Palmer filed that away for a later discussion. "He was scheduled to testify before a congressional committee next week."

"Yes, I know," she told him.

"When did you know?"

"You're asking if I knew about his testimony before this...this happened?"

Palmer was not fond of rhetorical teeth-pulling, but her voice made it clear she was troubled, so he remained patient. "That's what I'm asking."

He could almost hear her nodding her head as she said, "Yes. I knew."

"Something you discussed with your husband?"

"Yes."

When there was nothing more coming, he asked, "Is there more you want to share?"

She paused a moment before saying, "I don't believe his death was a suicide."

Palmer's instincts had him wondering the same thing, even if the news reports were selling a different story. "You have something to back up that belief?"

After hesitating again, she said, "I do, but please don't ask me now."

"When should I ask you?"

"Can we meet this evening? For dinner?"

When Whyte arrived at the office that morning, Palmer recounted his discussion with Christina.

"Seems Platt was not only close to her parents," Palmer explained, "but even more interesting, she said he did some work with her husband."

"Such as?"

"Claims she doesn't have any details."

"That seems to be her very convenient mantra."

Palmer could not argue the point. "I'm meeting her for dinner this evening. I'll find out what I can."

"I see. You've already progressed from an initial consultation to dinner."

"She sounded upset, wanted to get together, and I thought I might learn some more about what's going on."

"Over cocktails and chateaubriand for two, I suppose."

"Have a little faith, will you?"

"Faith," Whyte repeated.

Palmer waved away his skepticism and said, "You know what I'm wondering about?"

"The investigation in Washington, where Platt was supposed to testify next week?"

"Precisely."

"You want to know what it's about and if any of that is related to our boy Franco."

"Those are my questions."

"If he's involved somehow?"

"You'll fill in the blanks," Palmer said.

"I appreciate your confidence in me."

"You get anything from Lawson?"

"Not much," Whyte admitted, then described what little Lawson had shared the day before, including his request that Whyte tell him why they were interested. "He certainly does not believe it was suicide."

"Christina said the same thing."

"Ah, it's Christina now. You going to be calling her Chrissie by the end of your dinner?"

Palmer laughed but said nothing.

"One thing I mentioned did get Hugh's attention."

"The possible involvement of Peter Frost?"

Whyte nodded. "Hope you know what you're getting us into, kiddo."

CHAPTER EIGHT

Le Bernardin was one of the finest and most elegant restaurants in Manhattan. The dining room featured a two-story high ceiling, walls adorned with post-modern coverings and large paintings, and a neutral-colored carpet, all of which framed a sea of cloth-covered tables served by an attentive staff.

Palmer had allowed Christina to choose the site for their dinner, and he arrived early, punctuality being one of his numerous compulsions. Dressed in a dark gray suit with a pressed white dress shirt, open at the collar, he waited patiently at the table with a vodka on the rocks for company, using the time to discreetly polish his silverware with a napkin, just in case the dishwasher missed anything.

Christina showed up twenty minutes late, waving to him as she entered.

She wore a simple black dress of some clingy fabric and, as she glided across the room, he watched as she was repeatedly intercepted by other patrons with whom Christina engaged in greetings and a ballet of air kisses. As she finally approached, Palmer could hear various members of the staff addressing her by name.

Quite a show, Palmer thought.

Despite a lousy won-lost record in the romance sweepstakes, Palmer generally found women more interesting than men. He also found, when it came to people with serious wealth, women wore it better. Not the chic clothing, glittering jewelry, and expensive hairstyles. *It was about attitude*, he told himself. That intangible sense of confidence and the aura of privilege that was evident whether they were in a designer gown or jeans and a T-shirt—attributes he felt were magnified if the woman also happened to be naturally attractive. And Christina Franco was certainly all of that.

He was on his feet by the time she reached the table, where she offered no apology for her late arrival. "So good of you to meet with me," she said, her smile one of her more genuine efforts.

"As the saying goes, you obviously come here often," he observed as they took their seats.

"Often enough."

A waiter was already at the table. "Your usual, Mrs. Franco?"

She nodded and he went off to bring her a glass of rosé Champagne.

"How are you doing?" Palmer asked.

"Vernon Platt," she said softly, as if that answered his question.

"Quite a shock for anyone who knew him."

"Did you? I don't think you mentioned that when we spoke on the phone this morning."

"Our paths crossed," Palmer told her. "All business, nothing personal."

She nodded. "He and my parents knew each other forever. Vernon and mother were so close." It appeared she was about to say something else but stopped.

"Were he and your mother ever, uh—"

"Oh no," she said, "nothing like that."

The waiter returned with a delicate Champagne flute, poured Christina the sparkling wine, and handed them menus. When he walked off, they touched glasses and each had a taste of their drinks.

Then Christina said, "I'll never believe Vernon committed suicide."

"You said that this morning. The police are looking into it. If there's any chance—"

She waved away the idea. "No offense to the locals, but this needs more than some standard investigation. I promise you, Vernon could never have done such a thing."

Palmer studied her for a moment. She wore her blonde hair pulled back, her skin was creamy smooth, the makeup flawless, altogether an appealing picture. But what he found himself speculating about was what she might know that she was not telling him. He said, “The media is focused on his scheduled appearance before congress next week.”

“Vultures,” she said, then had another taste of wine.

“You mentioned that he did work for your husband.”

“He helped Edward more than once.”

“As you mentioned, Platt wasn’t just an attorney,” Palmer said. “He was a deal maker, involved in government contracts, private equity, all that.”

Her jewel-like eyes met his gaze. “We’re back to that? Something I might know that could be dangerous for Edward?”

Palmer leaned toward her. “Or to you,” he suggested with a serious look.

She stared at him without responding.

“Your husband’s threat, his mention of Peter Frost, and now Platt turning up dead—all sounds dangerous to me.”

Before she had an opportunity to respond, their waiter returned. Palmer watched as she made a show of looking over the menu, which turned out to be a superfluous gesture as the man suggested a choice for each course, and she agreed.

When that was done, Palmer gave his order and the man glided off.

“I was hoping you were about to share what little you know of the dealings Platt had with your husband.”

“Was I?” She gently brushed away some imaginary piece of lint from her dark dress. “I do know that Edward gets involved in buying and selling companies,” she said. “Or at least parts of companies. He never runs any of them, he just arranges financing, then cashes out when the companies become more valuable.”

Palmer laughed. “You make it sound simple.”

“It’s not, I realize that,” Christina said. “But he makes it look easy. They’re all high-stakes gambles, and I suppose even one false step could be disastrous.”

“Would Platt’s appearance in congress have been one of those disasters?”

She responded with her best imitation of a blank stare

"Did your husband ever say anything about the subpoena they served on Platt?"

"Not something Edward would discuss with me," she said with a bemused look, then polished off her drink.

Palmer sat back and took a moment. Almost on cue, their waiter was back, this time with a bottle of Meursault they hadn't ordered.

"One of my favorites," Christina told Palmer as the white wine was uncorked and the waiter offered them each a small pour.

Palmer lifted his glass. "I'm not much for white wine," he admitted, "but Meursault is special."

They tasted the small samples provided, nodded their approval, then watched as their glasses were filled and they were left to themselves again.

"There's going to be more information coming out about this investigation," he said. "In case you haven't noticed, DC is as leaky as an old rowboat."

"I might be able to find out something from mother." She picked up her crystal glass. "Although I hate to trouble her right now." After she had a taste of wine, she went on. "I cannot begin to tell you how devastated she is. Mother doesn't do well with upset. And she knows he would never have taken his own life."

"Well," Palmer said after he had his own go at the wine, "I doubt he wandered onto his balcony and stumbled over the railing in the middle of the night. If the two of you are right, you realize the implications."

Her look revealed that she had already thought it through. "It would mean he was murdered."

"That would be the logical conclusion and a part of what I meant about things being dangerous."

"I don't believe Vernon was capable of doing anything illegal, but he might have known things that could have been a problem for others."

"Your husband, for instance?"

"Vernon would never have done anything to hurt my family."

"Maybe not willingly, but you tell me you have no idea what was going on between him and your husband, and yet you've done all you can to convince me your husband is capable of violence."

She looked directly into his light brown eyes as she said, "Or have someone else act for him."

"Someone like Peter Frost."

Christina nodded slowly.

"Which means, if you want me to represent you, we need to figure out if there was an issue between your husband and Platt."

"I'm not sure that's a good idea," she said with a shake of her head.

"Maybe not," Palmer said, "but we'll have to find out. It's one thing for you to insist you know nothing about your husband's business, but it's something else entirely to not want to know. That's not how I operate."

"I need to be divorced from Edward, and the sooner the better. The deeper we dig, the more complicated things will become."

"Maybe, but complicated or not, there are realities we need to face." Leaning forward and lowering his voice, Palmer said, "Your husband threatened you. Why would you doubt he'd be capable of that same behavior if Platt posed a risk?"

"Why do we have to go there at all? What would it have to do with my divorce?"

"What if your husband's assets are at risk because of this congressional probe? Where would that leave you?"

"Vernon and mother loved each other. If there was a serious problem—the kind you're describing—she would have known."

"Then perhaps speaking with your mother is a good idea."

Christina shook her head again but said nothing.

"You mentioned a trust fund the other day, something Platt had to do with creating."

"Yes, he drew it up when I was a child. She's the trustee, all the decisions are hers, but she would rely on Vernon for advice." She paused, as if a thought had just occurred to her. "Now that he's gone, maybe she'll be willing to turn everything over to me. Especially if I'm divorced."

"Wouldn't that depend on what you get from your husband?"

"I suppose so," she said.

"I assume the trust holds substantial assets."

"That depends on what you consider—"

"Millions?"

"Yes," she said, "millions."

Palmer took a moment before asking, "Do you know Henry Carrigan?"

"Henry? Yes, why?"

"He a friend of your husband's?"

"He's worked for Edward for several years, sort of a right-hand man."

"What's your relationship with him?"

"What do you mean?"

"You know him well?"

"Sort of."

"You socialize together, beyond his work with your husband?"

"We've socialized, yes."

"What do you think of him?"

She looked as if she'd been asked to solve a riddle. "He's all right, I guess. Not my favorite person. Where did you hear his name?"

"Not important," Palmer said. "At least not for now."

He could see Christina was unhappy with his answer, but let it go.

"I know you want to explore Edward's investments," she said. "I realize that's your job in a normal divorce, but it may not be a good idea. I believe we should let him think his threat has scared me into only going after the property that's easy to reach. If I agree to stay away from his company interests and take less than what I might be entitled to, well, he might change his mind about letting me go."

"When you say 'easy to reach'—"

"Personal bank accounts, our apartment, the place in the Hamptons."

Palmer nodded slowly. *Makes sense*, he thought, although it all sounded a bit too easy.

"That's one of the reasons Beryl recommended you," Christina told him. "She said you know how to wrap cases up quickly. Difficult cases."

"I'm a lawyer, not a magician. Every case is different, and there are things beyond my control in every one of them. Including my ethical obligations to you as a client. And even if you want to limit the assets we go after, the more restrictions you place on what I can do, the tougher the negotiation will be."

"I'll be flexible," she told him. "But I know Edward, and I know how he'll react if we push too hard." She stared at him. "I take my husband's threat very seriously, but once you file, if he sees we're willing to make the sort of deal I'm suggesting, I believe things will work out."

"A deal that stays away from his business holdings?"

"Exactly. For Edward, that will change the game."

"The game," Palmer repeated, finding her optimism at odds with the concerns she expressed in their meeting yesterday. "Someone once said that divorce is nothing more than a game played by lawyers."

"I actually think it was Cary Grant," she said.

Palmer was impressed, and was about to say so, but she went on.

"Once you come to know Edward, you'll realize everything is some kind of game to him."

Palmer turned their discussion to her children, family background, and other less provocative subjects.

Later, after they finished dinner, Christina went to the ladies' room, giving Palmer an opportunity to call for the check.

The waiter smiled at the request. "It has already been taken care of," he replied politely.

Palmer watched as the man sauntered away, wondering how many things in life Christina and Edward Franco believed they could control by simply paying the bill.

Which led him back to the death of Vernon Platt, and his understanding that Robbie Whyte needed to find out all he could about that before they made a decision about getting involved with the Francos. Whyte was convinced there was some connection there.

And Palmer was certain there were things Christina was not revealing.

CHAPTER NINE

It was well after midnight as Joey D'Angelo made his way on foot along the dark streets of the East Village and let himself into the entry of the brick tenement on East 10th Street, reflecting for a moment on where he might live once the real money started rolling in. *Someplace better than this rat trap*, he thought.

He was thrilled over the events of the past two nights, his exhilaration after completing both assignments now intensified by the effects of the cocaine and Courvoisier he had stopped off to enjoy on the way home. Most of all, he was excited about the rewards that would be coming his way.

For once, he was not dealing with the petty-ante types that had defined too much of his life. This time he was working for powerful people who had made promises that were good enough for Joey. This was his chance for entry into another world, the start of an entirely new direction in his life.

Joey was pleased with himself.

Two nights ago, he had been flawless in dispatching Vernon Platt. After knocking him unconscious from behind, Joey moved swiftly, with only the light he left on in the bathroom to help guide him. Pulling on the latex surgical gloves he had in his jacket, he reached under Platt's arms and dragged him across the room and through the doors that led to the large, tiled balcony where he left the man's inert body seated on the cool, stone floor, leaning it against the wrought iron railing. Then he returned to the bedroom where he picked up the fallen book Platt had been holding, opened it, and placed it on the table face down. After ensuring there were no blood stains on the carpet, he took the brass sculpture he had used as the murder weapon into the bathroom. There, he washed away all traces of blood, cleaned and dried it with the towel he had already used to wipe the bathroom clean of fingerprints, then returned the small statue to its place on a glass shelf. Rushing into the living room, he grabbed the glass he had been drinking from all evening, washed and dried it, and replaced it on the shelf above the bar.

With all that done, he turned off the bathroom light and returned to the balcony. He took time to have a look around, to his left and right, at the building across the street, and then at the pavement beneath. At this hour, there was little concern about a witness to the events taking place on this small terrace, so high above the street. Lifting Platt's unconscious body, he hoisted it over the railing and shoved it to the street, twenty-two floors below.

From there, he rapidly made his way back inside, then hurried out of the apartment, quietly shutting the door behind him, walking quickly down the corridor, and entering the silence of the stairwell. Without stopping, he removed his gloves and replaced them in his pocket. Still carrying the towel he had used to wipe away all traces of his efforts, he stuffed it inside his jacket which he now zipped up as he raced down the steps.

In preparing for that night, he had already identified the placement of all the CCTV security cameras in the building and was now careful to stay out of their view as he reached the garage level. From there, he left through the service exit, feeling a sense of relief wash over him as he made his way along the darkened city streets.

This evening, he completed the second task, which was much easier and posed far less risk. Joey was indeed satisfied with himself.

Unfortunately, he had made one serious miscalculation. When you deal with real power, you need to maintain some sort of leverage to protect your destiny. There is no such thing as gratitude when evil deeds already done have no future value. He failed to realize how quickly he would outlive his usefulness and, at the moment, was too stoned and too full of himself to comprehend the danger when it appeared.

Inside the small vestibule of his building, as he turned to make his way up the staircase, a man, who had been waiting in the dark foyer, stepped out from behind the partition that led to the basement. Hearing the footsteps behind him, Joey turned quickly, relieved to recognize the intruder, even in the dimly lit hallway.

"Hey, what are you doing here?" Joey asked blankly, more surprised than concerned to see him in the tiny lobby, at this hour.

"The boss wants to see you."

"Now?" In his current state of intoxication Joey was incapable of hiding his confusion.

"What else would I be doing here in the middle of the fucking night?"

"Why would he want to see me now?" D'Angelo asked again.

"He wants to know how things worked out tonight. Everything go according to plan with Taub?"

If the man knew about Taub, Joey reasoned, he must be all right. Smiling, D'Angelo told him, "It was perfect."

"That's great," the man said. "Let's go."

Joey shrugged his shoulders, then followed the man outside to a car parked around the corner from his building and got in the passenger side.

"Where are we heading?" Joey asked.

"Uptown," the man told him as he settled into the driver's seat. "But first, he wants me to give you something." The man calmly reached into his sports jacket and pulled out a pistol fitted with a silencer at the end of the barrel. D'Angelo watched without moving, as if paralyzed for the moment by his own abject stupidity.

As that instant passed, Joey made a desperate move for the door handle, but it was too late. He turned away from the gun as the shooter fired one shot into the side of his head, sending D'Angelo's body into a contortion that left it slumped against the dashboard. A second shot made certain he was dead. Then the man started the car and drove off.

D'Angelo was dead, but his usefulness was far from over.

CHAPTER TEN

The following morning, Palmer was in his office with Whyte, comparing notes.

"From what I'm reading and seeing, there's a growing list of people who don't believe Platt's death was a suicide," he said. "But there's still no evidence it was murder, at least according to your pal Lawson. And apparently no suspects." He pulled the small bottle of Purell from his desk drawer and began cleaning his hands.

Whyte smiled.

"What's so funny?"

"Lawson thinks you're a screwball."

Palmer laughed. "Who am I to argue? Especially if he's going to help us."

"He will, as soon as I fess up about why we're interested."

"As you predicted."

Whyte nodded. "Off the record, he did tell me there was no suicide note. Hasn't been reported in the press yet."

"Interesting," Palmer said. "You'd think a man like Platt would leave one, no?"

"I do. And so does Lawson."

"You trust him, right?"

"Completely."

"Then let him know why we're in the mix. What the hell, right? Just keep it to a minimum, tell him we've been asked to take Christina Franco's divorce case, but so far we're just gathering information."

Before Whyte could respond, Maureen called them on the intercom to say Sloane Taylor was on the line asking for Palmer.

"The gossip reporter?" Whyte asked.

"Television personality," Palmer corrected him. "And I'm impressed you've heard of her. You still have a television up there in the burbs?"

"Only to watch the Yankees and the Giants."

He picked up the phone and said, "Russell Palmer here."

"This is Sloane Taylor, Mr. Palmer. I'm calling about the Franco case."

"There's a Franco case?" he replied, looking at Whyte.

"Word has it that the Francos' marriage is on the rocks, that you're representing her, and that this could become the divorce of the year. I'd like to discuss it with you, if you're willing." Before Palmer could interrupt, she added, "I understand your professional obligations. I only want some background so I can give your client a fair shake when we run with the story."

"A fair shake?" he asked with a short chuckle. "You haven't even given me a chance to say whether she's my client."

Sloane moved right past that, as if it were some technicality she need not address. "I can come to your office, or meet you for a drink, whatever works for you. I'm sure you want the best possible treatment in the media for Mrs. Franco. How the coverage starts in these things is usually a predictor of how it plays out."

Still staring at Whyte, Palmer said, "I'm not sure what we'll talk about, but I can certainly meet you for a drink. How about the King Cole Bar at six?"

"Perfect. See you there."

As Palmer hung up, Whyte was already shaking his head. "You're kidding me."

"What do you mean? A beautiful woman invited me out for a drink. Happens all the time."

"Ten minutes ago, we were discussing how much information I should give Hugh Lawson, a cop I know and trust. Now you're going to chat with a rumor peddler, where everything you say can wind up on tonight's news."

"You know me better than that," Palmer said. "I'll be discreet. And she may have more to tell me than I share with her. For instance, who told her Christina had spoken with us? And how much dirt does she have on Edward Franco?"

"You're so full of shit, Palmer. I've seen her on television. All she had to do was bat her eyelashes and you're off to the races."

"May I point out that one cannot possibly bat their eyelashes on a phone call, unless of course her lashes are so thick I could hear them."

Whyte frowned. "Just be careful. I felt lousy when I brought it up the other day, but your track record with women is a little worse than wretched."

Palmer could still feel the ache of his last disappointment, but said, "Not always."

"Shall I mention a few names?"

"How about we skip it."

"All right, but I'm serious. You really think meeting with this woman is a good idea?"

"This is all business, and I really think I might learn something," Palmer replied.

Their debate was interrupted by another call.

"Marvin Taub," Maureen called to them over the intercom.

Palmer picked up the phone. "Long time, Marvin, glad you called back. How are you?"

"Not sure. You remember a creep name of Joey D'Angelo?"

"Joey D? Sure. Party boy. Popular with the scuzzy and infamous. Specializes in ripping off gay men, as I recall."

"That's the one."

"What about him?"

"He showed up at my bar last night and picked a fight with me. Out of the blue. I know the guy's a lowlife, but there was something odd—like he was forcing the whole thing."

"Why would he do that?"

"How the hell would I know, Palmer? What I *do* know is that he made a scene, my bouncers tossed him, and this morning he turned up dead. Now the police are calling to say they're coming here to question me about what happened."

"Dead?"

"That's what they tell me. And what about this message your secretary left the other day?"

"We got an anonymous call saying you were going to be in some sort of trouble."

"Before any of this happened?"

"The day we reached out to you."

"The caller say anything else?"

"Nothing. No specifics, no name, untraceable call."

"Well I don't have any other problems I'm aware of, which means someone knew what was going down before this happened."

"Someone, but obviously not Joey D," Palmer finished the thought.

"Damn," Taub said.

"You have no idea what this is about?"

"None."

"Well," Palmer replied, "we're going to find out. You at your bar?"

"I am."

"Don't say a word to the police if they get there before I do. I'm on my way."

After he hung up, Whyte said, "You want me to come along?"

"Not this time. I know you're not a fan of Taub's, and we don't need any side issues. Let me find out what's happening before you get involved." He stood, and Whyte gave him the once over.

"You may want to change into something that makes you look a little more like a lawyer."

Palmer looked down, having forgotten he was still in the sweatpants and T-shirt he had exercised in early that morning. "Hazards of working where you live," he said. Then he hurried upstairs to take a shower, after which he put on a gray suit, white shirt, and sky-blue tie, as he wondered, *What has Marvin gotten himself into this time?*

CHAPTER ELEVEN

Taub's place on West 46th Street was a dive, a former gin mill that had been converted into a topless bar, the renovation evidently involving as little expense and effort as possible. The three-foot high stage in the center of the room had been constructed of two-by-sixes and heavy plywood, then covered on the sides with black fabric, the top sanded, stained, and lacquered to a high gloss. It was fitted with four vertical stainless-steel poles, anchored into the ceiling, secure enough for the ladies to swing around on for the amusement of patrons settled into the surrounding chairs. Hanging from above was a makeshift series of floodlights that washed the area below and the darkly painted walls. The bar itself was from the saloon's prior incarnation, its wood now pock-marked and dull from decades of use. Behind it was a huge mirror that provided a reflection of the entire tawdry scene.

The overall impression would best be described as a dump when compared to the high-end lust palaces uptown, and especially if one remembered The Honey Pot, the famous and far classier operation Marvin ran almost twenty years ago. But fortunes change, that location was long gone, and, for now, this was what he knew how to do.

The grimy environment sent Palmer's germophobia into high alert, and he promptly pulled out his handkerchief and began wiping his hands when he arrived just after eleven. A few characters were seated around, happy to get a snootful of booze and ogle the silicone sensations Marvin put on display. At the moment, there were two young women of generous bosom and dubious beauty strutting their stuff for the shabby group of patrons on hand. The customers watched as the girls gyrated and undulated and convulsed in a rhythm that didn't exactly match the music but was good enough to accomplish the intended purpose. From time to time, one of these so-called dancers would come to the edge of the platform and push her breasts right in a guy's face, or even better, turn around and bend over, offering a close up view of the delicate flesh barely hidden by her G-string. All of this would earn her a few bucks, shoved ever so tenderly under her garter belt, and then she'd be on her way to find another victim.

Marvin Taub was standing in the back, leaning against the bar. Beside him, his manager Richie Phelps was seated on a stool. Already waiting with them were two plainclothes police detectives.

Marvin was better than six feet tall, broad-shouldered, and too thick around the middle for a man in his sixties who had any hope of making it past seventy. He wore tinted glasses, required for his sensitive eyes, which also helped to create the shadowy image he liked to foster. There wasn't much hair left atop his large head, but he found enough every day to comb from left to right, pretending he wasn't bald. He was more intelligent than his circumstances might suggest, and Palmer had long held the view that the man should have done something better with his life.

Phelps was taller and beefier than his boss, ten years younger, far more muscular, and not anywhere near as smart.

None of the four men were speaking as they absently watched the girls, obviously waiting for him.

"Welcome to the party," Taub said as Palmer approached.

After acknowledging Taub and Phelps, Palmer introduced himself to each of the policemen. Then he asked, "What have we got here gentlemen?"

One of the detectives, after showing an ID displaying the name Kevin Chambers, said, "Following up on a tip."

"I'm listening."

"A couple of uniforms got a lead, found a body in a dumpster near the Hudson River this morning."

"Joey D'Angelo," Taub said.

"That's right," Chambers said. "Two shots in head. Then we got an anonymous tip, said this D'Angelo had an argument here last night with Marvin. Also claimed there were several witnesses."

"Anonymous. How convenient," Palmer said.

"Kevin and I have known each other a long time," Taub told Palmer, nodding in the officer's direction. "He's a right guy. Which, by the way, Joey D was not."

Palmer nodded. "Mind if Marvin and I have a private chat before we start answering your questions?"

"Go for it," the detective said.

Taub led Palmer into his small office in the back of the place, Phelps right behind them. The room had only two seats, so Phelps stood just inside the closed door.

Palmer began by informing them, "Having Richie here destroys the confidential nature of this discussion." Looking up at him, he said, "No offense."

Phelps shrugged.

Taub said he understood. "But Richie was here when Joey showed up last night. He may be able to fill in anything I miss. After we go through all that, you and I can have a private conversation."

Palmer nodded at Phelps. "You start."

"Joey D walked in last night, just after one," the manager began. "Acted even more hyper than usual, like he had a nose full of blow."

"Joey worked for me, on and off, over the years," Taub told Palmer. "Never liked the guy, but he was useful. Knew a lot of people—some were the right sort, others not so much. As you know, in this business, in this city, contacts are like currency and, as I say, Joey had a lot of them. We had our share of arguments, but I made allowances. You couldn't be around Joey without arguing."

"Same could be said about you," Palmer said.

Taub frowned. "Last night there was something different going on. He had an attitude as soon as he walked in."

"It's true," Phelps said. "I tried to stop him before he got to Marvin, but he was on some kinda mission. Got to the bar where Marvin was standing, where we were just now with the cops."

"I got it," Palmer said. "At the bar. Go on."

"He started right in," Phelps continued. "Called Marvin a miserable Jew. Then said something like, 'You're really doing great, running this shithouse. What's next? You gonna enter your girls in an ugly contest?' All kinda trash talk like that. Made some more nasty cracks, asked if we were gonna turn this place into an old age home. That sorta of bullshit." Turning to his boss, he asked, "Am I right?"

"That's about it," Taub said.

"And what did you say?" Palmer asked Taub.

"Nothing. I just stared at him like he was a piece of shit, which he is."

"Which he *was*," Palmer corrected him. "Then what?"

Phelps said, "He looked at me, asked 'What is it, Richie? The Jew went mute on us?' Something like that."

"I'm still listening." Palmer said.

Phelps shook his head in disgust. "I told him to take a fuckin' walk before he had a serious problem. I said, 'Good to see ya, really. Now get the fuck outta here.' All he did was start laughing. Said something like, 'Hey, I haven't seen you guys in a while. This the way you treat an old friend?' I told him as soon as an old friend shows up, we'll know how to treat him."

"This was some snappy repartee," Palmer said. "Then what?"

"He forced another crazy laugh, told me I'm a funny guy, then asked Marvin when I got so funny."

"When I didn't respond," Taub said, "he reached in his pocket and pulled out a vial, looked like coke. Said he didn't need assholes like us to have a good time. When he went to open the small bottle, Richic grabbed his hand. Told him hc was crazy if he thought we were going to let him do blow in our place. It seemed like he might be setting us up. The cops are always on our ass here anyway. All we need is a drug bust and they'll close us down for sure. Richie took the thing and got rid of it."

"When it was all done, I flushed it down the toilet," Phelps added.

"Get back to Joey," Palmer said. "What'd he do next?"

"Richie was still holding his wrist, so Joey started yelling and cursing at him. Loud enough so everyone in the place could hear. I'd had it by then, called him a sleazy little faggot, told him to watch his mouth or I'd kick his ass across the room and onto the street."

"Charming. Did you hit him?"

"What was I supposed to do, he wouldn't knock it off," Taub said. "I got off my stool and smacked the little prick, hard, across the face. He just smiled and told me to go fuck myself. That's when I was sure something wasn't right. Joey was too eager to push me, too fast pulling out the coke. I told him to get the hell out before I broke him into little pieces."

Phelps was nodding. "He insulted Marvin some more, called me some names, said our bouncer was a gorilla, so Marvin smacked him across the face again, this time with the back of his hand."

"By now," Taub said, "the girls and the customers were all watching, so I told Richie to throw him out. Richie let go of his wrist, and that's when he lunged at me. I'm a lot bigger than he is—*was*—so I grabbed his arm and swung him sideways into the bar, knocked him to the floor along with a stool he'd grabbed. By then, the bouncer came back, yanked Joey up by his jacket, and dragged him through the place and threw him out the front door."

"He try and come back in?"

"No."

"Okay," Palmer said. "Then what?"

"I told everyone the show's over. Called two more girls out of the dressing room, gave our customers more to look at, and it was over."

Palmer paused. "You think he was just stoned?"

"No way. It wasn't just the coke talking, he wasn't that high. Someone put him up to it, I'm sure of it."

Phelps nodded as he said, "Yeah."

"I spoke to the dancers and the barmaids," Taub said. "Told them it was a setup, warned them we should be expecting a visit from the locals so they should be careful. Everything by the book. Keep the G-strings on, no quickies in the back, and definitely no drugs."

"You're quite the citizen," Palmer said.

This time Taub scowled at him. "Now the creep is dead, I have no idea what his act was all about, but they want to tie it to me because he came in here last night and picked this fight. What do we do?"

"They already know D'Angelo was here, so we tell the police exactly what you told me. Since you can't be sure what he had in the vial, and it's gone anyway, I would skip that part for now. Let's wait for the autopsy to see what was in his system. Meanwhile, the fact there was a brawl doesn't connect you to his murder. These witnesses all saw he was alive when you had him tossed out, and you say he never came back. We're sure about that last part?"

"A hundred percent."

"Good. Let's go out there and speak with the detectives, be as cooperative as possible. I'll find out about the time of his death and whether they have anything else tying you to this."

"How are you going to do that?"

"Whyte will handle it, he's still got friends in the department."

Taub was clearly not happy about that. "He doesn't like me."

"Apparently he's not the only one," Palmer said, "but he'll take care of it. Now, if there's anything about this you're not telling me—"

"That's everything, I swear. Richie?"

"That's the whole story," Phelps said.

"All right. Let's go."

Palmer led them back to the bar, where he orchestrated the description by Taub and Phelps of all that had occurred the previous night.

When they were done, the two detectives admitted they didn't have enough to press charges. Palmer waited, knowing all they would have left was to give the usual warning about not leaving town, which they did.

Taub tilted his large head to the side, had a look around his shoddy kingdom, and asked, "I'm in paradise boys. Where the hell would I go?"

After the police left, Palmer said, "If either of you can recall anything you haven't shared yet, now would be a good time to share."

"I already told you," Taub said. "You've got the whole picture."

Palmer stared at him. "Why do I find myself hoping that's true?" Then he told Taub he would be in touch and left.

Outside, Palmer felt the desperate need for a couple of deep breaths to clear away the bar's stale air. Pulling out his phone, he called Whyte and brought him up to speed.

"D'Angelo? Why would Taub murder that punk?"

"He wouldn't," Palmer told him. "But you and I have an idea who would."

CHAPTER TWELVE

The King Cole Bar at the St. Regis Hotel is a classic Manhattan cocktail lounge, the mural behind the bar worthy of a fine museum, the ambience of the room refined, and the service top notch. That evening, when Palmer arrived there, he found Sloane Taylor was already waiting at a small round table in the corner. Given his own penchant for being early, he was both pleased and surprised to find her there.

She had shoulder-length dirty blonde hair and the sort of fine features and full lips that play well on television. Tall and athletic looking, her royal blue dress complemented the color of her eyes and hugged her in all the right places. The neckline alone provided a distraction even the most disciplined of men would find hard to ignore, and Palmer's first impression was that she looked even better in person than on the small screen.

His second impression was the same.

As he approached, she was sipping from a martini glass filled with a colorful liquid he guessed was a Cosmopolitan.

"Sorry," he said, taking the seat opposite her. "I had an emergency."

"You're not late. I was early," she told him with a relaxed smile.

"Couldn't wait to see me?"

"That might be it," she said.

"I get that a lot," Palmer told her with a slight laugh, then said how pleased he was to meet her and took a seat as the waiter arrived to take his order.

"Belvedere, straight up, as cold as you can make it, with olives."

The man nodded and sidled away.

"I'm surprised our paths haven't crossed before," Sloane said.

"How's that?"

"You've had your share of high profile cases."

"High profile," Palmer repeated. "That expression always makes me wonder if I should be flattered or worried."

"That's up to you, but it seems you've been involved in some interesting matters over the past several years. A sole practitioner in New York is a dying breed, especially one with your roster of clients."

"I'm not entirely on my own."

"Ah yes, Robbie Whyte, your very own Archie Goodwin."

Palmer smiled. "I appreciate the Nero Wolfe reference, since he was a genius. Although he was obese."

She had a sip of her drink. "You want to tell me how you manage to land these cases?"

The most sacred rule of the secret arrangement that funded Palmer's law practice was that it remained a secret. Palmer said, "We're not here to discuss my career, are we?"

"How about your newest client, then?"

"Right down to business, eh? What a shame. When I meet an interesting woman, I like to think she might have some interest in me. You know, some opening chitchat, piercing questions, a little personal interaction."

Sloane's eyes narrowed slightly as she asked, "Christina Franco is an interesting woman, is that how you and she began?"

Palmer was shaking his head before she finished. "She's a potential client, which is an entirely different type of relationship. You, on the other hand, are most definitely not a potential client."

"I see." Sloane studied him for a moment, and Palmer guessed she was trying to decide if he was serious or just teasing her. "I may not be client material, but this is a business discussion," she told him. "Don't you think things should be gender neutral?"

Palmer stuck out his lower lip as he thought it over. "You are indeed a provocative woman, since you've now raised two more issues."

"Such as?"

"Well first, whether this is a business discussion. You're not here looking for a lawyer, so there's no business on the line for me. Second, what does 'gender neutral' mean? Am I supposed to ignore that you're an attractive woman? Are you supposed to dismiss that I'm an incredibly appealing man?"

Now Sloane laughed. "I can see why you became an attorney."

"You married? Attached? Gay?"

"None of the above."

"Me either, so there you have it. What's wrong with a bit of flirting? If I had to take a position on the battle of the sexes, I would always give women the edge." The waiter returned with his martini, and Palmer told him, "Perfect timing." Turning back to Sloane, he hoisted his cocktail and said, "Here's to us, and *vive la différence*."

They clinked glasses and each had a taste of their drinks.

"It remains to be seen whether there is an *us*," Sloane said with a smile.

"Fair enough," Palmer agreed. "So why aren't you married?"

"Not giving up on the personal approach yet?"

"Never give up, never surrender."

"All right. Let's say I never found the right man."

"You mean, not yet."

That earned him a smile. "Not yet."

"Good," Palmer said.

"Now how about we get to what you're willing to tell me about Christina Franco?"

"That depends," he said. "You go first."

She responded with a look of feigned confusion.

"I'll be more specific," he said. "Let's start with who told you I'm representing her?"

"How about, a little birdie?"

"Unless there's a parrot in my office I've never noticed, that's not good enough."

"All right, I got an anonymous call. That's the truth."

"A lot of that going around lately."

"How's that?"

"Never mind. Man or woman?"

"Man, if it matters."

"You try and trace it?"

"I did. No luck."

Palmer was not sure he believed her, but had another taste of his vodka before asking, "And based on that, you called me and set up this meeting?"

"In my line of work, rumor is cryptocurrency. Now, how about you tell me whether it's true?"

Palmer stuck out his lower lip and thought it over. "Yes, Mrs. Franco came to see me."

"About a divorce?"

"That would be privileged, as you know. Let's just say she has some issues she wants me to help her resolve."

"Have you agreed?"

"Not yet, I'm still studying the situation," Palmer told her.

"We're going to run a story about the Francos," she told him, "with or without your input. I can keep anything you say anonymous, but it might help your client if you put a positive spin on her situation."

"There we go again with anonymity. Isn't anyone willing to stand behind what they say anymore?"

"That's also up to you."

"Then let's keep going and see where this discussion takes us."

"There you go with that 'us' again," she said with another short laugh. "All right, let's drop the Francos for now and you tell me about the other developing story that might involve you."

"Which story is that?"

"Marvin Taub."

She stared at him without blinking, and Palmer looked into her shimmering hazel eyes. "You really do have your ear to the ground."

She responded with an appreciative nod.

After another taste of vodka, he said, "That can be a rather vulnerable position, don't you think?"

"You are something, Mr. Palmer."

"Just Palmer is fine." Then he asked, "How do you feel about gay bars?"

"Excuse me?"

"I called an old friend, said I'd be stopping by to have a drink with him. Interested?"

"Should I be?"

"I think you should," Palmer said with a sly grin.

"This have anything to do with the Francos?"

"That remains to be seen," he told her. "But it should have something to do with the murder of Joey D'Angelo."

"You going to share?"

"On the way," Palmer replied, then turned and called for the check.

CHAPTER THIRTEEN

Palmer arranged for an Uber and they headed south toward the West Village, to a cozy tavern on Christopher Street. Benny Parsons was a regular there, and when Palmer called, this was where he suggested they meet.

As a young man, Parsons worked for Taub back in the heyday of Marvin's first club, The Honey Pot. It was an elegant topless bar in an era where there was no other place like it in New York City. Benny ran the back office in the beginning—he was capable, reliable, and had no interest in women, a perfect trifecta for that role. Regrettably for Taub, Benny tired of his unofficial position of modern eunuch and, after a couple of years, abandoned the night life and began a successful career as an interior designer for a midtown architectural firm. Some time later, when a legal problem arose there, Taub introduced Benny to Palmer, the issue was resolved, and Parsons had been grateful to Palmer ever since.

Palmer found Parsons far more intelligent and dependable than most of the people in Taub's orbit. Palmer also learned that Benny was always candid about his homosexuality, even when it was not as acceptable as it was finally becoming. Palmer respected him for that too.

When Palmer escorted Sloane into the place, Benny spotted them immediately, as did everyone else there—Sloane was only the second woman to stop in that week, the other having been lost and asking for directions.

"Russell Palmer," Benny called out, quickly making his way down the length of the oak bar to greet Palmer with a warm embrace. "How are you?"

"I'm all right, Benny. Say hello to Sloane Taylor. Sloane, Benny Parsons."

Benny kissed her hand. "Pleased to meet you, Sloane. Especially after seeing so much of you on television," he added. "And I must say, you are even more beautiful in person."

"That's what I told her," Palmer said before she could thank Parsons for the compliment.

"No you didn't," she said.

"Maybe I just thought it."

"Palmer, you'll never change," Benny said with a laugh. "Come, let's get a table."

Parsons was short of stature, slight of build, and his style strictly old world. He was well groomed, his nails manicured and buffed to a shine, his mustache always trimmed to a narrow line of geometric perfection, and his clothes, which tended toward a traditional British style, never seemed to wrinkle. Even his movements were precise.

After he left Taub's employ to pursue his design career, Parsons also embarked on a personal relationship that was still going strong. He stayed away from the pickup bars on the lower west side where single gays congregated, avoiding the scourge of AIDS that sent too many of his friends to the hospital, or worse.

Palmer thought monogamy suited him well and said so. "You're looking good, Benny."

Parsons smiled. "You're only saying that because it's true." Then, turning to Sloane, he added, "And because he wants something." Then he pointed them to the back of the restaurant, stopping along the way to whisper a few words to someone standing at the bar.

When Benny caught up with them again, Palmer teased him. "Are we interrupting anything? That's not Mark."

"I was just having a drink with a friend," Benny said as he gestured toward a small round table in the far corner of the room. "Don't be a troublemaker."

"So how are things with you two?" Palmer asked as they sat down.

"All good between us, Mark and I are just a bit older." Parsons instinctively reached up to smooth his thinning hair. "We've all got to give out somewhere. Better to lose it on top than—" he began, then hesitated. "Sorry, Sloane."

"No worries," she replied with a warm smile.

"So, Mr. Palmer," Benny said, "I've been half expecting your phone call."

"About Joey."

Palmer watched as Benny's smile disappeared and sadness filled his eyes. "Just awful."

"And one hell of a mess."

"Especially for you, with Marvin implicated."

"Bad news travels fast."

"Especially in this community," Benny agreed.

"I think someone is trying to set him up."

"Marvin has quite the list of enemies, as you know only too well. Any clue who might be behind such a thing?"

"Not yet. You have any guesses?"

"Wish I could help, but no. You going to represent him?"

Before Palmer could respond, a waiter came by, and Benny suggested they all have cognac. Palmer requested Cordon Bleu, Benny held up his hand, but Palmer insisted the drinks were on him.

"Show off," Benny said, then sent the young man to fetch their drinks. "And, by the way, you haven't answered my question."

"About representing Marvin? He expects me to."

"Of course he does."

"Why *of course*?" asked Sloane. "Other than the obvious brilliance of Palmer's legal talents."

Parsons chuckled. "This one is trouble, RP. Watch out for her."

"Don't worry," Palmer assured him, "I've got my guard up. She already accused me of sexism, just for wanting to flirt."

"Oooh, that's strict."

Sloane laughed.

"But that's not our boy Palmer," Benny said a bit more seriously. "Not his style."

"So he claims."

Palmer looked from Benny to Sloane with an amused smile but said nothing.

"To answer your question, Sloane," Benny said, returning to the issue at hand, "Palmer is the only lawyer Marvin trusts. Which is true for a lot of us."

They were quiet until Palmer asked him, "What do you think?"

"About Joey?"

"Yes," Palmer said. "You think there's any chance Taub killed him?"

"In a word, no. Marvin, for all his many and varied faults, is no murderer. Even if he were, I can't imagine any reason Joey would be that important to him." Turning back to Sloane he said, "I regret having to speak badly of the departed, but Joey wasn't that important to anyone." He sighed as Palmer saw the sadness return. "Joey and I were close at one time," Benny told her. "Very close. Then he got involved in stupid things and we went our separate ways. Everyone says he was a liar, a drug dealer, the scum of the earth, all of that, and maybe he became those things. But he wasn't always that way, not with me. That's why Russell Palmer is here tonight. Because of what Joey and I were to each other."

Sloane looked across the table at Palmer. "Is that why we're here?"

"Is *what* why we're here?"

"To drag up sad memories," she said.

It was Benny who responded. "Memories are never sad, Sloane. They're just memories. It's how we hold them that matters." He managed a slight smile. "Joey and I had some wonderful adventures, back in another lifetime, when we both worked for Marvin. He was exciting, and fun, and that's what I choose to remember now. The rest doesn't matter. For Palmer however," he said with a slight tilt of his head, "it's a different story. That's why I said this case would be tough for him, as it is with all his clients. He never knows what to hold onto and when to let go. He'll represent Marvin, he'll worry about Marvin, he'll even feel sorry for Joey. And he'll live every detail of the case over and over. That's the Palmer curse, if you don't know. Caring about everything too damned much."

Sloane turned to Palmer but said nothing.

"He's not like other attorneys," Benny went on. "Your television spots call you an investigative reporter. Maybe you can figure out the how and why of who Russell Palmer is. It'd make an interesting story. As for those of us he's helped, we just know he's special and leave it at that."

"I would blush," Palmer said, "if it weren't all so true."

Sloane uttered a soft groan.

The drinks were served, and Benny made a toast. "To friends, old and new, gone and undiscovered." Then the three of them resumed talking, which went on through another round of cognacs and some appetizers.

Benny reminisced about Taub's original topless bar. "No one had ever seen anything like it, and it's never been duplicated. Certainly not those expensive clip joints they run uptown these days, not even the places in Vegas. The Honey Pot was top shelf in every way, strictly on the up and up. The girls were gorgeous, and not for hire, if you catch my drift."

"Is that true?" Sloane asked.

"There was no funny business in back rooms, no pay for play, none of that. And the clientele was unbelievable. Politicians, celebrities, even diplomats from the UN, which was just a short walk from here. I wish I had a dollar for every dancer who ended up marrying one of the customers."

"I remember hearing about it when I first came to New York," she said, "but that was long after it closed down."

"It was legendary," Benny told her, then lifted his snifter.

Palmer felt it was time to address the reason he was there. "Sorry to return to the unpleasant matter of Joey's death," he said, "but do you know what Joey was up to recently? Who he was associating with, spending time with—"

"What might've gotten him killed?" Benny suggested.

"For instance."

Parsons shook his head. "I haven't had any contact with him for a long time, but I did hear he was still close to Sammy Burdick."

"The bookmaker?"

"The one and only. Lives on City Island, I think. I'll get you the address and phone number. Least I can do, if it'll help you find out who killed Joey."

Later, when Sloane and Palmer were ready to leave, Benny said he'd like to see the two of them again. Perhaps, he suggested, his partner Mark would join them and they could all have dinner. He also said how much he appreciated a woman who could sit in a restaurant filled with homosexual men and not appear the least bit uncomfortable or out of place.

"Never occurred to me," Sloane replied with a radiant smile, then leaned forward and kissed him on the cheek.

Sloane and Palmer stepped out into the warm June evening on Christopher Street. "I like Benny," she said, "and I had a fine time. But I do have a question."

Palmer waited.

"Why did you bring me here?"

"You were looking for a lead, right? You called me because you wanted to know about Christina Franco, said you were open to treating her fairly when you air the gossip about a possible divorce."

"That's right."

"Well, the murder of Joey D'Angelo might end up an even bigger headline, because I'm convinced there's a lot more to it than we know right now. And Marvin Taub is also going to need some fair treatment in the media." When she didn't respond, he said, "The owner of a grubby topless bar is the prime suspect in a murder. They'll be trashing him as soon as the story comes out tomorrow."

She nodded slowly, studying him with a curious smile. "I think Benny may be right, there may be an even bigger story than that."

Palmer looked into her beautiful eyes. "Such as?"

"You, your practice, your personal life. You're unattached. Romantically, I mean. Why is that?"

Palmer laughed. "When I tried to ask you the same thing earlier tonight, you accused me of sexism."

"Not true. You wanted to flirt. I'm asking a serious question."

Palmer took a moment. "I recently had a relationship, or thought I did. She didn't share my views on things like loyalty, trust, the basics."

"I'm sorry."

"So was I. Although it's best to find out sooner than later."

"I agree with that," she said with an unexpected trace of sadness. "How about we get back to the mystery of your odd collection of clients? People like Taub don't seem to fit with Christina Franco or that billionaire you represented in a divorce years ago. Or some of the other corporate types I've read about."

Palmer felt an odd mix of concern and appreciation. "You read about me?"

"I'm a reporter," she reminded him, "which means curiosity is my starting point. I want to know how you get these clients and why they're so loyal? Benny said you become committed to them in ways other lawyers are not. What's that about?"

"You should have spent more time flirting with me, you might have learned something useful." He followed that with a smile, not admitting that he was impressed at how she remained on the job, even after all the cognac.

"Then maybe next time," she said.

"I'll be pleased if there's a next time."

"There's something about you, your practice, something that makes me want to know more. Including Detective Whyte."

Palmer shrugged. "We'll see," he told her, knowing it was not something he was ever going to share with her, regardless of how beautiful she might be.

It was the story that had come to define his life, a series of events that had changed everything for him and Robbie Whyte.

PART TWO
MONEY

CHAPTER FOURTEEN

The origin of the story Palmer was not willing to share with Sloane Taylor began almost ten years before.

At the time, Robbie Whyte was a detective assigned to the 17th Precinct of the NYPD with almost twenty years on the force, having recently celebrated his forty-second birthday. Palmer wasn't yet thirty and had just left the Wall Street firm he joined straight out of law school.

Palmer had become disillusioned with the large firm approach to litigation, which was essentially the same for every case. Associates would be assigned to years of document review, mind-numbing research, and an endless string of depositions. Eventually the senior partners would step in and begin negotiating with their adversaries to hammer out a settlement. Throughout the process, they would bill their clients senseless until—after generating as much in fees as they could—they reached a deal and moved on to the next cash cow.

"I'm a trial lawyer," Palmer would tell anyone who cared to listen. "Doesn't that mean I should actually go to court and try cases?"

People who knew him were not surprised by his resignation, but they were concerned about his decision to establish a solo practice. Lawyers working alone had become increasingly rare, especially those with no family influence or political contacts. He struggled for the first couple of years, building a small roster of clients, some of whom could pay his fees and others who did their best to keep up. He could not afford to be choosy about which matters he took and, along the way, handled a number of criminal cases.

Whyte and Palmer had absolutely nothing in common back then, which is not unusual for a Manhattan police officer and a defense attorney. Cops are trained to respond to illicit activities, minimize the danger to the public, and identify the perpetrators. Criminal defense lawyers are on the other side of that equation. Most are not concerned with the truth—their only interest is determining how much the prosecution can prove. They seek to convince a judge or jury that the defendant is innocent, or at least create enough uncertainty to reach that mythical touchstone—reasonable doubt—so their client can go free.

This natural adversity was not a promising basis for a close friendship, but right from the start Whyte realized there was something different about Palmer. He came to learn that Palmer never took a case for the money, but only when he believed the defendant had been wronged, a concept the detective found fascinating. Whyte also came to understand, over the ensuing years, that once Palmer was convinced his client was right, whether the matter was civil or criminal, he saw it as his absolute responsibility to ensure a just result.

Evildoers were simply not his business.

They met for the first time during a murder investigation, when a young black woman was found dead in the room of a midtown hotel. She was beautiful, or had been before someone put a bullet in the back of her head that exited through the front, taking most of her face with it. It did not require much detecting for Whyte to discover she was working for an escort service and to identify the out-of-towner who had rented the room where she was found.

That young man was obviously the prime suspect.

Whyte had no idea who referred the accused to Palmer, but the young lawyer made it clear from the start that he would not entertain any sort of plea deal. He was convinced his client was innocent.

One afternoon, a few days after the arrest, Palmer came to see Whyte at the precinct on East 51st Street. That was not how these things generally go—arresting officers and defense counsel typically meet in court on days the case is scheduled for one sort of procedure or another—but from their first encounter it was clear Palmer did not do things in the usual way.

When Palmer arrived, he was escorted to Whyte's desk on the second floor. He introduced himself and identified the case he was there to talk about—even though he knew the desk sergeant would have called ahead to give Whyte the heads up.

Palmer was tall and trim, giving Whyte the impression he had been some sort of college athlete who wasn't ready to surrender to the realities of real life—which he would later discover was a bad read. The young man had dark hair that was cut short and light brown eyes that displayed far more intelligence than the detective experienced from most of the courthouse hustlers he dealt with. There was also nothing flashy about the young lawyer. He wore the sort of conservative suit and tie that had been mandatory in his prior firm and carried himself in a polite and respectful manner, which cops generally appreciated.

Palmer offered his hand, which Whyte took without standing, then sat in the chair beside the green metal desk. "I don't want to take up a lot of your time, I just have two questions I'd like you to consider."

"Go ahead," Whyte told him.

"What possible motive could my client have for murdering this young woman?"

"What's the other?"

"Where did he get the gun?"

Whyte liked his reference to the victim as a "young woman," rather than a hooker or something else a shyster might have said to demean the victim. All the same, Palmer was representing the suspect they had in custody, and Whyte was not there to make friends. Since no weapon was found at the scene, he decided to answer the second question first. "This is New York City. Pick the right neighborhood, and you can buy a gun on any corner."

"That may be true," Palmer conceded, "but it assumes a young guy from Lima, Ohio, in New York for only the second time in his life, knew the sort of neighborhood where he could find that corner." Then he asked, "Even if he did, why would he?"

Whyte didn't have a good answer, so he waited him out.

"We know he has absolutely no priors, nothing violent in his past," Palmer went on. "We know he contacted an online service that sent this young woman to his hotel room. Since there's no evidence he and the young woman had ever met before, there was no existing motive for murder. That means, whatever went wrong happened after she got there. Maybe she wouldn't do what he wanted, asked for too much money, maybe the sex got rough, whatever. So they have an argument, he pulls a gun, and shoots her. That the working theory?"

"That's as good as any we have right now," Whyte admitted.

"That would mean he had to buy the gun some time before she got there, right? I mean, if something went bad between them, he wouldn't ask her to wait in the room while he took a subway out to Bed-Stuy and got himself a Saturday night special."

Whyte could not suppress a grin, but he said nothing.

"And supposing something like that happened, she wasn't going to stick around until he got back, was she?"

Whyte did not argue the point. "He must have bought the gun beforehand. Or brought it with him. Maybe he's the nervous type. Maybe the big city scares him. Maybe he'd never done anything like this before. Hiring a prostitute, I mean. Maybe he wanted protection, just in case."

"That's a lot of maybes," Palmer said.

It wasn't a question, so Whyte waited again.

"I assume you're aware he went to a business dinner that evening. A little more than an hour after she came to his room."

"That's what I'm told."

"I interviewed the two men he met with that night. They said there was nothing odd or nervous about him, nothing out of the ordinary."

"So what?"

"So a guy with no priors, after having sex with this woman, shoots her in the face, then showers, dresses, and goes to dinner as if nothing happened? Leaving the body on the bed in his own hotel room for the maid to find when she came in for turn-down? I'm asking you, Detective, does that make any sense?"

"Murder doesn't always make sense."

Palmer frowned. "That's it?"

"Look Counselor, he contacted the escort service, as you say. Her body was found in his room. What else am I supposed to think?"

"I have two theories."

"Only two?"

Palmer ignored the crack. "Have you checked with the outfit that sent her? Maybe she had a history of problems. Maybe she worked for a pimp before she went upscale and signed with their service. Maybe that pimp was unhappy she went to work for someone else."

"Now you're the one with a handful of maybes, all of them a bit of a stretch, don't you think?"

"No, I don't."

"What's your second angle?"

"The victim's personal life. How about a husband, or a jealous boyfriend?"

Whyte shook his head. "If you think someone else pulled the trigger, that means your client left a call girl alone in his room when he went to dinner. In my experience, the john sends the girl on her way after they're done, he doesn't leave her in the room to rummage through his things."

"But he was an amateur. You met him and you have to admit, he's something of a rube. She was the pro here. Let's say he was in a hurry to get to his dinner meeting, and she told him she wanted to take a shower before she left. He can't be late for his appointment, and he knows he's leaving nothing valuable behind. This guy is not a high roller, knows there's nothing in the room but his clothing. So he tells her it's okay and she stays, has a look around, hoping to find a watch or some cash. A few minutes later there's a knock on the door and she makes the mistake of opening up. Whoever was there shoves her inside, caps her, and walks out, leaving my guy to take the fall."

Whyte stared at him for a moment. "You believe all this CSI bullshit?"

Palmer did not blink. "Have you spoken with my client? I mean, really listened to what he has to say?"

"Of course."

"He's facing a murder charge, but has he told you what his biggest concern is?"

Whyte sat back. "He's worried his wife is going to find out he had a call girl in his room."

"That's right. He's trying to figure out how to save his marriage, Detective. He knows he's not guilty of murder, he figures that'll all get sorted out. He's just petrified his wife is going to leave him because he was with another woman."

Whyte studied Palmer for what felt like a long time. At last, he said, "All right. Let me check some things out."

"Will you get back to me?" Palmer asked as he handed over his business card.

"Only if there's something worth discussing," Whyte told him.

That afternoon Whyte paid another visit to the hotel where the young woman was murdered. Security had no closed-circuit camera covering the door to the room, but they did have video from the lobby. He focused on the time just before and after their suspect left for his dinner meeting. Then he had them make a copy and took it with him. Afterwards he stopped by the victim's apartment building in Harlem. He was gathering information from some of the people she knew when a neighbor provided a description of the young woman's boyfriend. Which just happened to match one of the men Whyte had seen in the recording of the hotel lobby on the night of the murder. The man had entered after his suspect was gone and left shortly after. Whyte got his name, picked him up and took him to the 17th for questioning. The interrogation did not take long before the man broke down in tears, admitting he could not bear that the woman he loved was a prostitute, then confessed to the murder.

In the detection business, as with most things in life, people tend to take the easy route. At least until they hit a dead end. Only then are they forced to reverse direction and travel the more difficult path. It is not an admirable approach, especially in police work, and Whyte could offer all sorts of excuses—large caseloads, shortage of manpower, and a claim that the most obvious answer is usually the correct one. But sometimes mistakes are made—or, as in this matter, almost made—and he felt he owed the young lawyer something.

Palmer was renting space in a suite of lawyers at 777 Third Avenue, not far from the precinct, and Whyte decided to stop by with the news.

There were several different ways the young attorney could have reacted, but he took the high road. He told Whyte how grateful he was that the detective was willing to entertain his ideas and to do the legwork necessary to exonerate his client and identify the murderer.

Then he took Whyte to P.J. Clarke's on 55th Street, treated him to lunch, and they remained friends ever since, a relationship that underwent an astonishing turn just a couple of years later.

During those two years, Palmer remained in Manhattan, working his way through a series of failed romances. His law practice grew increasingly active, although not as successful as it might have been if he were not so selective about the matters he took. He continued to take on some criminal cases, civil matters and, reluctantly, the occasional divorce.

Including Robbie Whyte's.

Whyte resigned from the NYPD, took his pension, and moved to Connecticut, taking a job with the Darien Police Department—a decision actually made by his wife.

After years of living in Queens, she told Whyte it was time to change their lives. She constantly lectured him about the needs of their two teenaged daughters and how there were better places to raise them than Astoria. The suburbs beckoned and, after numerous debates that did little to allay his misgivings, Whyte agreed to the move.

Relocating with his family to Connecticut meant a substantial pay cut for Whyte, as well as an increase in their cost of living, which his new salary and pension checks barely covered. Unfortunately, he soon discovered those financial concerns were the least of his problems.

First there was the adjustment at work, which was like going from a rock concert to a library reading room. Darien was not exactly a hotbed of crime, and there was not much of consequence to investigate, not for a cop of his experience. Taken together, all of the incidents of vandalism and burglary he handled in the course of a year were less dangerous than a single midnight-to-eight tour in a tough New York neighborhood.

Next were the changes in his personal life, which ultimately turned upside down. It began in subtle ways, as these things often do, such as losing contact with old friends from the city. His wife discouraged those get-togethers, asking, "What's the point?" convinced their old crowd from Queens resented them for moving away.

Meanwhile, she was mingling with new people—locals who were living the affluent lifestyle she envied. She didn't care that casting away old relationships was tough for Whyte, or that making new friends was difficult for him in an area where he was regarded as the hired help. That was his problem, not hers.

Never a materialistic type, Whyte did not understand her fascination with the wealth around them, nor did he properly read the intensity of her growing disenchantment with his career and their limited means.

As he later told Palmer, "Some detective I turned out to be."

There were more and more evenings when she would go out on her own, something she never did in the city. She claimed to be meeting with other women for dinner or participating in charitable functions and community activities.

He tried to be understanding but was ultimately confronted by the truth. She was having an affair.

"I was a regular Sherlock Holmes," he told Palmer.

When she finally left him, she told him there was nothing for them to discuss. It was over. She was in love with some real estate investor she'd been sleeping with for the past year, during those evenings when Whyte stayed home with their daughters or worked late for the extra income.

The divorce that followed was as cut and dry as her attitude. Palmer advised his friend that any sort of court battle would get him nowhere and only upset his children. She was asking for minimal alimony and statutory child support, which Palmer told him was as good as it was going to get. She had already taken the two girls and moved into her boyfriend's large house in Westport.

And that was that.

Whyte did a lot of soul-searching, wishing there was something to fight for. After a few sad and angry nights, when he had a few too many drinks, and then a couple more, he finally gave up. A judge in Stamford brought the gavel down on their marriage and that was how Whyte ended up alone.

Palmer urged him to move back to the city, "Where you belong."

But Whyte wanted to remain close to his daughters. He moved from the Cape Cod style home they had been renting in Darien to a small townhouse on the outskirts of town. He kept his job with the local force, not interested in starting over again in New York. He met an interesting woman during the only murder investigation he handled during his entire tenure with the Darien PD. It was a widely publicized case involving the death of a prominent surgeon's wife, a local politician, and a diary that was hot enough to steam the paint off a Mercedes. The woman he met was the victim's psychologist, and they hit it off for a while, but his wife's betrayal was still an open wound, and the relationship faded.

Palmer remained close to Whyte, throughout his ordeal and afterwards. To Palmer, loyalty was the bedrock of friendship, and the loyalty was mutual. Palmer suffered through his own romantic issues, Whyte telling him, "You need a little of my cynicism, kiddo. You're just too damn sincere."

"I thought sincere was good," Palmer said, realizing it had not worked out for him. At least not yet.

Over those two years, Palmer had Whyte help him with various matters. It was, therefore, not unusual when Palmer phoned one afternoon to ask if Whyte would meet with him to discuss a new case. What *was* unusual was the urgency of the request and the unique nature of the case.

That was several years ago, the result of that case life-changing, and the story behind it a closely guarded secret.

CHAPTER FIFTEEN

The morning after Palmer took Sloane Taylor to meet Benny Parsons in Greenwich Village, he awoke in the master bedroom on the third floor of his 64th Street brownstone. The room was large and comfortably furnished, with a king-sized bed, cherrywood furniture, and blackout shades. Despite the late night and several rounds of cognac Benny had ordered, he arose at his usual hour.

Palmer was nothing if not habitual.

As he descended the three flights of stairs that led to the basement gym, he felt the same sense of gratitude and excitement he experienced since he had moved into this brownstone several years ago. Palmer was not someone who would ever forget how fortunate he had been on so many levels in life.

As for the gym, he had been no sort of athlete as a child and had difficulty with his build and conditioning until college. Only then, with the help of a generous physical education instructor, did he begin to understand the importance of achieving and maintaining a healthy physique.

After a vigorous workout and refreshing shower, he gulped down some orange juice—he was not much of a breakfaster—just as his telephone rang. It was just before eight o'clock and Palmer saw that it was coming into his main business line, which was connected throughout the brownstone.

He picked up the phone and asked, "Who might be calling me at this ungodly hour?"

"Get off the case, Palmer," an unfamiliar voice told him.

"Excuse me?"

"I'm talking about Taub. Stay away from it, you hear me?"

"I hear you, all right. Why not tell me who you are and what the hell you're talking about?"

"I'm just a stranger doing you a favor." Then the line went dead, and Palmer slowly replaced the phone in its cradle.

This was not the sort of thing that normally bothered him, he had handled other cases that inspired crank calls. *Lately*, he thought, *it was becoming an epidemic.*

First there was the Franco matter, which inspired a call from Henry Carrigan, followed by the claim from Sloane Taylor that she learned he was representing Christina from an anonymous message of her own. As for Taub, there was the first tip Palmer received, telling him his former client was going to need help. That was particularly interesting since it came before D'Angelo was murdered. Now, from another source, he was being warned off the Taub case altogether.

Maybe I should set up a straw poll, he thought, *get a reading on public sentiment.*

The first question would be, *How the hell did all these people know about cases that didn't even exist yet?*

The even bigger question was, *What do all these people know that Robbie and I have not figured out yet?*

Palmer shook his head. As he wondered how he and Whyte would tighten things up, a Washington correspondent appeared on television to report an announcement from the Department of Justice.

"*An investigation has begun into RDMO, a pharmaceutical company engaged in genetic engineering. There may be allegations of insider trading as well as possible improper interference with FDA procedures. It is also rumored that Vernon Platt had information about these issues, and his death may delay the currently scheduled congressional hearings, but the DOJ says its own review of these transactions is ongoing.*"

"RDMO," Palmer repeated aloud, then hurried downstairs to his office.

* * *

A LITTLE WHILE later, seated behind his desk, Palmer looked up from his computer when Whyte walked in. "You're early."

"It's going to be a busy day," Whyte told him, then set down his Starbucks coffee cup, a decaf for Palmer, and took his usual seat across the desk.

"Do tell."

"You heard about this drug company, RDMO?"

"I did."

"News reports may be pointing to the missing link in our investigation," Whyte said.

"That company and Vernon Platt."

"How about Edward Franco?"

"Nothing about that, but we should get a list of their officers and directors," Palmer said.

"Already found some on their website, including Franco and your new pal Henry Carrigan."

"You went online? I'm impressed."

"Spare me, it's too early for sarcasm."

Palmer picked up the coffee. "All right. Let's get the full list of officers and directors. And some background into what they're investigating, especially these DOJ and FDA charges?"

"Already on that too," Whyte told him, "and it gets better. Who do you think is on the oversight committee monitoring FDA approvals?"

"I'm afraid to guess."

"None other than Congressman Eugene Scott, father of our almost client Christina."

"If his son-in-law is on the board, he should have recused himself from anything pertaining to RDMO."

"One would think," Whyte agreed, "especially since a recusal would mean so little, since all of his friends would still be on the committee."

Palmer shook his head. "Does your cynicism know no bounds?"

"None."

"He should have stepped down for the sake of appearances, if nothing else."

"Appearances," Whyte said with one of his patented scowls. "How do you think all these people in Congress get so rich? Anyway, I have more."

Palmer waited.

"Hugh Lawson called me at the crack of dawn, says there's a break in the D'Angelo murder case."

"I'm all ears."

"They found the murder weapon in the same dumpster D'Angelo was tossed into, near the Hudson. No prints, but they ran the serial number and guess who it belongs to?"

"Don't tell me Marvin Taub."

"But I must. An S&W .38, registered in his name."

"You've got to be kidding. They don't see this as a setup? Who the hell would throw his own gun along with a dead body in the same garbage bin?"

"Someone who wanted to be sure the murder weapon was found?"

"Precisely," Palmer said.

"For once, you get no argument from me. Or from Lawson, for that matter. You know I don't think much of Taub, but I never said he was stupid. This is a paint-by-numbers frame if ever I saw one. The best part is that they found the gun during what was politely described as a follow-up inspection of the crime scene."

"Lawson is saying it wasn't there when they found D'Angelo?"

"If it was," Whyte said, "no one saw it."

"Ridiculous. And now they're going to arrest Taub?"

"As we speak. He should be making his one phone call to you after they book him downtown."

"Unbelievable."

"That's one word to describe it. What did you get from Parsons?"

"A name," Palmer said. "You ever run across Sammy Burdick?"

Whyte took a moment to run through his memory bank. "Oh yeah, small time bookmaker to the gay crowd. Been picked up a couple of times, never charged with anything serious. How does he fit in this drama?"

"Recently close with Joey D, or so Benny tells me. I think you need to pay him a visit."

"Any idea where this gentleman might be found?"

"Runs around town, tending to his clients. Lives on City Island, which is probably your best starting place."

"Address?"

"Benny texted it to me, with his cell phone number."

"You think he'll take my call?" Whyte took a deep breath and let it out slowly. "No matter, I'll find him. What are you up to?"

"According to what Lawson told you, I assume I'll be at Taub's bail hearing after they process him. First, I have a date."

"Let me guess, your new friend Sloane Taylor."

"Guess again."

"Christina Franco?"

"Close, but wrong again. Since you're out of guesses I'll have to turn all the cards over and tell you, but thanks for playing. I am, in fact, meeting our client's mother."

"The congressman's wife?"

"One and the same. Jeanette Scott and I will be getting together for a little chat this afternoon."

"How nice for you. You have an agenda or is this just a meet and greet?"

"She called early this morning," Palmer said. "Wants to speak with me about Vernon Platt. Since Christina claims he and Mrs. Scott were the best of friends, I intend to find out what she knows."

"She mention her daughter?"

"Not a word."

"I find that a bit odd."

Palmer stuck out his lower lip. "So do I," he said.

"How did she get to you, then?"

Palmer fixed him with concerned look. "Claims she heard about me from our old friend."

CHAPTER SIXTEEN

One of the myriad benefits of Palmer's brownstone was the street-level garage where Palmer kept his black Porsche Cayenne. It also featured a recessed driveway, set far enough back from the street for Whyte to leave his Ford SUV there when he drove in from Connecticut.

This morning, just after eleven, Whyte backed out his Explorer and headed downtown, as Palmer set off in his SUV to meet Jeanette Scott at her home in Westchester County.

Palmer had a pleasant drive, the northbound traffic light at that time of day, and he arrived in the tony Westchester suburb of Bedford ahead of schedule. Pulling into a large circular driveway, he came to a stop and prepared to get out when he saw Jeanette Scott walking toward him.

Aristocratic. That was the first word that occurred to him as he watched her approach. She exuded a patrician air that Palmer figured can only be inborn, a senior version of her daughter.

A thin woman of average height, Jeanette was exceedingly well groomed, coiffed in a glossy hairstyle that was a couple of decades behind the current trends. She was wearing a summer dress of cottony pastels, carrying herself with a stiff bearing and natural formality. But there was also a sense of fragility and, as he stepped out of his vehicle and she came nearer, he could see the lines etched deeply in her face, forming a pattern of sadness around her pale blue eyes. He had difficulty finding any resemblance to Christina, but he realized time can be merciless.

"Mr. Palmer," she said as she reached him.

"Just Palmer is fine," he told her.

"Don't you like your first name?" she asked.

"Not much, to tell you the truth. I've just been called Palmer forever."

"Well, I'm Jeanette," she replied as she held out her hand. "It's very good of you to meet with me." Before he could respond, she said, "Let me show you my gardens."

She led him along a slate path, around the side of the huge colonial-style house, to a vast expanse of property featuring a staggering array of flora. Rhododendrons, azaleas, rose bushes, and hyacinths were in full bloom, and Jeanette took time to point out a few of the other, more unusual plantings as they walked along. She then directed him past a clay tennis court and an enormous greenhouse, explaining that their chef took pride in the fresh vegetables grown there year-round. They ended their walk at a table that had been prepared for them beside the swimming pool.

"Hot as it is today, I should have told you to bring your bathing suit," Mrs. Scott said.

"That's all right," Palmer assured her, "but I hope you don't mind if I take off my sport jacket."

Jeanette Scott smiled, but Palmer could see happiness was not something that came easily to her. He had heard stories about her personal problems and wondered if what he first judged as her upper-class reserve, might be owed in part to something else entirely. After the brief tour of her estate, seated across from Jeanette at the lattice patterned cast iron table, he had another good look at her. Maybe it was the extent of her frailty, or the slight tremor in her upper lip as she spoke. Or perhaps it was the way she appeared to momentarily lose the flow of their conversation and then struggle to regain it. Whatever it was, Palmer recognized an alcoholic in need of a drink, doing her best to maintain control.

When a butler appeared, as if from nowhere, Jeanette said, "Lawrence can bring you a cocktail, whatever your taste may be." Then, looking up at Lawrence, she said, "I'll have a lemonade."

"I think I'll join you," Palmer said, offering the tall butler a pleasant smile. When Jeanette responded with a disappointed look, he said, "As you mentioned, it's a hot day, and I have to drive back to the city."

As they settled into a polite discussion about the gardens, Palmer found something touching about the privileged but miserable life she was living, the sorrow in her eyes, the wasted elegance of her face. She was the sort of woman who could evoke in him every protective instinct he possessed, neither age nor beauty having anything to do with it. Her palpable sense of need was the catalyst that intrigued him, and his belief that he could save her was the thing that drove him.

The Marilyn Monroe Syndrome, Robbie Whyte called it.

After Lawrence walked away, Palmer found himself biting at his lower lip. Trying to sound as casual as possible, he said, "This is a big place. With your husband spending so much time in Washington, it must get lonely up here."

Someone else might have been put off by the comment, but Mrs. Scott seemed pleased he bothered to notice. "It can be, although we have a lovely staff. You've met Henry. Sybil works with Enrique in the kitchen, and Carmen is our housekeeper. As well as my resident den mother and parole officer," she added with a diffident smile.

When Palmer nodded his understanding, they shared a look like co-conspirators but said nothing.

"Nice girl, Carmen, although she can certainly be strict," she went on. "Still, I admire a cleaning woman who's managing to put two children through college. We live in a wonderful age, don't we Mr. Palmer?"

"Yes, we do. And please, just plain Palmer."

"Palmer," she said, considering the name again. "I like that. It really is sort of a first name, isn't it?"

"Depends where you're from," he said with a grin. "Where I grew up in the Bronx, Palmer as a first name would have been a problem. There were times even Russell was pushing my luck."

She appeared to be thinking it over. "Around here people name their sons things like McBundy or Granville. Wouldn't get very far with a name like that in the Bronx, would you?"

"Not unless I learned how to fight really well, which I never did."

After a brief laugh she paused, and it looked to him as if she was trying to recall what they'd been talking about. "Ah yes," she said, obviously relieved that her memory had not failed her. "It *is* a big home. And it *can* become lonely, servants notwithstanding."

"What do you do for fun here in Bedford? You get on that tennis court much?"

"Me? Oh, heavens no, not for years. Are you a tennis player, Palmer?"

"I like to think so."

"Then I must have you up some time. I'll have some tennis playing friends over." She hesitated before saying, "I wouldn't think tennis was something you played as a child. Growing up where you did."

Now it was Palmer's turn to be put off by a comment, but he was not, since it was coming from her. "You're absolutely right," he said. "There weren't a lot of tennis courts in my neighborhood. Learned to play in college, still catching up. On the other hand, if stickball ever becomes a professional sport, I'll be a valuable free agent."

"So other than tennis and stickball, what do you do for fun?"

"I asked first."

Jeanette Scott nodded. "Nothing has been fun for me lately," she admitted. "Not since I heard about Vernon."

Palmer waited, but the melancholy in her eyes told him she wasn't about to say anything more about it, at least not yet. "That's what you wanted to see me about."

"We'll discuss it after lunch is served." She turned and Palmer followed her gaze, watching Lawrence come across the lush, manicured lawn with their lemonade. He was followed by a woman armed with a platter containing poached salmon, assorted vegetables, and a bowl of fresh cut fruit.

Since the table had already been set, it only took a few moments for their meal to be laid out, after which Lawrence and the woman were gone.

"That was Carmen?"

"No, that was Sybil." With a rueful look, she lowered her voice and confessed, "Carmen would only have come out here if one of us had ordered cocktails." Then she said, "Please, help yourself."

They filled their plates and began to eat when Palmer asked the obvious question. "Why me?"

Jeanette blinked. "I'm sorry?"

"Why would you want to speak with me about the death of Vernon Platt?"

Instead of answering the question, she said, "It was a terrible moment, when I heard about Vernon. Broke my heart."

"I understand the two of you were very close."

"It's not too much to say he was the best friend I've ever had. Old friends are irreplaceable Palmer, especially the loyal ones."

"I couldn't agree more," he said, then studied her for another few seconds. "Are you aware your daughter has come to see me?" He paused, adding, "For some advice."

She nodded. "She wants to divorce Edward."

Palmer did not respond, instead tasting the cold poached salmon with mustard sauce. "It's delicious," he said.

"Good. Now, where was I? Oh yes, friends. I receive upsetting news from time to time. At my age it's understandable. Someone getting divorced, or taken ill, or failing in business. But death—" she said, then stopped, laying down her fork and staring at it, as if she had no idea what to do with it.

"Your daughter told me you knew Platt most of your life."

"Oh yes. Since we were teenagers, can you believe it? Vernon was a beautiful man." She looked up from her silverware. "Did you know him?"

"Worked on a matter with him several years ago."

"It's a horrible thing, for him to be murdered that way."

Palmer noted the certainty of her statement, and how Jeanette now met his even gaze. Suddenly, she was no longer a lost soul looking for salvation in a bottle. Her intensity was unmistakable, and those pale blue eyes told Palmer that her moments of lucidity only made her awareness more painful.

"You met Vernon," she finally said, "you must have had a sense of what kind of man he was. His integrity. His intelligence."

Palmer watched and waited.

"Do you believe he would take his own life?"

Palmer was struck by the way she asked it, as if it were not a question at all, that the conclusion was obvious. He said, "Suicide is a strange thing, Jeanette. People do it for many different reasons, in many different ways. I admit I don't understand how anyone can take their own life. Perhaps if someone has a terminal illness with no remaining hope." He paused. "But people do kill themselves, and we often don't know why, do we?"

"Too true. Some may even feel they have good reason to end things and lack the necessary courage," she observed wistfully. "But I can tell you this, Vernon was not a man who would take his own life. He was murdered. I could never be convinced otherwise. Do you agree?"

Palmer was not going to share what little he knew about the case from Whyte's discussion with Hugh Lawson. All he would say was, "For what it's worth, I believe you're right."

Mrs. Scott managed a smile and picked up her fork.

"But you didn't have me up here only to ask my opinion," Palmer said. "You could have done that on the phone."

"You're right," she admitted. "I needed to see if everything Cameron Pinckney thought about you is true."

The mention of that name caught Palmer by surprise. "You knew Mr. Pinckney?"

"My dear young man," she said with an amused smile, "I know everyone worth knowing."

He was uncomfortable discussing Pinckney, but resisted the impulse to ask what details, if any, she might know about his relationship with the man. All he said was, "That's quite a claim."

"It happens to be true. Which provides the benefit of knowing whom I can trust and whom I cannot. Some years ago, Cameron told me you were a lawyer I could count on if I ever had a problem. Which is why I've asked you here."

"I just assumed you heard that your daughter had come to see me."

"Of course I did, which is when I recalled Cameron speaking so highly of you."

Palmer decided to let that go, at least for now.

"But I have no interest in discussing Christina. Not now." She looked directly into his eyes as she said, "You must understand. I am not willing to allow Vernon's death to remain some unsolved riddle. If left to the wrong people, it will not even rate a footnote in the annals of corruption."

Palmer found it difficult to believe her decision to call him, and her daughter's interest in having him represent her, was a coincidence. He hated coincidences, especially if Cameron Pinckney was involved. For now, he simply repeated, "Corruption?"

"Yes, Palmer, corruption. Or political expediency. Or power brokering. Call it anything you like, but if you're half the lawyer Cameron believed you to be, then you already know what I'm talking about." Her eyes became alive again, this time with anger and determination and something else he could not quite make out—perhaps hatred—as she said, "It all leads to the same conclusion. Vernon was an important man, which means someone had to have an important reason to have him murdered. And then go to the trouble of having it staged as a suicide. I know that sounds awfully melodramatic, but there you have it."

"And you want to find out who and why."

She relaxed. "That's correct. My loneliness, as you perceive it, has advantages. I have the luxury of caring and ruminating and speculating, all without interference. And I have my gardens."

"Your gardens?"

"You asked what I do for fun. I love to see things grow, which is why winter is truly so bleak for me. Thank heavens for the greenhouse."

"I don't know anything about gardening, but I know more than I'd like to about corruption and deceit and crime."

"That's what I've been led to believe. Which is why I want you to investigate Vernon's death for me."

Palmer took a deep breath and let it out slowly before responding. "It's a little outside my line of work."

"Your partner is an accomplished private investigator. Former police detective. The two of you take on difficult and unusual cases and, as you know, I have no concern about finances. I'll pay you for your time and for any professional support you require."

Palmer shook his head. "I'm an attorney, Jeanette. As you say, I do my best for people in need of legal assistance. Unfortunately, Vernon Platt is beyond my help."

"But I'm not. Please remember, Palmer, I knew Vernon before I knew my husband. The pain I feel in losing him is indescribable."

Palmer realized he was gnawing at his lower lip again. He couldn't think of a single logical reason to do what she asked, yet he knew he was not going to refuse. "You have to tell me everything you know, everything you suspect. You mentioned corruption."

"I did."

"There are a lot of rumors swirling around the testimony Platt was going to give."

"I'm aware of that."

"The fallout might have harmed a lot of people, destroyed reputations, even some of those close to you. Have you considered that?"

The look of grief returned to her eyes. "Have you met my husband?"

"I have not."

"You're certain?"

"I think I'd remember meeting a United States congressman," he told her with a smile.

"But you have met my daughter. You've agreed to represent her."

"Nothing official yet. Let's just say we've been having discussions about her issues."

"It's all utter nonsense," she said with a dismissive wave of the hand. "She and Edward have some growing up to do, nothing more."

Palmer waited again without speaking.

"It's rubbish, you know, the idea the two of them divorcing. Just one of the high-stakes games they like to play."

"I'm sure you know I can't discuss any of that with you, even though you are her mother."

"Of course," Jeanette said, "and that's a knife that cuts both ways." She leaned forward slightly as she said, "I don't want my daughter or my husband to know you're looking into Vernon's death for me. That's critical to me."

Palmer resisted the impulse to smile again. He hadn't agreed to do anything for her concerning Platt's death, and she was already creating conditions. *Wealthy people*, he said to himself, but all he did was nod.

"If you can't promise me that, I ask that this discussion be held in total confidence and you can forget my request. But I do want help. *Your* help, Palmer. And the fact that you don't know my husband is an added benefit."

In that instant she had gone from making demands to pleading with him, this woman who was not accustomed to requesting things she might not receive.

"You don't have to concern yourself with confidentiality, I take my professional ethics very seriously."

"Well then?"

"Your daughter knows we're meeting today?"

"Of course she does," Jeanette said with a dismissive wave of her hand. "But Christina will naturally believe we'll be talking about her. She and Edward assume everything is about them."

Palmer could not stifle a laugh.

"Let her think what she wants," Jeanette said. "She knows that I'm devastated by what's occurred, but my family must not know I'm having you look into Vernon's murder."

Palmer wondered if he could insulate himself from the trouble this might create. What he could not escape was her determination, her certainty, and the desperate way she looked at him.

He said, "What you told me earlier, about things cutting both ways—"

"That I will not disclose the true nature of our relationship? You have my word."

"Then I return to my earlier concern. I may uncover things that impact your family, are you prepared for that?"

"I am," she said without hesitation.

"Then there's a corollary to that. You have to tell me everything you know about why Vernon Platt was subpoenaed by congress."

He watched as she thought it over. "First you find out what you can. If you come back to me with something meaningful, I may be able to provide some insight."

"All right," Palmer said as he sank his fork into a piece of fish, "let me see what I can find out for you."

Then his thoughts turned to the name Jeanette brought up earlier in their discussion, the man she claimed as the reason she trusted Palmer.

Cameron Pinckney.

CHAPTER SEVENTEEN

The unusual matter involving Cameron Pinckney took place several years ago and was all over the news at the time.

As Whyte described it back then, when Palmer asked if he had heard of the case, "Sure. Pinckney is a ninety-year-old gazillionaire. Married to a young wannabe actress from L.A. Charlotte something or other, with Double D's and pouty lips."

"I suppose you also know he's asked this young woman for a divorce."

"Those are the headlines in the *Post*. What about it?"

Palmer paused for effect, then told him, "I met with Pinckney. He may want to retain me for the divorce."

Whyte emitted a low whistle and said, "What the hell."

"Really something, right?" Palmer replied.

"No offense but, regardless of the help you gave me, you don't exactly specialize in family law. What brought him to your door?"

"I still have some friends at my old firm downtown who throw me an occasional referral. They were in the middle of some billion-dollar M&A deal for Pinckney when this came up. They wouldn't touch a contested divorce with a whaling harpoon—such crude matters are beneath them. When they recommended a few big-time divorce lawyers, Pinckney shot them all down."

"Why?"

"Not his first rodeo. This young woman is his fourth wife, and he regards the matrimonial bar as a bunch of diseased bottom-feeders."

"Who could argue?"

"I'm told there were three senior partners in the room, and they all agreed he should speak with me."

Whyte couldn't suppress a smile, and Palmer felt like he was looking at a proud uncle who just saw his nephew knock in the winning run in a little league game. "Look how far you've come," Whyte said.

"We'll see. I haven't signed him up yet, but he and I covered a lot of ground in our meeting. Pinckney isn't kidding when he told me this will not be a typical divorce."

"Not with the amount of money involved, and a woman on the other side of the equation about sixty years younger than he is."

"It's more than that. This also has some nasty twists to it."

"Such as?"

"It appears there's a bit of blackmail here."

"Just a bit?"

"Pinckney says she's got some pretty embarrassing pictures of him and no doubt she'll use them."

"When you say embarrassing—"

"Let's just say sexually explicit and leave it at that."

Whyte waited a beat, then began laughing. "Ninety years old and he's worried about sexually explicit photos? He ought to pay to have them published."

Palmer shook his head. "He's a captain of industry. He's a father, a grandfather, and a great-grandfather several times over. This is extortion, and I need to stop her before she gets any traction."

"Sorry to be so critical, but there's no fool like an old fool," Whyte said.

"Not critical at all." Then he held up his hand. "He said as much himself."

"What can I do to help?"

"I need you to run down a lead."

"Let's have it."

"I've been looking into Charlotte Pinckney's background. As you said, she was in Hollywood when they met, trying to become an actress, but all I've found so far is some soft-core porn."

"How soft?"

"Nothing that's going to stop her from trying to squeeze him, not with this much money up for grabs. She took her clothes off then, I doubt she's going to be worried about her reputation now. I need something more."

"Like what?"

"I have information that could lead to something useful."

"And whatever it is, you want me to find it."

"I *expect* you to find it."

"What makes you so sure there's something to find?"

The way Palmer looked at Whyte was all the answer he needed.

"Where do I start?"

"I'll give you what I have," Palmer told him.

Over the course of the next two weeks, Palmer continued to look into the case on his end, while Whyte traveled to the west coast to check out Charlotte's background. What they found turned the case upside down and ended, not with a divorce—but an annulment. Not only did they arrange for Pinckney to walk away without having to pay a dime, but they had enough leverage to force Charlotte into turning over all the photos and agreeing to a non-disclosure and non-disparagement agreement.

It was more than a victory, it was an absolute triumph.

After it was all done, Pinckney visited Palmer and Whyte to discuss the end game. In those days, Palmer was still sharing the suite with other attorneys on Third Avenue. His office was small and plain, the furniture nouveau cheap, featuring Formica and chrome, the sole redeeming feature being a large window providing a generous view of New York's east side. When Pinckney joined them, all three chairs were taken.

As the conversation began, Palmer found his client to be far more merciful than anticipated. "People think I'm a skinflint," he told them. "It's not true."

Palmer was not about to judge what a man does with billions of dollars and offered no reaction. He studied his client, seeing that the man was wrestling with all that had occurred.

At ninety, Pinckney looked his age. He was thin and frail, his skin almost translucent, the collar of his shirt too big for his wrinkled neck. But his pale blue eyes were as vibrant as a young man's and his voice was firm and clear. "I give more money away than you can imagine, all of it anonymously. Learned long ago it's easier that way. You start making a fuss about what you donate, and everyone lines up with their hands out. Who needs that bullshit?"

Palmer smiled. "Never been in that position, I wouldn't know."

"Trust me boys, it's a lot of hooey. You give them a barrel of dough, they put your name on a museum or a theatre, then you drop dead and someone else comes along with a bigger check and your huge sign gets tossed in the dumpster. And what does it matter anyway? You're already dead, right? The point is to do good deeds when you can. Not for the credit, just for the satisfaction of helping. Make sense?"

"Does to me," Palmer replied.

Now Pinckney studied Palmer for a moment. "I believe you. Checked you out plenty before I let you handle this case. Had helluva lot at risk." He uttered a short, raspy laugh. "Have to admit, didn't expect things to go down *this* way."

"You also have Mr. Whyte to thank for that," Palmer said with a nod in his friend's direction.

"I suppose I do," Pinckney said. "So now what?"

Palmer was careful about what he said next. "As I understand it, she's still living in your apartment on Fifth Avenue. We can have her removed and you won't owe her a thing."

His gaze narrowing, Pinckney asked, "You figure that's what I oughtta do?"

Palmer took a deep breath before saying, "No sir, I don't."

Pinckney allowed himself a thin smile. "Neither do I. Had some fun with that girl, believe me. At my age, pharmaceuticals are a miraculous thing."

Whyte did not bother to stifle his laugh, and it was clear the old man did not mind.

Pinckney said, "I've got plenty of other houses I can live in. Got them all over the place. I think she should stay in the apartment for a year or so, give her time to figure things out."

"That's very good of you."

Pinckney thought it over. "I suppose so. I'll write her a check, let her keep the clothes and jewelry I bought her. Then, I suppose, that's it."

Palmer took a moment to examine him. "If you don't mind me saying so, it sounds like you'll miss her."

"Hell yeah, I will. Been married a few times, had a lot of women in between those wives. Let me tell you boys something, that girl knows her way around the bedroom. Don't want to be any more graphic than that, but believe me, I'll miss her all right." After a pause, he went on. "But she betrayed me, and you know what they say about a woman who's done you wrong. There's no going back."

Palmer and Whyte waited.

"Shame of it is, she played me for a payday. Shit, if she had just hung in there, I'll be gone soon enough, and even with the prenup she signed, she would've been set for life." He thought it over. "Instead, she made me a punch line for the tabloids. No, I don't care how good she is in bed, we're finished."

"I understand," Palmer said.

"I know you do," the old man said, followed by a deep sigh. "Which brings me to the matter of you fellas. I got your bill, and it's ridiculously low."

Palmer shrugged. "We did what we did, and it worked out. A lot faster than we imagined, I admit that, but I charged our time and expenses. That's all we're entitled to."

"Not so." Pinckney shook his head. "You have a pretty good idea how much money was involved."

Palmer laughed. "It's difficult for me to get my mind around it, but yes, I have an idea."

"What I'm saying, is there's billing your time and then there's getting paid for a result. You turned the tables, made her the joke, and I came away looking like a prince for not pressing charges against her. There's tremendous value in all that, not to mention how difficult a contested divorce would have been for me at my age. And for my family."

"We're glad it worked out."

Pinckney nodded. "I told you, I had you checked out. Seems you have an unusual attitude towards the law."

"It's not unusual to me."

"Maybe so. But I know a lot of lawyers, and almost every one of them is all about the money. You have a reputation for actually trying to help people. The way you helped me."

"That's nice of you to say."

"The hell with nice. I'll bet if I hadn't been a billionaire, you would've taken my case and done the same thing anyway."

Palmer smiled. "Maybe, but if you weren't wealthy there wouldn't have been a case like this."

Pinckney laughed again. "I guess that's true. But you know what I'm saying." He leaned forward in the chair, both hands resting on the desk. "You use your skills to solve problems for people who need help, and I intend to work out something to make it possible for you to continue doing just that."

Then they said their goodbyes, and Pinckney left.

But, as it turned out, that was not the end of their story.

A week later, a lawyer from a large trusts and estates firm showed up at Palmer's small office. He had made an appointment, explaining that he represented Cameron Pinckney and had a proposal to make on his client's behalf.

Palmer watched as the man took a seat. In his three-piece suit, striped tie, and rimless glasses, he looked as conservative as any of the partners in Palmer's old firm. Opening his briefcase, the man pulled out a sheaf of papers and got right down to business.

"Mr. Pinckney owns a three-story brownstone at 113 East 64th Street, between Lexington and Park Avenues. There's a comfortable three-bedroom residence on the top two floors. The main floor has a suite of offices. The building is currently vacant."

Palmer waited.

"Mr. Pinckney wants to give you the building."

"Excuse me?"

"We are aware of your financial circumstances, so Mr. Pinckney will pay all of the taxes and conveyance fees involved in the transfer. In addition, he is arranging a trust that my firm will administer. You will be a beneficiary of that trust for life." He handed some of the documents across the desk to Palmer. "This sets out the monthly payments you'll receive, which include an annual cost of living increase."

Palmer stared at the papers for a few seconds, then looked up. "Is this some sort of prank? Did Robbie Whyte put you up to this?"

"No indeed," the man said without a trace of mirth. "In fact, Mr. Whyte is the other beneficiary of the trust." Producing another set of contracts, he said, "These are the financial arrangements for Mr. Whyte."

Palmer sat back in his chair, feeling as if he were in a free fall.

"Mr. Pinckney has a proviso to all of this."

"I'm listening."

"He believes your law practice has been geared to help people in trouble, rather than to simply enrich yourself. This trust is intended to remove the necessity for you to earn fees or pay for offices or lodging. You can obviously earn whatever income you like, but this will enable you to take cases where you provide a benefit to those most in need of your assistance, including those who cannot afford to pay. Either way, rich or poor, it will not matter. The only things that matter are the circumstances of the client and the integrity of your work."

Palmer shook his head. "How do you judge such a thing? And who's going to make that determination?"

The man smiled for the first time since he arrived, then pulled out another document. "As you can see, Mr. Pinckney has laid out some ground rules, but in the end, he believes it will be up to you."

"I'm going to monitor my own actions?"

"My firm will be keeping an eye on you, you can be sure of that," he said, returning to his serious demeanor. Holding out the last of the papers, the lawyer said, "This agreement describes the arrangement. Once you sign, we will immediately put all of this in place."

"The brownstone, the trust—"

"Exactly."

"Shouldn't I speak with Mr. Pinckney—"

"He prefers you sign everything first. As strange as this may seem," the man said, with a look that betrayed his own fascination, "Mr. Pinckney thinks you may try and talk him out of this."

The lawyer waited as Palmer read the agreement, which had already been signed by Cameron Pinckney. And with that, Palmer's life—and Whyte's along with him—were changed forever.

When Jeanette Scott used Pinckney's name as the reason she had called Palmer, it sent up a red flag. The Trust was confidential and, if Pinckney was ever going to reveal any of the details, Palmer doubted he would share them with Mrs. Scott—for more than one reason, all of which seemed obvious.

If Palmer and Whyte were going to continue with the Franco case, not to mention providing information to Jeanette, they now had one more reason to tread carefully.

CHAPTER EIGHTEEN

Federal Plaza in downtown Manhattan is a monolith that houses innumerable government agencies, most identified by an assortment of acronyms. Robbie Whyte went there to look into the RDMO investigation, starting with an agent he knew at the local office of the FBI.

The agent he spoke with, name of Brian Smith, had worked with him years back on a joint task force sting, but this afternoon Whyte found their past cooperation did not count for much. As soon as Whyte explained why he had come, Smith told him he was in the wrong place.

"This is not the NYPD, Robbie. You have less pull down here than the cleaning lady."

"Never sell a cleaning lady short," Whyte told him. "They see and hear a lot more than you think."

"Very amusing," Smith replied with a blank look.

"All I want is a heads up on this probe that earned Platt a subpoena from DC."

"No can do. As soon as Platt took that swan dive, the lid on this case got screwed on tight."

"I assume the hearings are going forward anyway, is that true?"

"Nice try. Maybe you'll have better luck with one of your old cronies in the US Attorney's office."

Whyte thanked him for nothing, then followed Smith's advice. Unfortunately, the temperature he encountered in the federal prosecutor's officer was even chillier. Platt's death was hanging over their investigation, and no one wanted to be the source of a leak, regardless of their prior dealings with Whyte and his well-deserved reputation for discretion.

"You can read about it in the papers," he was told by one of the Assistant AG's he knew. "That is, after we make our next announcement."

After striking out there, Whyte hoped he might get some traction in the FDA compliance office, where his contact was of a more personal nature.

Vera Alexander was a sharp, attractive African American woman in her late-forties. Years ago, just before he left the NYPD, Whyte teamed up with Vera and a group of other feds on a case involving a large shipment of opioids entering the Port of New York from China. Whyte helped track the purchasers, a band of Triads who were planning to take delivery of the goods in Chinatown. The joint task force successfully brought the operation down, he and Vera dated for a while, but she ended the affair, concluding he was still not over his divorce.

As she bluntly put it to him one night during dinner, "You're a great guy, Robbie, but you're damaged goods. Straighten yourself out and you'll make some woman very happy."

"But not you."

"Not anyone, not now."

He knew she was right. They went their separate ways, managing to remain friends, getting together every now and then to catch up. Some time ago, Vera found a better candidate for her life partner. As she explained one evening when she and Whyte met for drinks, her new beau was neither damaged nor any sort of cop, which she saw as two beautiful things.

Whyte called ahead and, when he arrived, Vera was waiting for him in the entry area. She walked him through security and showed him into her office, closed the door, and got right to it. "You said you want to know about RDMO."

"That's why I'm here."

"Any particular reason for your curiosity, or have you developed a sudden interest in medical research?"

"You could guess."

"Vernon Platt."

Whyte nodded. "He was slated to testify before congress next week. It just came out that RDMO was one of the featured topics."

"Why would that matter to you?"

"We have a client that could be affected by the investigation."

"We? Does that refer to you and your friend Palmer?"

"It does."

She nodded. "And when you say *affected*, might this client of yours potentially be one of the bad deed doers?"

Whyte shook his head. "Innocent bystander."

"And I should take your word for that?"

Whyte paused for a moment. He thought she still looked very good, her cocoa skin smooth, her features even, her eyes dark and intelligent. *Might have made a mistake letting you go*, he thought, but all he said was, "You know you can trust me."

She only paused for a moment before saying, "All right, here's what I can tell you. Our application process is the toughest in the world. Everyone knows that, especially Big Pharma, since they're constantly bitching about how we're hung up on tests, tests, and more tests. My answer is, excuse the hell out of us for protecting the public."

Whyte grinned. "Seems I've heard that speech from you before."

Vera returned the smile. "Yes, you have. But this bunch of jokers at RDMO, they're another story entirely. Strictly off the record, all right?"

Whyte held up three fingers. "Scout's honor," he said.

"They've tried every conceivable end run, attempting to shortcut our protocols and exaggerating positive test results. The worst is how they use political connections to strong-arm our compliance officers. Everything they do comes at us with an angle or a twist, they couldn't draw a straight line with a ruler."

"I hear the company is involved in genetic engineering, trying to create treatments for some serious diseases. Don't get upset with me for asking, but that should be a good thing, right?"

"When could you ever get me upset, Robbie?"

Whyte narrowed his gaze. "There was that night at Raoul's, after too many martinis."

Vera laughed. "That's the best you could come up with?"

"It was one of several moments that came to mind."

She allowed her smile to slowly fade, then said, "Look, I admit the medical technology they're pushing will obviously be wonderful if it works, but that's a big *if.* It's what the FDA is here to determine. It's why we have strict procedures, so we're sure there are no unintended side effects. We don't want them using a bunch of very sick people as human guinea pigs."

"Understood."

"Our people in DC believe RDMO may have some good ideas, but they also think the company takes shortcuts that make a marathon look like a sprint. They even tried to take advantage of the coronavirus epidemic."

"How did they do that?"

"When the government worked to fast track the search for a vaccine for Covid-19, that was a good idea, within reason, and we worked with big and small pharma to make Operation Warp Speed happen. These jokers tried to piggyback on all that, as if it opened the door to speeding up the process for every new drug in the pipeline going forward."

"That seems low to me."

"Low is right. You should dig deep on them, you'll find plenty of dirt down there."

"You have names?"

"Names? All you need is an annual report."

"You happen to have one you could share?"

"You can get it online, you know."

"I did the best I could." With a shrug, he added, "You've seen me in front of a computer, Vera."

"All right," she said, then went to a file cabinet and handed him a copy. "Just remember that—"

"I know the drill. I didn't get any of this from you."

She smiled.

Whyte had a quick look at the list of officers and directors, several of the names having already become familiar to him. Shoving the report into his jacket pocket, he asked, "How are things with William?"

"Walter," she said. "They're fine, but that doesn't mean you don't owe me dinner."

"A debt I'll be happy to pay. And if you ever get tired of him—"

"Good luck with your case, Robbie," she said, cutting him off. "Just keep me informed."

After he was done with Vera, Whyte got back in his car, headed over the Third Avenue Bridge, and traveled the Bruckner Expressway to the Thruway, exiting onto the access road to City Island. He was there to see Sammy Burdick, the friend of Joey D'Angelo who Benny Parsons had mentioned to Palmer.

City Island is an odd little chunk of land just off the eastern tip of the Bronx. It's a bit of New England with a New York accent, devoted to marinas, seafood restaurants, and a collection of modest homes. The small island is bisected by one long avenue crossed by streets running left and right to the water on both sides. Whyte drove along that main road, City Island Avenue, until he came to the street name Palmer had been given by Benny Parsons. Turning left, he came to a stop before the bulkhead at the end of the short lane.

Whyte was early for the appointment he made with Burdick, which turned out to be a good thing. When he walked up to the little cottage and knocked on the screen door, he found Burdick preparing to leave.

"Sammy?" he inquired through the screen. "I'm Robbie Whyte."

"Uh, yeah. I tried your number just now, turns out I've gotta go meet someone."

Without being asked, Whyte opened the door and stepped inside the rustic little cape style home. It was decorated in an utterly predictable marine motif, with large shells for ashtrays, cheap prints of sailboats on the wall, and various other nautical touches.

Burdick looked to be in his late fifties, about the same height as Whyte, five-foot-seven or so. He had light brown hair, a protruding gut, and a face that was positively Delancey Street. From what he had been told, Whyte was surprised to find that the man did not look to be gay in the slightest, as if that might be some universal quality.

"I didn't get your call," Whyte lied.

Burdick hesitated before saying, "Look, I really shouldn't be talking to you." Then he began nervously rearranging what appeared to be a pile of betting slips on his dining room table.

Eyeing the paperwork, Whyte said, "You run a fairly casual operation for a bookmaker. If a cop ever walks up to your door he'll probably have to stop laughing before he makes the arrest."

"Arrest me?" Burdick looked up from the papers. "I've been here for years. With all the online sites they have nowadays, I'm not important enough for them to bother with."

"From what I hear, someone thinks you're important for other reasons."

Burdick blinked but said nothing.

"Benny Parsons is worried you may be in trouble."

Burdick picked up an envelope from the top of a knotty pine bookcase beside the table. "I just found this at my door. After I spoke with you."

Whyte took the envelope and peered inside. There was nothing there but a bullet. No note, no writing inside or out. "No greeting card?"

Burdick responded with a miserable look. "I think the message is clear enough."

The detective nodded.

"Look, Benny Parsons is a good friend of mine. We'll remain good friends. But I'm sorry he gave you my name. And I don't want to talk with you."

Holding up the envelope, Whyte said, "I may be the one person you *should* talk with."

Burdick shook his head. "This has nothing to do with me. It has to do with Joey. So if you don't mind—" He did not finish, instead watching as Whyte walked over to the sofa and sat down.

"I'm suggesting you could use some help," the detective said.

"That's not how I see it."

"Enlighten me," Whyte said.

"It's clear that whoever left this wants me to keep my mouth shut, which I'm taking as good advice. Which also means you shouldn't think I'm rude if I ask you to get the hell out of my house."

"I'm already here. What's the difference if we talk for a few minutes? Your place isn't bugged, is it?"

Burdick remained standing. "What do you want to know?"

"Like you already mentioned, it's all about Joey D'Angelo."

After wavering one last time, Burdick said, "Okay, but let's make it fast."

"Fast as you want."

Burdick pulled a chair out from under the table and sat facing Whyte. "Joey and I were friends, what of it?"

"Lovers," Whyte corrected him, curious to see how he might react.

"Yes, lovers," Burdick admitted, as if the distinction did not matter. "Joey was a piece of shit, but he was an appealing piece of shit. And he could charm the bark off a birch. He used me, took money from me, then he'd be gone. I wouldn't see him for weeks, then he'd show up again. Walk in here like he owned the place. 'Hiya Sammy. How are ya Sammy? There's a party downtown, Sammy.' And I'd go with him, have some fun, you get the drift. He'd be around for a coupla weeks, then he'd be off again. I hadn't seen him for a month when I heard he was dead. I'm sorry about it, I am, but Joey was a bad habit."

"I'm still listening."

"He always wanted more than what he had. Something better, something different. He used his access to coke like a passport. He moved between a low-life crowd and some high rollers, went with the action, always on the take."

Whyte glanced at the man's generous middle. "You don't look like a cocaine user."

"I'm not. I became Joey's safe haven, that's really what I was to him. He'd come here to chill every once in a while. That's why I always knew he'd be back." He paused, and Whyte wondered if he was reflecting on the fact that Joey would not be returning. "I'm better off," he concluded, as if confirming the thought.

"Do you think Marvin Taub killed him?"

"Taub?" he reacted with a snort. "Not my favorite person, but no, I don't think he killed Joey. Why would he?" He stopped again. "But who the hell knows what people will do anymore? The world's become a crazy place." Burdick had relaxed, at least slightly. "Joey had a lot of enemies. I'd warn him that he was running with a bad crowd. That he was going to get himself in a fix. But he never listened. He wanted to be a superstar."

"A superstar? At what?"

"At anything. Everything was appearances with Joey. How you looked. What you wore. Who you were with. That was the big one, who you were with. Joey had all the character of a cold knish. All starch, no substance."

If Sammy Burdick was Joey's lover, Whyte wondered how his enemies felt about him. "If Taub didn't kill him, who do you think did?"

That question brought Burdick back to the present. "Whoever sent me that message," he said, pointing at the envelope that was still in Whyte's hand.

"You say he liked to run with a fancy crowd. You ever know him to get close to anyone like that?"

Burdick smiled. "Sure. He was attractive and gay. He had a great line of bullshit and, like I told you, contacts for all sorts of quality drugs. That's how he made himself valuable to people." He got to his feet. "But enough already. I don't know who killed him, and I don't know why Benny sent you here. All I know from that bullet is that someone thinks

I should dummy up," he said, nodding at the envelope. "And that's exactly what I'm gonna do. Now I'd like you to go."

Whyte stood. "Just a couple more questions. Did you know the names of any of these bigshots Joey ran with?"

"Not really. I mean, I met a few of them. Most of the time Joey thought I wasn't glitzy enough for that part of his life, but I went to a few of those parties."

"You ever meet a man named Vernon Platt?"

"No," he said, but the look on his face made it clear he knew the name, and it made him nervous.

"You ever hear Joey mention him?"

"They got together once in a while I think. He's the one who jumped off his balcony the other night."

"That's him."

"Never met the guy," Burdick said, then asked, "Did you know him?"

Whyte thought it an odd question, but said, "I met him."

"Smallest town in the world, New York City."

Whyte smiled. "I've heard it said."

"Look, I'm sorry to be rude, but it's not as if I know anything, so what else is there for me to say?"

"You could give me some other names."

Burdick was shaking his head before Whyte finished the request. "I don't know anything and I'm not saying anything more."

"How about Peter Frost?"

Whyte saw the name send a flash of fear across Burdick's face, but he said nothing.

"Well," Whyte said with a nod, "whatever you say to me, it's obvious someone dangerous thinks you know something. You better be careful."

"Yeah, sure," Burdick replied glumly.

"You have my number if you think of anything," Whyte told him. Then he handed Burdick the envelope and left.

CHAPTER NINETEEN

Palmer was driving back from his lunch with Jeanette Scott when Maureen called. Marvin Taub had phoned the office. He had been processed through the system and was set for arraignment in the criminal court at 100 Centre Street, so Palmer turned toward the West Side Highway and headed downtown.

It was almost four o'clock by the time he was standing at the counsel table in the dingy old courtroom on the main floor of the Criminal Court Building. He was reading the information form on the charges when two officers brought Taub in from the holding cell.

The bailiff called out the docket number and announced the name of the case. "People of the State of New York against Marvin Taub."

"Defendant over here," the court officer said to Taub, pointing him to a spot beside Palmer.

"Counselor, state your appearance for the record," the court clerk instructed.

Palmer recited his name and address for the stenographer, then had a good look at his client. Taub was in his street clothes, appearing paler than when they met at his bar a couple of days ago. His arrogant smile had been replaced by a look of concern.

"Does counsel waive the reading of the rights and charges?" the judge inquired.

"If it please the court," Palmer said, "I would like to approach the bench."

"Come forward," the judge directed.

Palmer was joined by the assistant district attorney who was handling courtroom AR2 that afternoon. She was a young woman Palmer had never met, but the presiding judge was someone he had appeared before several times over the years.

"Good morning, Judge."

"Good morning, Mr. Palmer. What have we got here?" Taub's arraignment was one of several on the calendar this afternoon, and the judge wanted to move things along.

"What we have here, Judge, is a minor travesty. My client was arrested on suspicion of manslaughter. According to the criminal information, the only connection he has to the homicide is that a handgun registered to him was found at the crime scene. No fingerprints were on the weapon and, incredibly, the revolver did not even turn up until the day *after* the body of the victim was discovered." He held up his copy of the charges. "There is no other nexus between my client and the incident in question."

The judge managed a tired grin. "Are you arguing for a summary dismissal, Mr. Palmer?"

"That would work, Judge, but before I even make such an argument, I would like to know why my client has been held in custody for more than twenty-four hours while the DA's office was trying to invent a charge against him?"

Staring down at Palmer, the judge said, "The fact that your client's gun appears to be the murder weapon, whether it was found at the scene a day after the shooting or tomorrow, is reasonably incriminating." He then looked to the young assistant prosecutor.

"Your Honor," the woman began, "this arraignment is being conducted within the statutory period. Defense counsel is aware that the issue of his client's involvement in this homicide will be reviewed by a Grand Jury. We see no impropriety in the way this case is being handled."

Palmer responded with a frown. "Since when can the police hold a citizen in jail while they try to make a case against him? And while we're at it, since when does it make sense for a murderer to take the trouble of wiping his fingerprints off a murder weapon registered in his own name and then leave the gun behind? Which weapon, as I've said, was not noticed by anyone the day the victim was found. It magically appeared the day *after* the body was carted off. Come on, Counselor, this a frame that belongs in the Metropolitan Museum of Art."

Now it was the judge's turn to frown. "A bit trite, Mr. Palmer. Anything else before I hear argument on bail?"

"No, your Honor."

"Very well, your impromptu motion for dismissal will be ignored at this time," the judge advised him. "You will have the right to file a formal motion at a later date. As to bail, I want those arguments on the record, if you would return to your places."

Back at the counsel table, Palmer made his statement, insisting that Taub should be released on his own recognizance. "He has no history of violence, is a life-long resident of this city, and conducts his business here."

"The defendant's business," the prosecutor advised the court, "is a topless bar."

"Why is that relevant to the pending charges?" the judge asked sternly. "I will not permit that sort of sniping in my courtroom. What bail are you requesting?"

"One million dollars," the young prosecutor replied.

After some back and forth, the judge imposed a bail of $250,000. Then a motion date was set, and Taub was remanded to custody until a bond could be posted.

In the hallway, Palmer met with Sal Levine, the bail bondsman he used.

"Haven't seen much of you lately," Levine said. "Keeping your clients out of trouble?"

"Maybe I'm just avoiding troublesome clients."

"Not Marvin, though."

"No, not Marvin. What's the word down here?"

"They want him," Levine said. "But they're going to be patient. Nice and slow, build the case, then bury him."

Palmer nodded. "Line up the bond, will you, Sal?"

"From you I'd usually take your word and twenty-five grand in cash against the quarter million, but what's my security going to be from Taub? A box of G-strings?"

"How much security do you want?"

"The whole thing," Levine told him. "This is a homicide, Palmer. If he owns an apartment or has a bank account, okay, I don't need the green. But I'm concerned about Marvin, everything he's got is probably in a suitcase. And what happens when they indict him? The next day he could be living in Brazil." Levine placed a hand on Palmer's shoulder. "You're a sweetheart, and I'd do anything for you. But if Marvin doesn't want to show the cash, I've gotta be protected."

Palmer smiled. "I don't expect you to front that kind of money on Taub's signature. Draw up the papers and I'll get you the twenty-five cash and some real security."

"Consider it done. And Palmer—watch yourself on this one," Levine warned him.

"That's what everyone keeps telling me," Palmer said.

When Palmer stepped outside the courthouse he found Whyte waiting for him on the street.

"What happened?" the detective asked.

"Judge set bail at a quarter million. Now Marvin needs to figure out how to make Sal feel warm and fuzzy enough to write the bond."

Whyte nodded. "How'd it go with the old lady?"

"The old lady? Aren't you Mr. Charm."

"Sorry. Just tired is all."

"Me too," Palmer said, then recounted his discussion with Jeanette Scott.

Whyte shook his head. "First the Franco divorce, then Taub on a murder rap, and now you want to play Sherlock Homes on the Platt case? You sure about all this?"

"I'm not sure about anything, except Taub. I've known him a long time."

"A relationship that doesn't exactly dress up your résumé."

"I need your help here," Palmer said. "Don't let your personal feelings get in the way."

"You know I won't."

"What about Sammy Burdick?"

"Scared to death," Whyte said. He told him about the envelope with the bullet in it and how reluctant Sammy was to speak with him. Then he related the details of his meeting with Vera about RDMO. "There's a lot more to all this than we're seeing so far."

"So far," Palmer agreed.

"It seems Vera wants me to dig deeper."

"Jeanette is basically asking me to do the same. Says if I come up with anything, she may be able to fill in some blanks."

"Even if it involves her family?"

"That's what she says."

"You believe her?"

Palmer took a moment. "I think she meant it when she said it. I'm not so sure."

CHAPTER TWENTY

On his drive back to the office, Palmer checked his phone for messages. The first call he returned was to Christina Franco.

"Have you filed the divorce papers?" she asked to begin the discussion.

"Not yet. I'll need some more information from you, assuming you're determined to go through with this."

"Determined? Whatever would make you doubt I'm determined?"

"Divorce is a big—"

"You had lunch with mother," she cut him off. "What did she have to say?"

"About what?"

"About me, obviously. About the divorce?"

Jeanette Scott had predicted her daughter would assume their meeting was all about her, and Palmer had agreed not to tell Christina her mother actually asked to see him about Platt's death. But there was nothing privileged about Jeanette's opinions concerning her daughter's marriage. On that subject, only his discretion would dictate how much he was willing to share.

"Your mother agrees with what I was just about to say, that divorce as a big step. She thinks that you and your husband ought to take some time to work on your marriage."

"My mother has no idea what really goes on in my relationship, Palmer, or what I've been living with. She certainly knows nothing about the threats Edward has made." The tension in her voice rising, she said, "Mother would never be able to handle it."

"She'll never hear any of that from me," Palmer assured her.

"Good, because I don't want her to worry, which leads me to the next issue."

"Which is?"

"I'm being followed."

"By whom?"

"How on earth would I know? Isn't that something your partner should be finding out?"

"This is the first I'm hearing of it, and—"

"I told you the first day we met that I'm in danger. What has to happen for you to believe me?"

Keeping his tone even, Palmer said, "I'm an attorney. Whyte is an investigator. As I explained that day—"

"I know," she cut him off again. "You think I should hire an expensive divorce lawyer and have some goons around to protect me twenty-four-seven. Well, you can forget that, I'm not going into hiding because my husband is a sociopath."

Palmer shook his head. "You can't have it both ways."

"What is that supposed to mean?"

"It means, on the one hand you're telling me you don't want anyone, such as a security detail, to interfere with your comfortable life, but on the other you're telling me you're worried about being followed." When Christina offered no reply, Palmer said, "All right, tell me what makes you think you're being followed?"

Christina described a man she noticed standing at the bar of the restaurant where she was having lunch with her girlfriends the previous day. Later that evening, she saw the same man standing across the street from the building where she lives on Park Avenue.

"You're sure it was the same man?"

"No doubt. Evil looking. Made no effort to hide the fact he was watching me. Then this morning, as I was leaving my apartment building, I would swear he was there again. He hurried around the corner when I came outside, so I can't be sure." As Palmer wondered how that made any sense—either the man was trying to intimidate her or he was not—she said, "He could be following me right now, for all I know."

"Where are you?"

"I just had my hair done. I'm in the car heading home."

"Stop at my office first. Robbie and I are both on our way back. Let's get some more detail from you, and perhaps we'll also see if you're followed there. I want to make sure you're okay."

"All right. I can also give you any other information you need from me so you can file for my divorce."

* * *

Palmer, Whyte, and Christina converged at the 64th Street brownstone at about the same time, and Palmer led them to one of the monitors at Maureen's workstation.

"We handle some odd cases, as you know, so we're sensitive to security issues," Palmer explained as they all had a look at the split images on the large screen behind Maureen's desk. "We have six cameras in place. The two shots on the bottom are the patio out back and a wide-angle lens covering the front door. The two in the middle cover upstairs." Pointing to the top two feeds, he said, "These are views of the street outside, east and west. Any of the people out there look familiar?"

Having just come from her hairdresser, Christina was dressed in tight black slacks, a white halter top, and leopard-patterned high heels. When she leaned forward in front of him to get a closer look at the video feeds, Palmer kept his eyes on the monitor.

"You're asking if I see the man who's been following me?" she asked without turning away from the camera feed.

"Or anyone else you might recognize."

Watching the images of people strolling along, she shook her head. "I don't."

"All right, give Maureen whatever description you can, and she'll keep an eye on things while you're here."

Taking a moment to look at Palmer, Christina said, "Thanks. For caring, I mean."

What Christina then provided was not particularly useful. A man of average height and build, around fifty, gray hair, no distinguishing features. "Sorry, but it's not as if he ever came right up to me, I only saw him from a distance."

Maureen looked at Palmer with an expression that asked, "What do you expect me to do with that?"

"Do what you can," Palmer responded to her unspoken question, then led Christina and Whyte into his office.

Before she sat in the comfortable armchair Palmer gestured toward, Christina said, "I want to apologize. For the way I spoke to you before, I mean."

Palmer stood behind his oak desk, waiting.

"I know I sounded like a bitch, and that's not who I am. It's just, with this man following me, and Edward's threats.... I'm really not myself."

"Forget it," Palmer said, then lowered himself into his black leather chair.

Taking her seat, Christina said, "I really do want you to file papers for the divorce."

"I think I got that," Palmer said. "When we're done here, you can sit with Maureen. You'll need to sign a retainer agreement, a verification form, and fill out a basic questionnaire. While you work on that, you can continue to look at the closed-circuit feed, in case you recognize anyone."

"Tell me about this man," Whyte said.

"What do you mean?"

"You say he never approached you."

"That's right," Christina said.

"Describe exactly what you told me," Palmer said.

When she was done, Whyte asked, "What about this afternoon, outside your beauty parlor, or whatever you call it?"

"No, but I have a thought about that."

"Go ahead."

"There's a charity event tonight. Anyone who knows me knows I'm going to attend, and they would know I was going to see Alexandre this afternoon."

"Alexandre?" Whyte asked.

"My hairdresser."

"Your husband would know that?"

"Of course. And he would know what time I would be there."

"Assuming your husband is the one having you followed," Whyte said.

"Who else would it be?"

Whyte did not answer the question, instead telling her, "Whoever it is still wouldn't know where you'd be going next. Such as here."

Christina responded with an indulgent smile. "When I get my hair done for a big event, the only place I go is home."

Palmer laughed. "Not taking a chance you'll be caught in the rain, or that your hairdo is going to wilt in the humidity."

"Something like that," she allowed with the seriousness due her appearance. "I have someone coming to the apartment to help me with makeup and my outfit."

Whyte looked to Palmer as if he were listening to someone speaking a foreign language.

"But why have me followed at all?" Christina asked. "Where would he think I'm going, and why would he care?"

"Seems everyone in New York already knows you've been to see me," Palmer said, "so that's not it. But there's another possibility." He paused. "We've asked what you know of your husband's business dealings that might be dangerous to him. You say there's nothing, but his threat suggests otherwise. Perhaps he's afraid there's some sort of information you could take to the authorities?"

"Authorities?"

"Police, feds, IRS. Someone in the media."

Shaking her head, Christina said, "No way."

Palmer sighed. "Whether you think so or not, that may still be a reason to have you followed, to see if you're meeting with any of those people."

Christina looked as if that had never occurred to her, which Palmer was not buying.

"All right," he said, "let's get you set up with Maureen."

"Will it take long? I really do have to get home," she reminded him with a coy grin.

"I understand, makeup and wardrobe await." Standing, Palmer said, "It won't take long, but it will get me what I need to draw up the paperwork to file your action. Then I'd like Robbie to ride with you to your apartment."

"That would be wonderful," she said, but hesitated before getting up. "What did you think of mother?"

"I think she's charming," he said.

Christina appeared to be thinking that over before saying, "She really is a wonderful person," making it sound as if she was apologizing for something. Then she stood and followed Palmer to Maureen's desk.

Back in his office with Whyte, Palmer waited for what he knew was coming.

"You're going to have her sign a retainer agreement and file her case. Unbelievable," Whyte said.

"We're in it this far, I don't—"

"We don't *have* to be in it at all," Whyte interrupted, the frustration in his voice clear. "It's simple. Just tell her no."

"Hold on," Palmer said. "You have any doubt Taub is being framed?"

"I don't."

"Who do you think is behind the setup?"

"I don't have enough information yet. I couldn't even guess."

"Sure you could."

"You want me to say Peter Frost."

"That'd be nice."

Whyte said nothing.

"You have another guess?"

"Not yet, we simply don't have enough information. And I admit that Frost has some bad history with Taub. But what has that got to do with Christina Franco?"

"Maybe nothing, maybe everything."

"But you think there's *something*."

"We know her husband mentioned Frost when he threatened her on that video, right?"

Before Whyte could respond, Maureen buzzed them and said Benny Parsons was on the line and did not sound happy. Palmer took the call and placed it on speaker.

"I'm here with Robbie Whyte, Benny. What's up?"

"I've been trying to reach you all afternoon," Parsons told them. "Your partner went to see Sammy?"

"Yes, Robbie did. They had a nice little chat."

"Too nice."

"What's wrong? You sound like hell."

"I *feel* like hell, but Sammy's a lot worse. I just saw him in Montefiore."

"He's in the hospital?"

"An hour or so after Whyte left Sammy at his house, two punks showed up and beat the shit out of him."

"What?"

"You heard me. They left him with three broken ribs and a face you could make hamburger from."

"Jesus Christ."

"Sammy asked me to call. Please guys, stay away from him." Benny was practically in tears. "And do me a favor."

"I know. Stay away from you too."

"Just for a while," Parsons said. "Okay?"

"Sure."

Benny sighed. "What's going on, Palmer?"

"I don't know yet, and you don't want to know. Just watch yourself."

Palmer ended the call and turned to Whyte, who said, "There was no one tailing me, I'm sure of it."

"Which means they were going to visit Burdick whether or not you spoke with him."

"Maybe. Or someone knew I was going to see him."

Palmer thought it over. "But who?"

"I have some thoughts on that," Whyte said.

Palmer nodded. "After you get Christina home, please come back. We obviously have some things to sort out."

CHAPTER TWENTY-ONE

Palmer's brownstone had an enclosed garden in back with a stone patio bordered by a short hedgerow. It was just after seven that evening when Palmer, Whyte, and Maureen settled into three of the teak and navy blue mesh chairs, each of which faced a cast iron firepit in the center of the courtyard. The night air was warm, but the fire felt good.

Maureen was nursing vodka on the rocks, Palmer was on his second bourbon, and Whyte had switched from whiskey sour to iced tea.

"Can't fly on one wing," Palmer said.

"Can't drive back to Connecticut under the influence either."

Palmer looked to Maureen. "When is he going to give up this suburban pretense and move into the bedroom on the second floor?"

"I would guess after both of his daughters finish with school and move away from his ex."

"Point taken. Although, for all the driving he does back and forth, he might as well live here and drive up to Connecticut for their weekly dinners," Palmer told her. "In fact, I'd bet his girls would rather have dinners with him in New York than in Westport."

"You two *do* notice that I'm still here," Whyte said. "I'm only mentioning it in case you want me to weigh in on any of this."

"You're still here?" Palmer said.

"Putting aside my desire to live close to my daughters," Whyte explained, "both of whom I see a lot more often than just weekly dinners, what makes you think I'd ever want to live in the same building as you? Bad enough we have to work together. I need my personal space."

"Personal space? You going New Age on us?"

"The fact that I don't want to look at your mug all the time is not New Age. It's called common sense."

"When Pinckney gave me this brownstone, the idea was for both of us to benefit from it."

"And we do, we have our offices here, but I doubt he expected us to live together. I mean, you're not exactly my type, if you catch my drift."

"Enough, boys," Maureen interrupted. "How about we return to something important."

"Some *things*," Whyte corrected her.

"Right," Palmer said. "To begin with, what are we going to do about Sammy Burdick?"

"Nothing," Whyte said.

"You don't think we should tell the police you were there before those goons worked him over?" Palmer asked.

"I do not," Whyte said. "First, I never saw those goons, so I can't identify anyone. Second, I have no idea what they wanted from him, and I can't ask Burdick because Parsons made it clear he doesn't want to hear from us. Last, I'd be surprised if he tells the police about my visit, since that might only make things worse for him. But I'll deal with that if and when it happens. Burdick's likely to dummy up on all counts."

Palmer thought it over. "Nice analysis," he conceded.

"Thank you. Now, since you've decided to take Christina Franco's case," Whyte said, adding, "over my strong objection, why not tell us some more about your visit with her mother."

"Not much more to tell. She wants us to look into Vernon Platt's death. I didn't commit to anything more than making a few inquiries. I obviously didn't tell her you were already poking around the investigation."

"She's convinced he was murdered?" Maureen asked.

"Along with some other people, apparently," Palmer said.

"But, unlike everyone else," Maureen reminded them, "they were best of friends. Which means she knew a lot more about him than all those other folks. And never underestimate a woman's intuition."

Palmer shook his head. "Why is it not sexist to suggest that women have some special intuitive power that men do not?"

"It's not sexist because it's the truth," Maureen said.

"Of course."

"I never underestimate female intuition, if anyone cares," Whyte told them. "But what's the point of complicating matters by telling Jeanette Scott what we find?"

"Because we may reap more than we sow," Palmer said.

"How biblical of you."

Palmer held up his glass in appreciation. "I'm convinced Jeanette already knows more than she's told me, including things about her son-in-law, and that could become useful."

"Assuming she's willing to open up," Maureen said.

"Right," Palmer agreed. "And I believe she will."

"What about her daughter's situation?" Whyte asked.

Palmer had a taste of his drink. "What about it?"

"You think Mrs. Scott is willing to share anything about Christina?"

"Time will tell. Depends on the sort of relationship we build."

"Let me get this straight. You're building a relationship with our client's mother?"

Before Palmer could respond, Maureen said, "I'm still wondering about the relationship you think you're building with our client."

"There you two go again, a WWE tag-team."

Maureen responded with one of her *don't kid me* looks. "I saw you staring at her ass when she was bent over my desk this afternoon."

"She placed her ass in my line of sight, as it happened. And you really are something, you know that?"

"That's not much of a denial," Whyte said with a short laugh.

"For what it's worth," Palmer said, "I don't believe for a moment her little pose was without purpose. She's a woman accustomed to being looked at, but I did my best not to dwell on the view. What do you guys want from me?"

"She's not a woman," Maureen corrected him. Then, speaking slowly, she said, "Mrs. Franco is a *client*. A *married* client."

"Thanks, Jiminy."

"Little Mo is right," Whyte said. "You tend to get caught up in all the glitz and glamor—"

"And asses and breasts," Maureen added.

"She's right again," Whyte said.

"Enough," Palmer said, showing them the palms of his hands. "I get it. I'm lousy with women. Guilty as charged. But be assured, I have no designs on Christina Franco."

They both stared at him without speaking.

"Could we get back to her mother for a minute?" Palmer asked.

"Why?" Whyte asked. "What does the mother look like?"

All three of them laughed, then Maureen became serious again. "You're sure you want me to file the divorce papers?"

"She signed the retainer agreement, handed us a check, and gave you all the information we need, correct?"

"She did."

"Then let's file her divorce case tomorrow morning, get a docket number from the court, and arrange to have Mr. Franco served. We'll see what happens from there, right?" When neither of them answered, Palmer asked, "Any reason we shouldn't?"

Whyte lifted his left hand and used it to enumerate his points. "First, Vernon Platt may have been murdered. Second, Joey D'Angelo was definitely murdered, and Taub is charged with the crime. Now Joey's bookmaker boyfriend is having dinner through an IV tonight, maybe just for speaking with me. Meanwhile, Edward Franco and Christina's parents may end up neck-deep in the RDMO probe Platt was going to testify about. And then, in case anyone has forgotten, Peter Frost may be in the middle of all this."

Palmer appeared pleased. "You finally coming to believe all of these events are somehow connected?"

"I'm not sure," Whyte said. "And neither are you. But according to what we know from Christina Franco, Frost is involved with her husband. Then her husband used Frost's name to scare his wife. Meanwhile, Vernon Platt was going to testify about RDMO—a company in which Edward Franco is involved—and now Platt is dead, a classic Frost move." The detective shook his head. "Too many intersecting lines."

Palmer sighed. "We always say no coincidences, right?"

Maureen asked if they thought Frost might be behind the attack on Sammy Burdick.

"RP is convinced Taub is being framed, and I tend to agree," Whyte told her. "I admit that would also be vintage Frost, although I can't figure out how he would be involved there."

"He hates Taub," Palmer said, "which is the one possible thread that could tie some of this together."

Maureen was nodding as she said, "Frost would know that Taub would come to you for help."

"Yes," Whyte agreed. "But why would he want that? Other than spite work, which is not Frost's style. He's more clinical than that."

"True," Palmer said. "We've got too little information and too many intersecting lines."

"And a growing list of clients looking for your help," Maureen said.

Whyte leaned forward. "Mo is right again. Christina Franco, her mother, your old pal Marvin Taub." He fixed his friend with a stern look. "Peter Frost is a very dangerous man. You dueled with him before, came out on top, and lived. That last part is good, the first not so much."

"We parted on fairly decent terms."

"Because it was the only way for him to save face." Whyte sat back. "Now we're into a whole lot of who knows what." Whyte stood up. "I'm heading home. I've had enough brain damage for one night." Looking at Maureen, he asked if he could drop her off.

"Sure," she said, getting to her feet. "Just let me clean this up first."

"Forget it," Palmer said. "I've got it."

Before she could respond, they heard something being tossed over the tall brick wall facing the back of the property, as it landed with a thud among the shrubs. It instantly ignited, sending off an explosive flash, followed by the release of a dark, noxious cloud.

Palmer immediately dove toward Maureen, pulling her to the ground and shielding her with his body, as Whyte dropped to a knee, his S & W revolver already in hand. Everything was silent, until a second missile came flying through the air, this time just a rock with paper taped to it.

"It was only a smoke bomb," Whyte told them as he got his feet, gun still at the ready, and walked toward the rock. He picked it up, pulled off the note, and read it aloud. "Back off or next time it will be the real thing."

Palmer stood and helped Maureen to her feet. "What the hell?" he said.

But instead of responding with a look of concern, Whyte was smiling at him. "Nice move kiddo, protecting our girl," he said. "You never know who a man really is until the first shot is fired."

After Whyte took Maureen home, Palmer cleared their glasses away, then went upstairs and did something he almost never felt the need to do—he removed the Walther automatic from the lockbox in his nightstand drawer, checked to see that it was loaded, then slid it back into its leather holster and placed it on the marble top beside his bed.

CHAPTER TWENTY-TWO

After Whyte dropped Christina at her apartment building, she went upstairs and spent the better part of three hours preparing for the night ahead. With hair and makeup done to her exacting standards, she dressed in an elegant blood-red designer gown, then balanced herself atop a pair of impossibly high stiletto heels, looking ready to present an Oscar.

Her elite corner of the world already knew about her pending separation from Edward, and Christina had the pick of several suitable and willing escorts for this event. But she decided to attend alone. It was an opportunity to make a statement about her independence, and to avoid having the tabloids suggest she had found a new mate who might have been the cause of the breakup. Edward was the villain, and she was going to do what she could to make that clear to one and all.

Leaving her apartment, she rode the elevator to the lobby, where she was greeted by admiring eyes and compliments from the doorman and building security guard. Emerging onto the street, the driver helped her into the back of the black Bentley sedan and navigated the few blocks to the Metropolitan Museum for its annual gala.

The area around Fifth Avenue and Eighty-First Street was bright with klieg lights and thick with reporters, cameramen, and photographers from print and television, flanked by thousands of dazzled spectators. The rich, famous, and beautiful were congregating to enjoy the festivities at this coveted charity event, the colossal proceeds of which would be divided among a handful of causes, lest anyone claim favoritism.

When Christina arrived, there were a few young men in black-tie assigned to escort any unaccompanied women up the long flight of carpeted stairs leading into the museum. As she prepared to exit her vehicle, Christina took the arm offered by one of the handsome ushers and stepped onto the street. She moved slowly, in part because her gown and heels made it impossible to do otherwise, and in part because she was there to be seen by the assembled crowd and was not about to let them down.

When she began her measured ascent, she did not appear to notice her husband's car dropping him off at the curb shortly after she arrived. Not hampered by yards of rich fabric or the need for a chaperone, Edward Franco moved quickly up the stone steps until he reached her.

"Hello babe," he said with a malicious grin.

Turning to him, Christina's eyes filled with fury. "You? *You?*" she demanded. "How dare you show up here?"

Edward Franco was good-looking, just over six feet tall, and athletically built. His eyes and hair were dark, his complexion tanned, and his custom-tailored tuxedo suited him well.

"Good to see you too," he said.

She made a show of looking past him, then asked, "Didn't bring one of your whores with you? What happened, you short of cash this week?"

He stared at her without speaking for a moment, the two of them impeding the flow of other attendees who were also slowly making their way up the stairs. At last, he said, "I don't think this is the time or place," beginning to turn away.

But Christina reached out, grabbed his arm, and spun him back toward her. "Don't you walk away from me, you bastard," she snarled.

Edward had no difficulty pulling away from her grasp, but never saw her other hand as it lashed out and slapped him hard across the face. Although he did his best not to react, the gasps from the people all around them were audible and flashes from dozens of cameras and hundreds of smartphones were blinding.

"Have a nice evening, Christina," he said, then hurried past her toward the entrance.

* * *

Around the same time Christina was confronting her wayward husband outside the Met, Palmer remained on the patio, enjoying the balmy night air. After a while he got up, cleared away the glasses, and brought them to the small kitchen on the main floor of the brownstone. When he heard the office phone ring, he looked at the caller ID and saw it was Sloane Taylor.

"Good evening," he said.

"Working late?"

"You too, it seems. The city that never sleeps."

"So they say. Have you been watching the evening news?"

"Why would I do that when I have you to keep me up to date?"

"You obviously haven't heard about the brawl your client had a little while ago with her husband at the gala tonight."

"Come again?"

"Mr. and Mrs. Franco ran into each other as they were entering the museum this evening. Bad timing for both. They had some angry words, then she slugged him."

"Slugged him?"

"Am I not speaking the King's English? She hit him flush across the face."

"In front of an audience, I take it."

"Very much so. As I said, they were outside, on the steps, with cameras flashing and video rolling."

"And then what?"

"I wasn't invited to the festivities inside, but from what I hear, she tracked him down a few minutes later and added a few choice comments about his ethics as a husband."

"Perfect."

"Thought you'd want to know."

"I'd like to say I appreciate it, but—"

"Understood. Will you give me an exclusive statement? After you speak with her?"

Palmer paused. "Let's just say I won't give a statement to anyone but you."

"Drinks tomorrow?"

"I'll get back to you," he said, then hung up.

Staring at his phone, he now had to wonder about Sloane Taylor.

"What next?" he said aloud to the empty room.

CHAPTER TWENTY-THREE

Early the following morning, Palmer worked out, showered, dressed, and made his way to his office. As he was arranging some paperwork on the Marvin Taub bond, he received a call from an attorney who informed him that she represented Edward Franco.

"Lillian Bartz," the nasal voice told him. "I don't believe we've ever met."

"I don't think so," he agreed.

"I'm told you represent Mrs. Franco."

Since the divorce papers were yet to be filed that morning, Palmer asked, "Who might've told you that?"

Ignoring the question, she said, "Either you do, or you don't. May I have an answer?"

"Might I?"

"If that's how you want to play this, it's fine with me. If you *do* represent Mrs. Franco, you should be aware that she assaulted my client last night. In front of thousands of witnesses."

"That so?"

"Are you telling me you are not aware of the incident?"

"I'm not telling you anything, Ms. Bartz. So far, I'm just listening."

Attorney Bartz proceeded to offer a lurid rendition of what had occurred between the Francos. When she was done with her breathless account, she said, "That sort of behavior is entirely unacceptable. Thus far, I have persuaded my client not to press criminal charges, but we need to get their situation under control."

"Under control? I'm an attorney, not a therapist, but I will have a discussion with Mrs. Franco and get back to you. Let me have your number."

Bartz recited her contact information, then said, "Whatever you believe you know about Mrs. Franco, you should have a second look. I'm sure she's provided you a list of negative things about my client and their personal life, but Christina Franco has a nasty little background of her own."

Palmer waited.

"You know anything about Henry Carrigan?" she asked.

"The name rings a bell," Palmer said, not telling her about the call he received from Carrigan about Christina Franco.

"When you have a moment, you'll want to ask Mrs. Franco about their relationship, although I wonder how much she'll tell you." Bartz paused, but when Palmer offered no response, she said, "I expect to hear back from you soon," and hung up.

Maureen arrived at work just as Palmer finished the call.

"Seems Mr. Franco has lawyered up."

"You hear about their little spat?" Maureen asked.

"Got a call from Sloane Taylor last night, then saw it on the news this morning. She slapped him across the face, that was clear. The media is trying to make it sound like a prizefight."

"You'll have time to worry about all that later. This morning you need to spring Marvin Taub, as I believe the saying goes."

Palmer laughed. "Where's Robbie?"

"On his way."

"Good. Please call Sal Levine and tell him I have the paperwork done for the bond." He paused. "Or maybe just tell him we've got the green ready for the swap."

CHAPTER TWENTY-FOUR

Christina Franco called Palmer, they picked a time to meet, and she arrived at the office a couple of hours later, beginning her rant as soon as she walked in, before he could even pose a few obvious questions about the previous night.

She finished her tirade by angrily repeating the statement, "Edward knew I was going to be there," and slumped back in the armchair.

"Understood," he calmly replied, as it appeared she had run out of steam. "Did you know *he* was going to attend?"

"I didn't give it any thought."

Palmer took a moment to look her over. She was dressed in tight jeans and a red silk blouse, apparently her attempt at a casual look, although he noticed that her hair and makeup were perfect and the top a half-size too small.

"I have to say, that seems odd to me," he admitted, "given what's going on between the two of you. You told me he bought the tickets way back when, and that they were very expensive. I realize at that point it was with the expectation you would be going as a couple—"

"We are no longer a couple," she reminded him. "We're certainly not comparing social calendars at this point."

"You had to realize there was at least a possibility he would show up. The idea it did not even occur to you—"

"What does it matter?" she demanded as she sat up again. "And whose side are you on?"

Palmer took a deep breath. "If I'm going to represent you effectively, I need to know the truth. About everything. Your actions, your motivations, your plans."

"All right, maybe it did cross my mind he would be there, but there were hundreds of people attending. There was no way to know we'd run into each other, and when we did, well, I just didn't expect to feel so upset. This was a major party, and I had to go alone, like some old maid, because he's a cheating slimeball who's chosen to destroy our marriage. The moment I saw him, I became furious." Coming up for air, she added, "It wasn't something I planned, if that's what you're suggesting."

"I'm not suggesting anything, I'm inquiring," Palmer responded with a dismissive shake of the head. "We were going to have him served with the divorce papers this morning, but I decided to hold off. The timing felt a bit melodramatic, all things considered."

"I think the timing would've been perfect," Christina said. "Serve him as soon as possible. It'll put an exclamation point on things, don't you think?"

Palmer decided not to tell her what he thought. Instead, he said, "An attorney called me this morning, says she represents him, claims she's considering filing criminal charges against you for assault."

"What?"

"Don't sound so shocked, you hit him in front of hundreds of witnesses, with a television audience to boot."

"I know what I did. And I've seen the video enough times to remind me."

"Me too. Although, I must say," Palmer told her with a grin, "you looked quite lovely in that dress."

Christina frowned. "Who was the attorney, that woman Bartz?"

"You know her?"

"I know *of* her. Handled divorces for a couple of Edward's friends. He told me they figured having a woman representing the husband was good optics."

"Good optics," Palmer repeated. "Maybe it is."

"What else did she say?"

"It was a brief discussion although, curiously, she never mentioned anything about a divorce."

"Of course not. I've already told you, he'll do anything to keep me from leaving him." When Palmer responded with a puzzled look, she again asked, "What?"

"If he really doesn't want the divorce, why would he have an aggressive divorce lawyer call me and threaten criminal charges? She certainly didn't mention anything about reconciliation."

"Don't worry, she will."

"What makes you so—"

"When she was representing one of those friends I mentioned, Edward kept me up to date on her tactics. He found her strategy amusing. She uses a sort of, what do you call it, bait and switch? She'll hold out an olive branch, talk about counseling, the usual nonsense, then she'll hit the wife's lawyer with a lot of motions and depositions and all that."

"But, in the end, these friends of your husband wanted to be divorced, correct?"

"They did."

"In your case, you're saying he'll do anything to prevent it."

"Believe me, Palmer, the games are only beginning. You still want me to call you Palmer, right?"

"Palmer is fine," he said, distractedly. "What sort of games?"

"Who knows, but Edward is a clever man. He may let some time pass. Offer me gifts or a trip, who knows what?"

"After he threatened you the way he did, would he really believe that's how he's going to lure you back?"

Palmer watched as she seemed to be thinking it over. "Good point. He'd probably opt for a tougher approach."

"Such as his attorney threatening to file criminal charges?"

"Maybe. Let's face it, this isn't just about him and me. My father is a congressman, my mother has personal issues, my family had ties to Vernon that might prove embarrassing. All of that."

"You're saying he might blackmail you, somehow threaten your family?"

"I wouldn't put it past him."

"What would your mother's friendship with Platt have to do with any of this?"

"I was thinking more about the business relationships Edward had with Vernon and my family."

At their dinner together at Le Bernardin, Palmer had asked her about Henry Carrigan but had not told her about the call he received from the man and the unpleasant things he had to say about her. Based on the prompting from Lillian Bartz, he figured it was time to push that issue. He simply stated the name and waited for her to react.

"You asked me about him the other night. What about him?"

Palmer bit at his lower lip, watching her. "You said you know him."

"Of course, he works with Edward."

"You said you had something of a casual, social relationship with him."

"That's right, what of it?"

"Was that always the case?"

"I beg your pardon."

"He called me a few days ago, warned me that you're a dangerous woman. Why would he have that opinion of you?"

"He called you a few days ago, said nasty things about me, and you're just telling me now?"

"It seemed irrelevant until this attorney Bartz mentioned him this morning."

"She did?"

"Why would Carrigan want to warn me about you?"

She looked away, saying, "I have no idea."

"Truth, remember? You want me to represent you, you always have to tell me the truth. That's the deal."

Christina turned back to him. "Henry's hit on me more than once and I never showed the slightest interest. You fill in the blanks."

"I'm a bit confused. Carrigan works for your husband, correct?"

"That's right."

"And this guy is making a play on his boss's wife? Help me out here."

Christina smiled. "You want the truth? I thought Edward might have put him up to it. Probably told Henry to call you, too."

Palmer sat back and stared at her. "This is quite the fun group."

"I keep telling you, but you don't seem to believe me. You have no idea who you're dealing with."

"All right, I'll bite. Why do you think your husband would play that card?"

"Come on, Palmer, you're a smart lawyer. I'm sure you can figure it out."

"I'll come up with my own theories. I want to hear yours."

She shrugged. "He wanted to have something on me, hoping I would be tasteless enough to get back at him by sleeping with Henry. He might even have wanted something on Henry. That's how Edward lives, always looking for an edge."

"Even in his marriage?"

"Especially in his marriage."

"And people say romance is dead in the Internet age."

Christina frowned. "We have other things to discuss."

"Other than—"

"Other than the incident with Edward last night and all the hoopla since." She hesitated. "I received a phone call this morning."

Palmer waited.

"From Peter Frost."

"You have my attention," he said.

"He pretended he was looking for Edward, but that's utter nonsense. After Edward's threat, Frost would be one of the first people my husband would tell about our separation. Frost knew Edward wouldn't be in the apartment this morning."

"What did you say?"

"I told him Edward was not at home, used those exact words, and was about to slam the phone down, but it was almost like he could see me doing it. He said, 'Don't hang up.' I waited, sort of a reflex if you know what I mean."

"Go on."

"He said I was making a mistake, or words to that effect. That I should think twice before I went past the point of no return. He actually used that expression. Trite, no?"

Palmer knew enough about Frost to agree that his call was no casual accident. "Did he get specific about what mistake you were making? Pursuing a divorce, for example?"

"He didn't have to."

"All right, then what?"

"Then he mentioned you."

"How flattering," Palmer said, not revealing his surprise. "What did he say?"

"Said he knew I had been to see you. Said you're a smart lawyer. And tough. He used that word. Then he said you also have common sense and that we should think about what we're doing before it's too late for both of us. Then he hung up."

"That was it?"

"That's everything. I hardly got to say a word."

"So, he's saying we're *both* making a mistake, not just you."

"That was clearly the message he wanted me to deliver."

"Then mission accomplished," Palmer said, managing a smile. Doing his best to sound positive, he told her, "We can get back to Mr. Frost later. For now, I want to be sure you want the divorce papers served."

"You mean, in spite of this new warning."

"I'm not worried about Peter Frost," Palmer lied, "but you know the media is going to have a field day. They'll link our filing of the case to your confrontation last night. And there are all the other issues that will come up, the things you've mentioned about your family."

"I can handle all that, as long as I know you and your partner are going to protect me. I mean, really protect me. If you can promise that, as Edward likes to say, let the circus begin."

Palmer nodded, although the image that came to mind was far more ominous than a circus.

PART THREE
MURDER

CHAPTER TWENTY-FIVE

As Palmer wrapped up his discussion with Christina, Robbie Whyte was meeting with Lt. Hugh Lawson in the corner of the small, dark bar at Lusardi's, on the Upper East Side.

"No whiskey sour?" Lawson asked when Whyte ordered a draft.

Whyte shook his head. "Miles to go before I sleep."

Lawson nodded.

"Hear any news on Taub?"

"I already told you," Lawson said, "that case is outside my jurisdiction."

Whyte smiled, had a sip of beer, then said, "But not outside your sphere of curiosity."

"I'll give you that."

"All I want to know is what you're hearing."

"First you need to come clean about your interest in Vernon Platt's death."

Whyte placed his glass on the bar. "Palmer's handling Christina Franco's divorce."

Lawson allowed himself another wheezy chuckle. "Palmer handling a divorce. You guys short of cash?"

"It wasn't my idea, believe me. But it turns out her case is more complicated than just splitting up the silverware."

"Especially because there's a lot more than silverware to split."

"And because her old family friend took a dive off his twenty-second-floor balcony."

"Or was pushed," Lawson said.

"Right," Whyte agreed. "Which leads us to the questionable activities of our client's husband."

"I hear he may end up front and center at that Washington hearing, where Platt was supposed to testify."

"That's the word," Whyte said.

"And you think all that is somehow tied to Joey D'Angelo's murder?"

"I do."

Lawson took a moment. "I know that Taub and D'Angelo have crossed paths, heard about the argument they had the night Joey was shot, but I don't have anything tying Taub to the Francos."

"Neither do I," Whyte admitted. "What about Joey D and Platt?"

"What's the link there?"

"Some things one of Joey's friends had to say."

"His sometime boyfriend on City Island?"

"That's right," Whyte said, picking up his glass again. "Sammy Burdick, who had the shape of his head rearranged just for speaking with me."

Lawson drew back slightly. "I heard about Burdick getting roughed up, didn't know it had anything to do with you."

"You asked me to come clean and I'm giving you everything I have. I went to see Burdick. He wasn't too happy about the visit, but after a few minutes he warmed to the idea of trashing D'Angelo. Apparently, Joey didn't think Burdick was high class enough to mingle with some of his upper-crust friends and clients."

"When you say clients, you mean drug customers," Lawson suggested.

"Correct. And friends such as Platt."

"D'Angelo and Platt had some history?"

"Yes indeed," Whyte said. "And with Platt and Joey both dead, Sammy was a nervous man."

Lawson took some time to have a taste of his beer. "What do you and Palmer figure ties all of this together?"

"Not what, *who*. He thinks it's Peter Frost."

"You mentioned him last time we met. You agree?"

"I do," Whyte said. "His fingerprints seem to be on too many aspects of what's happened."

"For instance?"

"I have something that has got to be strictly on the downlow."

"Go ahead," Lawson said.

"When the Francos went at it one morning, Mr. Franco suggested that Frost was a resource he might turn to if she became a problem."

"His wife recognized the name?"

"She sure did. Says Frost has helped her husband fix some problems in the past. No specifics, but Mrs. Franco knew enough to be frightened at the mention of his name."

Lawson responded with a slow nod. "Shows good sense on her part."

"She made a tape of the argument, had her phone running without her husband knowing."

"How convenient."

Whyte smiled. "I said the same thing. Cynicism comes with the job, never goes away."

Lawson took another gulp of his beer, then said, "You believe Frost had something to do with Platt's death?"

"Not sure, but according to Mrs. Franco, Frost has some kind of involvement in her husband's business."

"Interesting," Lawson said. "What about D'Angelo's murder? You see Frost involved there?"

"Depends on what Joey did to get himself killed."

"An argument with Marvin Taub was certainly not the reason."

"Hell no," Whyte agreed. "Taub is not my favorite person, but he didn't off Joey."

"He is a sleazeball, though," said Lawson.

"Agreed. But not a murderer. And if something was going to drive him to homicide, it would take a lot more than D'Angelo acting up in his bar."

Lawson drew a deep breath and let it out slowly. "Makes no sense."

"What does?"

"I don't know," Lawson said. "D'Angelo was involved in a lot of seedy activities. He preyed on the gay community, pushed narcotics, was generally a lowlife. No telling who he might have pushed too far."

"What could he have done to Frost?"

Lawson shook his head. "Again, I haven't put it together yet. Maybe it wasn't Frost directly, maybe it was someone who works with him. Frost deals with professionals, not junkies."

"True, but my gut tells me these are not just a series of random events. Platt's death. Joey's murder. Burdick ending up in the hospital just for talking with me. Franco using Frost's name to intimidate his wife."

"Don't forget the investigation in DC."

"Exactly."

"My job, for the moment, is to wrap up the Platt situation," Lawson said. "My guess is that he didn't take that leap on his own, and I may have something that makes it more than a guess."

"Just let me know what you find."

The lieutenant regarded his old friend with a narrow gaze. "As long as you do the same for me," he said.

Then Whyte told him about the smoke bomb.

* * *

Later that evening, Palmer and Whyte were seated again on the rear patio in the brownstone garden. They had made the decision not to disclose the smoke bomb incident to the police. Their security cameras did not cover the area from which it was thrown, so there was no way to identify the perp. There would obviously be no chance of fingerprints on the rock or the note, so for now they would just have to keep their guard up. Lawson told Whyte they should at least file a report, but Whyte demurred. Instead, Maureen had already called Lawson's son Caleb, who did occasional tech work for Palmer and Whyte, and he was going to install a couple of new CCTV positions at the rear of the brownstone. That was all they would do for now.

For now.

After Whyte finished providing an update on the rest of his meeting with Lawson, he listened as Palmer shared the details of his discussion with Christina Franco. Then he said, "While I was waiting for you, I was thinking about where we go from here."

"How about we drop the Franco divorce?" Whyte suggested, giving that idea one more try. "We get rid of that, it simplifies our lives. And makes things a lot safer. All we'll have left out of this melodrama will be the defense of your pal Taub."

"We can't be sure that smoke bomb was about the Franco case. Given the calls we've received, it might actually have something to do with Marvin."

"True enough," Whyte reluctantly conceded.

"And what about Jeanette Scott? She asked me to help find out who murdered Platt."

Whyte shook his head. "You drop her daughter's case, I'm betting you'll never hear from her again. Regardless of her mentioning how Pinckney thought so highly of you. Which, I should add, may be another reason for us to get away from these people, and soon."

Palmer frowned.

"Anyway, it's not your job to solve Platt's death. You're a lawyer, not a cop. Leave the investigation to Lawson."

Palmer smiled. "You know me better."

Whyte groaned. "All right, there may be another way to go."

"Which is?"

"A global approach. Learn more about the starting point of all this trouble, maybe then we can discover what the hell this is all about."

"RDMO," Palmer said.

"Exactly."

"That's what I've been thinking. Which means you need to make some phone calls, pal."

"I will." Then, with a short nod in the direction of Palmer's sport coat, Whyte said, "And you need to lose the piece."

Palmer frowned. "Damn, I thought I had it covered up."

"Yeah, well, I'm the real detective here, in case you forgot. And you're lousy with a gun, in case you forgot that too."

"Hate the things," Palmer admitted.

"Then put it back in the drawer. I've got you covered."

CHAPTER TWENTY-SIX

The next day, Whyte began a deep dive into the RDMO story. Maureen guided him through an online review of the company and their pending applications with the FDA. Then he began making calls to various contacts who might help him flesh things out, especially with regard to the pending congressional investigation.

The most fruitful of those conversations was another brief chat with Vera Alexander, who referred him to Kevin Mahoney, an old friend from the NYPD, now working for a branch of the capitol police in Washington. Mahoney and Vera managed to arrange a meeting for Palmer and Whyte with someone from the FDA based in DC. The source knew and trusted both Vera and Mahoney, was familiar with RDMO, and was willing to discuss the current state of things—entirely off the record.

Palmer and Whyte spent the day reviewing and organizing the information they had accumulated, then, early the following morning, they headed to Penn Station to catch the Amtrak for Washington.

"First class?" Whyte asked as they settled into facing seats on the Acela Express.

"Why not?" Palmer responded as if the choice was obvious.

Whyte shook his head. "The fare is almost double, and what do you get for it?"

"You're so old school," Palmer replied with a large smile. "We can afford it, in case you forgot, and besides, we get bigger seats, free food, and free cocktails."

"We're having cocktails at this hour of the morning? On the way to this meeting?"

"Hell no, but we are on the way back."

Whyte could not suppress a slight laugh. "And I suppose we mingle with a better class of people here."

"I'll have you know I rode first class years ago when the only other person in the compartment was Henry Kissinger. And his bodyguard, of course."

"And that was valuable, why? Because you helped him shape our foreign policy?"

"We talked sports, tell you the truth, but it makes a great anecdote, don't you think?"

When Palmer and Whyte arrived in Washington, Mahoney was already waiting for them at The Palm, where he had arranged for a table in one of the smaller rooms. Whyte introduced the two men, and the three of them had time to order drinks and have a brief chat before Jon Speare showed up.

Mahoney was stocky, square-jawed, clear-eyed and—like Whyte—was never going to be mistaken for anything but a cop. Speare arrived and was something else entirely. Standing around five foot nine, he had the weary appearance and soft middle that comes from a lifetime of sitting in an office. Given that initial impression, Palmer was surprised when the man ordered a Tito's martini immediately after introductions were made.

While Speare waited for his drink, Palmer watched as their guest from the FDA had a look at each of them in turn, then said, "Vera and Kevin assured me this entire discussion would be strictly off the record."

"Absolutely," Palmer told him, but he could see his assurance was not good enough.

"I'm not just saying no recordings or notes. I mean, I don't want to read in the paper tomorrow that some unattributed source at the administration spilled his guts, or anything even close to that."

"Agreed," Palmer said. "We're just looking for some background that might relate to a matter we're working on. Maybe more than one matter."

Speare's martini arrived, and he had a generous taste of the clear, cold liquid. "Well then, since you expect candor from me, you want to start by telling me what these matters are about?"

Palmer glanced at Whyte and Mahoney, then turned back to Speare. "One involves Edward Franco. You know who that is?"

Speare responded with a "Don't bullshit a bullshitter" look, and Palmer found himself liking the guy.

Palmer said, "His wife has asked us to represent her in a divorce."

Speare nodded. "Saw their little to-do on television the other night. From what I know about the guy, I wish she'd hit him again."

Palmer smiled. "Just to be clear, Robbie and I don't take many divorce cases, not unless there's something unusual or compelling."

"Which there obviously is here. Not to mention a lot of coin."

"True, but I'm not referring to that," Palmer told him, "or the slap in the face, for that matter."

"Then I assume," Speare said, "you're referring to the death of Vernon Platt."

Palmer nodded. "That's correct."

Speare had another bracing gulp of his vodka and sat back. "Vera explained that you're an attorney and Mr. Whyte, who was previously a cop with Kevin in New York, is now a private investigator who works for you."

"*With* me."

"With you. What do the two of you have to do with Platt's death?"

Palmer grinned. "That wording is a little unfortunate. I assume you're asking why we're *interested* in it."

Speare allowed himself a slight smile. "Sorry, yes."

"We've been finding a lot of overlapping incidents and personalities, and we're trying to determine whether it's a series of incredible coincidences or not."

"I don't believe in coincidences."

"Neither do we."

"I did a little homework on you after I got the calls last night from Vera and Kevin." Looking at Mahoney, he added, "Both of whom I trust and respect, which is the only reason I agreed to this lunch."

Palmer nodded. "Got it."

"Seems you get high marks for integrity, you get involved in some difficult cases, and that currently—in addition to the Franco divorce—you're representing a rather sleazy individual accused of murdering someone just as sleazy."

This time it was Whyte who replied. "I couldn't have described those two better myself, but that's right, we're defending Marvin Taub against the charge he murdered Joey D'Angelo."

"And am I to understand you believe that matter contains some of those overlapping elements Mr. Palmer mentioned?"

"That's the idea," Whyte conceded.

"And you're here because you think RDMO somehow fits into all of this."

"We think it may be at the core of everything," Palmer told him.

Speare nodded thoughtfully, then polished off his drink. "Anyone having another?"

After Palmer signaled the waiter for a second round, he said, "Edward Franco's venture capital group became a major investor in RDMO. After that, Platt was called to testify before a congressional committee investigating the company—"

"And wound up dead," Speare completed the timeline.

"We understand that his testimony had to do with pending FDA applications."

"That's the scuttlebutt," Speare agreed.

"If I may ask, what's your role with the FDA, your position, background—however you want to explain it."

"I'm an analyst with a master's and a PhD in biochemistry. I review test results, working with Big Pharma, and Little Pharma as well. I'm not in a supervisory role, and I don't get to make the final decisions, but I do my best to make a difference."

"The people on the next level, do they have the same impressive credentials you do, or are they, uh—"

Speare's smile interrupted him, providing Palmer a good look at his uneven teeth. "You mean the political hacks? Civil servants with their heads screwed on backwards? Incompetents who don't know an aspirin from a narcotic?"

Palmer could not help laughing. "I think you've just described government inefficiency in a nutshell."

"There's some of that, sure, and I have the occasional run-in with them. But in fairness, most of them do their best to protect the American public from dangerous drugs."

Palmer nodded.

"I don't mean to get on a soapbox," Speare went on, "but pharmaceuticals are tricky. Tests may generate miraculous results, but what about the long-term effects? Think of the horrific consequences from thalidomide, or artificial sweeteners that turned out to be carcinogens. Whoever imagined talcum powder might cause cervical cancer?"

"Which is why the FDA takes such a conservative approach," Palmer said.

"That's correct. You have people demanding action and, sadly, some of them are seriously ill. They're willing to take chances we cannot. They want to know what takes us so long, branding us a bunch of lazy, obstructionist bureaucrats, but that's not true. We're the gatekeepers against the sort of problems I just mentioned, even if we don't always get it right."

"I've gotten that speech from Vera more than once," Whyte said with a friendly grin.

Their fresh cocktails were served, Speare lifted his glass, said, "Cheers," and then had a generous taste. Palmer figured the man was either a lush or just didn't get out to lunches like this very often.

"How does all this relate to RDMO?" Whyte asked.

"How about we order some food before I dive too far into this second martini," Speare suggested. "Then we can talk about our friends at RDMO."

They chose a variety of appetizers, ordered steaks for which The Palm was famous, and some classic sides. When that was done, Palmer said, "You have the floor."

"Before we get too deeply into the research they're doing at RDMO, we should start with the people who now control the company. You mentioned Franco, but do you know about Henry Carrigan?" When Palmer shot Whyte a glance, Speare said, "I see you've heard of him."

"Heard *from* him, to be accurate," Palmer said. "Works for Franco's venture capital firm."

"From what I've seen, he now works almost exclusively on RDMO, acting as their in-house pit bull."

"You've dealt with him directly?"

"Oh yeah. He's their point man, trying to ram approvals through our agency."

"Which you must deal with all the time," Whyte said.

"Sure, but he's a little more aggressive than most." Speare paused, pushing his glasses up the bridge of his nose. "As you may know, RDMO is working on genetic engineering. Fascinating work, of course, and it could result in some major breakthroughs, assuming they get it right."

"We've learned that a lot of companies are engaged in that sort of research," Whyte said, based on the previous day's research.

"True, but many are dedicated to specific diseases, some rare, others not. The RDMO model is a broad spectrum. They're experimenting with a range of genomes that can be tailored to a number of different diseases, which would obviously be groundbreaking."

"Sounds like you support what they're doing."

"I did," Speare admitted. "Until Franco's team became the major investor."

"We're listening."

"It's complicated," Speare said.

"That's what we live for," Whyte told him.

Speare nodded. "Once their group took over, the focus of the testing changed. They're investors, not scientists. They began identifying the drugs they might get approved fastest. Pump up the price of the stock and then—"

"Take the money and run," Palmer said.

"Exactly."

"There's nothing wrong with a profit motive, is there?"

"No, but there's more to it than that," Speare said. "We all know that hedge funds and investment houses manipulate stock prices all the time. They can make money either way, moving the numbers up or down, depending on their positions at any given moment. They're especially good at it in the pharmaceutical sector."

"But that money helps to finance companies doing the research."

"Also true. And a lot of good can be done if the trials are successful and a treatment is discovered. Or a cure, which is even better."

"Makes sense," Palmer said.

"That brings us to the underbelly of the relationship between the financial sector and the drug companies. Remember, we're talking about the biggest privately held industry in the country. Billions and billions of dollars are involved."

"When you say privately held—"

"I mean other than the military and other parts of the government sector."

"I see," Palmer said.

"Medications and health care taken together are a trillion-dollar industry, you agree?"

"Sounds right," Whyte said, once again trying to show off his knowledge while hoping Speare didn't press him for details.

"So far, there are certain diseases that cannot be cured—they can only be treated or, worst case, managed." Speare shook his head, and it was obvious the man felt genuinely sad about the dilemma he faced every day. "Some of these illnesses are rare, others affect millions. Take the coronavirus and how determined the government became to find a vaccine."

"We all know that story," Palmer said.

"The pressure on my agency was enormous."

My agency, Palmer noted, but all he said was, "Must have been."

"Well, our friends at RDMO used the crisis to demand that we move their applications along, even though their work had absolutely nothing to do with Covid-19."

"Vera mentioned that," Whyte told him. "Wasn't too happy about it."

"The financial side of all this is enormous," he said. "Just imagine if one or more of those major illnesses no longer existed, consider the fiscal consequences. Tens of thousands of medical professionals who were trained for the treatment and care of those patients are suddenly out of work. Any number of facilities would become obsolete, or at least require expensive renovations to be used for other purposes. Perhaps the largest impact of all would be a dramatic rise in the average life expectancy. The population would swell with elderly Americans living longer, maybe to the point where the economy couldn't handle it."

The other three men stared at him until Palmer asked, "Are you saying there are financial reasons why certain cures could be a bad thing?"

The man from the FDA looked back at him without responding.

"That's awfully cynical, Jon," Mahoney said. "Not only does it ignore all the good that sort of breakthrough would do, but what about the windfall a cure like that would provide to the company that finds it?"

"I'm not suggesting there's some evil group of scientists conspiring to prevent these discoveries," Speare told them. "To the contrary, there are countless scientists who work every day to find those answers, and I believe their motives are pure. I've become acquainted with hundreds, perhaps even thousands of them over the years. Most are underpaid, and almost all are underappreciated. But we're not talking about them, are we? We're talking about the people who control the money." He picked up the tail of an ice-cold shrimp and dipped it into the spicy red cocktail sauce in the middle of his plate.

"Such as the investors in RDMO," Palmer said.

"Far as I know, that's why we're here."

"I'm confused," Palmer admitted. "I thought the problem with RDMO was that they were pushing for approvals and that there are possible improprieties in how they report their trial results. Isn't that what Platt was being called before Congress to discuss?"

Speare responded with a smile worthy of the Cheshire cat. "Is it?" he asked and went for a second shrimp.

Palmer, who had not touched his salad and was still holding his drink, said, "Enlighten us, please."

"You're all sophisticated men."

"Not so much when it comes to your area of expertise," Whyte said.

"You don't have to be a biologist to understand what I'm saying about the business world."

"Go on," the detective said.

"There are many reasons why someone would invest in a business. To build it, to sell it, to break it up into parts, and in some instances, for less straightforward reasons. Not everyone is interested in running a stock price up. Some take a short position, intending to profit when the crash occurs."

Palmer finally placed his drink on the table and leaned forward. "You're suggesting that Franco and associates invested in RDMO with the purpose of destroying the company?"

"Not necessarily and not completely. As I say, there are trials they're still pushing. Preliminary approvals would help run the price of the stock up and easily disguise what comes next. They could take a position in the market expecting the stock to lose value, knowing they can cause the final tests to fail our standards. Short selling is not an unusual tactic. After all, whatever goes up—"

"I understand short selling," Palmer said. "But you're suggesting they could be creating an artificial increase in the price of their shares, knowing their ultimate test results might then be artificially made to fail."

"And therefore make their short position extremely valuable. Gentlemen, Kevin and Vera told me I should be blunt, and I'm happy to oblige since I do not like what's being done to that company. I thought the issue might be addressed in the congressional hearings, but with the death of Mr. Platt, there's no way to know what other proof they have. If you care about what's happening here, I suggest you dig into the portfolios of both Mr. Franco and Mr. Carrigan. Have a good look at other things they own, directly and indirectly. If you want to know what they're up to, I believe that will lead you to some of the answers you're seeking."

"What should we be looking for?" Whyte asked.

"Related investments," Speare said, apparently satisfied to leave it at that.

"What about other people? Anyone else we should be looking at?" Palmer asked.

Speare had picked up his drink, ready to have another go at it. "You have someone in mind?" he asked.

Palmer was looking directly into his eyes again as he said, "Peter Frost. His name ever come up?"

Speare shook his head, then had a taste of his vodka. "In regard to RDMO?"

"In regard to anything."

He shook his head again. "Not that I recall."

"You never heard the name?"

He took a moment, as if to think it over, before saying, "Don't think so."

Palmer glanced at Whyte, who responded with an almost imperceptible nod.

They knew Speare was lying and, with all the man had divulged up to then, the question might be, *Why?* Except Palmer already knew the answer—*Peter Frost cast a large and fearsome shadow.*

CHAPTER TWENTY-SEVEN

During the train ride back to New York, Palmer was on his cell phone, catching up with Maureen.

Whyte worked on his laptop, which the detective generally considered a mortal struggle between man and machine. Nothing about it felt intuitive to someone born before the dawn of the microchip era. "This is not going to be easy," Whyte said as he looked up from the screen.

Palmer told Maureen to hold on as he turned to Whyte. "Meaning what, the computer getting the best of you again?"

"No, I'm talking about what I'm finding. Speare said these holdings could be direct or indirect, and he wasn't kidding. Franco's companies have more layers than a French pastry."

"A French pastry?"

"What about a French pastry?" Maureen asked.

Ignoring her, Palmer told Whyte, "I know where we can get some help. Just pull together what you can." Turning back to his call with Maureen, he said, "Robbie is hungry, that's all. Who called?"

"The usual suspects," she told him. "Marvin Taub said, and I quote, 'What the hell is going on with my case?' Christina Franco phoned, basically asking the same thing, only a little more politely. Said she couldn't get through on your cell."

"I turned it off during my meeting," Palmer said. "Go on."

"Her mother called. I told her you were out and she said it would be fine if you called her tomorrow."

"That it?"

"The lawyer representing Christina's husband wants to speak with you."

"Lillian Bartz."

"Yes. A real charmer, by the way. Basically hung up on me after she left the message."

"All right, I'll return some calls. Be back to you soon."

The first person he phoned was Christina Franco.

"You served him with the divorce papers," she said.

"The process server got him at his office this morning. How did you hear?"

"He called my mother, can you believe it?"

"Your mother?"

"You've met her, you get who she is. Old-fashioned to the bone. Romantic in a misguided way."

Palmer was tempted to ask what she found misguided about being romantic.

"I'm sure Edward wants her to talk me out of it."

"Can she?"

"What do you think, Palmer?"

"All right, I'll speak with her. I also heard from your husband's lawyer."

"What did she want?"

"I'll get back to her and find out."

"What should I be doing in the meantime?"

"Whatever you normally do, except stay away from your husband. No more confrontations, no more fistfights." He hesitated before asking, "Any sign of that man who was tailing you?"

"I've seen him a couple of times," she said. "I think there may be others now, working some sort of rotation. No question about it, I'm being watched."

"It's time to get you some protection."

"I'm not giving into that, at least not yet. Let Edward play his sick games, I won't provide him the satisfaction."

"It could be useful to your case if we can intercept one of these characters and prove your husband is paying them. A judge is not going to like that, could help if they press the assault charge—"

"*Assault,*" she said, making it sound profane.

It was a rare talent she had displayed before, Palmer thought, *her ability to do that with a single word.* "Just be careful," he told her. "By the way, you know anything about your husband investing in nursing homes, medical providers, anything like that?"

"From the little I know about his business, I have to admit none of that sounds familiar."

"Okay," he said, "I'll be in touch."

After that call ended, Palmer told Whyte that Jeanette Scott had phoned the office.

"You two are becoming quite the item," Whyte said.

"I like her."

"I'm sure she's a delight. She's also got a reputation as an alcoholic, loaded with family money, who has nothing to do with her time. Her husband's been keeping her hidden for years, and now she's going to get you running in circles so she can feel relevant or involved or whatever the hell she needs to feel."

"Anyone ever tell you that you can be a real downer?"

"Almost everyone," Whyte said, then shut his laptop and sat back. "And speaking of alcoholics, I think you and I need to pump the brakes on all this boozing." He stared at the drinks sitting on the tray table between them.

"You're serious."

"Don't mean to sound like a wimp, but these liquid lunches and barroom meetings are taking a toll on my liver."

Palmer waited.

"And my brain."

"And mine, I assume."

Whyte nodded. "I know when you're over the line. Given what's at stake, we need you on top of your game. With no unnecessary complications."

"As opposed to necessary complications?"

"You need to stay sharp, kiddo."

"Point taken," Palmer said. "Now, what's really bothering you?"

"Peter Frost. Speare knew the name but denied it. You see that flicker of recognition in his eyes?"

"And fear," Palmer said. "Which is why he lied about it."

"Which is also why he may have more sense than you do."

"Thanks for that."

"Whatever he knows about Frost, it means it likely has something to do with RDMO."

"Or some other deal," Palmer suggested.

"Maybe, but if that were true, he could have told us what he knows about him. As far as any involvement by Frost with RDMO, Speare shut that discussion down like a toilet lid."

"A toilet lid? You're full of odd similes today."

"That's a simile not a metaphor?" Whyte asked, but Palmer shook his head. "All I'm saying is that we have enough to keep us busy without getting involved with a congressman's unstable wife."

"I've told you," Palmer insisted, "I'm helping her, because my plan is for her to also help us. What better place to get inside information on the Francos, Platt, and her husband?"

"That's a nifty rationalization. You're counting on inside information from the wobbly wife of a United States congressman?"

"It might be useful," Palmer said, then his phone buzzed.

"What's up?" he asked Maureen.

"Attorney Bartz called again. She said to tell you she's livid that you served papers on her client."

"I think 'livid' is her default gear. Anything else?"

"Oh my, yes," Maureen told him. "She said you better call her because she's about to file a motion for a protective order. She doesn't intend to allow Mrs. Franco to continue her violent assaults on Mr. Franco, nor does she intend to allow you to control the narrative."

"Did she actually say that, 'control the narrative?'"

"A direct quote."

"What's with everyone today?"

"As Christina Franco predicted," Whyte said, "the circus is about to begin."

"You going to get in touch with Bartz?" Maureen asked.

"Nah. Call her office and let her know I'm at meetings in Washington, coming back late tonight. It'll make me sound important. I'll call her in the morning."

"All right," Maureen replied, her tone letting him know she thought he was making a mistake.

"You don't approve?"

"I think you should make that call yourself, regardless of how important you are. What do I always tell you? Build bridges."

Palmer sighed. "All right, I will. Meantime, put together the forms for a cross-motion on temporary support. If she's going to file for a protective order, we should give the judge something else to think about."

"Much better," Maureen said cheerfully. "I was so looking for something to keep me busy. That it?"

"That's all for now," he said and rang off.

"Our divorce case heating up?" Whyte asked.

"It is. Now get back to your computer and let's figure out what the hell Edward Franco is up to."

CHAPTER TWENTY-EIGHT

The following afternoon, Palmer returned the call from Jeanette Scott. As he anticipated, she wanted an update.

"I'm still in the information gathering stage," he told her. "RDMO is an interesting company, doing research into things I don't understand, genetic engineering and so forth. Since your son-in-law and his group became large investors, it seems there's been a change of direction." When Jeanette did not respond he said, "It might help at this point if you told me what *you* know."

"I understand the company was doing some wonderful things," she began. "Then, as you say, some of that changed."

"Why?"

"Money, I suppose. He's all about the money."

"Edward?"

"Edward and his cronies. He had us invest with him, have I mentioned that?"

"No."

"That's why Vernon became involved. When Edward approached us about the company, I asked Vernon for his advice."

A light began to dawn, but Palmer simply said, "I obviously didn't know that either."

"Edward claimed the investment would multiply by five or even ten times. 'Five to ten X,' he would say. He convinced Gene it was a good idea, then Vernon too. We all invested."

"When you say all—"

"Vernon and I."

"We have a list of the major investors," Palmer told her. "Part of the FDA disclosure requirements. I didn't see your family's name there. Or Platt's."

"Of course not. Edward never does anything directly. He works through different entities, or so I'm told."

"I want to help you, Jeanette, not create problems, but your husband is a United States congressman. Are you saying—"

"That he might have been involved in something unethical? Heavens no, that's what he has me for," she said with hoarse laugh. "As I've already told you, the serious money is mine. We have all sorts of trusts, investment vehicles, things set up over the years by Vernon."

Palmer shook his head. "Then, you're one of the investors in RDMO, at least indirectly, but your husband is not."

"That's right."

"And when things went sideways, when they began changing the direction of the company, then—"

"Vernon did what he could to protect me."

"Such as?"

"He began asking why certain drug trials were being abandoned and others pushed." She paused again. "Like you, I don't understand much about all these medical things, although Vernon did his best to explain. That's when he advised me to sell what I had, but Edward told him it would be a bad idea. Something about optics." She laughed again. "What a wonderful expression, optics. My daughter loves that word."

"What did Platt know about RDMO that Congress wanted to question him about?"

"I assume it was all about politics. The Republicans want to tie my family to the company, embarrass Gene by exposing whatever Edward is up to."

Her statement that Edward was "up to" something was so casually provided, Palmer decided to let it go. But the message that lit up in his mind read, *Trust no one*. He said, "If Platt advised you to get out, he must have been concerned the investment was a problem. And I don't just mean the money involved."

"I don't see how. All I did was agree to buy some stock. I had nothing to do with running the company, did I?"

"The rumors I hear suggest Platt's testimony was expected to expose corruption inside the company. If you and he were both investors, that might look a little suspicious."

She took some time before saying, "That could be. But Vernon was a careful man. He would have known what was going on there and would have protected both of us."

"Do you know if he sold his interest in the company?

"I have no idea, but it's hard for me to believe he would have gotten out and left me there."

Palmer paused before asking, "Did you ever talk about RDMO with your daughter?"

"You mean Christina discussing something serious with me? About business? Heavens no. She and Edward would keep those things between them."

"She's involved in his investments?"

"Involved? I wouldn't describe it that way, no. I would simply say that she's informed."

"Informed. Is that so?" Palmer said, then repeated it, as if he needed to hear it again himself.

CHAPTER TWENTY-NINE

The Hart Building is the newest structure in Washington to house offices for the United States Senate. The modest exterior is balanced by an impressive interior that features marble and bronze and contains fifty large suites, each comprised of two floors and ranging in size from 4,000 to 6,000 square feet.

That evening, Senator Harlan Detweiler and Congressman Eugene Scott were seated in a corner room on the second floor of the senator's quarters. The space was decorated like an old English library, complete with large leather armchairs, beautifully crafted tables, muted lighting, and a well-stocked bar set against the wall.

Scott watched as Detweiler shifted his corpulent frame in the large armchair, vainly seeking a comfortable position that his excess weight and chronic sciatica appeared to make all but impossible. "I'm sorry we weren't able to meet yesterday," he apologized in his lazy, southern drawl. "That military appropriations bill has us burnin' the midnight oil on our side of the building."

"That's all right, Harlan," Scott said, glad he had not been put off any longer than this. "I just need some friendly advice. Nothing urgent."

Detweiler leaned forward in a gesture of intimacy, although there was no one else in the room. "I hope it's not urgent, Gene. I truly do." Then he sat back again, his heavy-lidded gaze remaining fixed on the representative from New York.

Anyone acquainted with Senator Detweiler knew he was extremely valuable to have as a friend and exceptionally dangerous to have as an enemy. His lethargic pose had long ago lost its dissembling effect on those who knew him, which included everyone in Congress and almost anyone else in business or government that mattered. He was working through his sixth term in the Senate, the embodiment of true power. Even so, he was loath to abandon the laconic act that had served him so well for so long. It was comfortable for him, and every now and again there might still be someone gulled into mistaking him for a slow-witted Southerner. Those familiar with his act, such as Eugene Scott, simply disregarded the façade. Such indulgence was a small price to pay for his patronage.

Scott was a Yankee through and through, the opposite of Detweiler in almost every way. He was taller, trimmer, and more refined. Though his looks had faded over time and his straight hair had thinned, he still made an impressive appearance. When it came to intellect, however, he was a lightweight compared to the wily senator from the South. Detweiler was welcome at any serious gathering on national or local issues. Scott was considered by most as a fine addition to any cocktail party or fundraiser. A career politician, his path had been paved with his wife's money, his loyalty to the party, and the social skills he had honed as a frat boy at Colgate.

"I only wish I had a better sense of what's coming down the pike," Scott said.

"Have you heard anything new?" the senator asked.

"Not a damned thing. That was part of my reason for calling you."

Detweiler grunted. "And what might be the other part?"

"Just as I've said. Some friendly advice."

Detweiler pressed his lips together before responding. "Seems your old friend, the federal prosecutor in New York, wants your butt in a sling. I suppose you've heard the same thing."

Scott's look of concern made it clear he had. "Is the push coming from up there or from the AG's office down here?"

"I'm told it's from up there, and for now, they'd like to keep it that way. The Attorney General seems to be givin' the office in New York free rein. And you know why."

"Yes," Scott said. He knew if the investigation into RDMO was approached on a national level, it might snare too many others in the net, something the Democrats wanted to avoid since they only held the House of Representatives by a razor thin margin. The party wanted to avoid yet another national scandal and having the matter handled in New York would limit the focus to Scott and his family. It was good politics for the party, bad for him.

Scott picked up his scotch and took a long swallow. "Seems I'm on my own," he said flatly.

Detweiler slowly nodded his leonine head. "That's what I'm hearing, which is why they've narrowed the scope of the inquiry. No other big fish in the barrel. And that son-in-law of yours," Detweiler began, then didn't bother to finish the thought, since the senator had already made his low opinion of Edward Franco known to Scott. Instead, Detweiler gulped down a generous part of his rye on the rocks before he delivered the rest of the bad news. "They may also be dredgin' up some dirt about you and that young lady who worked in your office last summer. So far they don't appear to have much, but soon there'll be some reporter lookin' into it, tryin' to sell the story." Detweiler's thesis was accompanied by a searching look from beneath his sleepy eyelids. "What can they prove, if it comes down to that?"

Scott smiled slightly at the question. Regardless of the senator's careless bearing, he knew that Detweiler always chose his words carefully. He cut his teeth as a trial lawyer in his home state and, as he had explained more than once, when dealing with the law, it rarely mattered what was true—it was all about what could be proved. In politics, the standard was even lower. It was all about the rumors you could spawn.

"I don't have any idea what they can prove, Harlan. I wish I did."

"We'll get to that another time, then, but it *is* an issue you're going to have to face."

"I know," Scott conceded. "Is there a way we can stop any of this before it gets that far?" There was no mistaking what the congressman was asking.

Detweiler slowly moved his gaze from the drink in his hand to the eyes of Eugene Scott. "We need some hard information before we try to answer that. Starting with the death of Vernon Platt. There's a stench comin' from there we can't turn away from." The senator's drawl tended to thicken as he moved closer to the heart of a matter. Right now, his accent was as dense as the mud along the Mississippi River.

Scott remained calm. "You have to know I had nothing to do with Vernon's suicide. He was my wife's best friend."

"Suicide," Detweiler repeated, slowly pronouncing the word as if he had no idea what it meant. "Platt negotiated several large contracts for your son-in-law. Then he became involved in this drug company, invested in it himself. There are some individuals who think he had information the committee would have found useful. Do I make my meanin' clear?"

"I'm not sure that you do."

Detweiler smiled patiently. "Come now, Gene. It's one thing for a man to insist he's innocent. That carries with it the hope of sympathy and ultimate vindication. On the other hand, one would be ill-advised to equate innocence with ignorance. One is the posture of the righteous, the other of a fool. Am I becomin' clearer?"

Scott did what he could to appear composed. "I don't believe Vernon would have done anything to hurt me."

"Maybe he wouldn't want to, but it might've depended on what was at stake for him personally. Not to mention which questions he was asked." Detweiler took a moment to shift in his seat again. "Loyalty is a wonderful quality, but it can become inconvenient, even for the best of men."

"If there was any wrongdoing, it was the work of Edward and his team, not me."

"See what I mean about loyalty," Detweiler responded with the knowing grin he had practiced for so long. "You talkin' about your son-in-law that way."

"I'm only saying that to you, for god's sake."

Detweiler exhaled slowly. "We've been on the same team for a lot of years, Gene. Fightin' the men and women across the aisle, even some inside our own party. A lotta years." He paused again, as if providing time for Scott to summon a few of those shared memories. Then he went on. "You came to me for advice and information. Unfortunately, I have little information, and my advice might not be worth much. My influence, such as it is, doesn't enjoy its strongest favor in New York."

Scott nodded his understanding.

"I'll do all I can, but I can tell you this much—do what *you* can to avoid an indictment. Once they charge you, a lot of your friends'll be runnin' for cover. Politically," he said, affording the word the full measure of each beat, "you'll be a toxic issue."

Scott knew he was right. "You think I should step forward and take an active role in the inquiry?"

"I think that may be your next move. You can't just keep giving these wishy-washy denials. The media will be lookin' to bury you before a grand jury gets the chance." The senator picked up his drink again. "You may even have to waive immunity and testify, if things get that far."

"Are you serious?"

"You know me better than to think I'd joke about such a thing after only one whiskey. It's gonna be rough if you're called to testify; I was a prosecutor long enough to know. They may serve a subpoena, just to embarrass you with the decision of whether to appear or not."

"I've thought of that," Scott admitted.

"Well think on it some more. And get your finances in order. Everyone knows your wife is a wealthy woman. That would seem to deprive you of a motive to be grabbin' money from that pharmaceutical company, unless what's hers isn't yours, if you see what I mean. That may be why they're harpin' on your relationship with that young woman, suggestin' your marriage may be on the rocks." At this point, Detweiler's tone was not allowing for the possibility Scott's affair was something invented by the press. "You better think about mendin' some fences at home. It may be of the utmost importance for you to rebut any claim you need to be chasin' money." Having said that, the senator finished his drink and climbed slowly to his feet. "Avoid an indictment, Gene. Once they file charges, even an acquittal at trial won't rescue your political career."

"American justice," Scott smiled grimly.

"You're too good a man to go down without a fight. Call me in a couple of days, I may know a bit more, have an idea or two. Then we'll see where things stand."

Scott nodded, not admitting that things were already far worse than Detweiler imagined.

CHAPTER THIRTY

Palmer spent the afternoon in his office catching up on paperwork and phone calls. Then he headed out to have dinner alone.

P.J. Clarke's on Third Avenue is one of New York's iconic taverns. It has been featured in any number of movies, with its dark wood, old mirrors, the raw bar up front, and dining room in the rear. As Detweiler and Scott were concluding their brief meeting, Palmer was polishing off a cheeseburger, fries, and a beer. He bid the bartender Jerry good night and began the walk home. It was dark, and the evening air was still warm. Strolling over to Lexington Avenue, he passed the large display windows of Bloomingdale's, continuing north.

It becomes relatively quiet in that part of the city after the stores close and, as Palmer made his way home, the streets were all but deserted. The quiet allowed him time to think about the Francos, Vernon Platt, Marvin Taub—all of that occupying his attention as he headed west on 64th Street when he suddenly heard someone rushing up from behind him. Before he could turn around, a man grabbed hold of his right elbow. Palmer pulled away, only to find a second man on his left.

"Just keep walking," the second man said. "No one has to get hurt, Counselor, not unless you insist on it."

Palmer saw that the first man, who now let go of his elbow, had the compact build and posture of a wrestler. He was not tall, but he had a broad chest, long arms, and large shoulders hunched slightly forward, his face putting the finishing touch on his simian appearance. Palmer thought he had the look of a moron.

The small gorilla gave him a shove forward, saying, "We just want to talk."

"Make an appointment with my office," Palmer told him, which was answered immediately by a quick, hard punch to his kidney.

"I told you no one has to get hurt," the man said. "Just don't try to be a smartass." Looking past Palmer to his accomplice, he said, "They told me he's a smartass."

Before Palmer could speak, he was hit with a second shot to the ribs and told, "Walk."

Palmer was feeling more than a little sorry he had listened to Whyte and placed his automatic back in the nightstand drawer. Catching his breath as they shoved him forward, he asked, "Where are we going?"

"You keep moving, we talk a little, that's all."

Palmer figured if they meant him serious harm they could have already done a lot worse than a couple of cheap shots. As he resumed walking, he asked, "What do you want to talk about?"

"Friends," the man on his right replied.

"Mine or yours?"

"Let's say both."

"We have friends in common?" Palmer asked, tempted to say how unlikely that possibility might be. Instead, he asked, "Who?"

"Coupla guys."

"Should I guess?"

"Sure, why not?" the man on his right said.

The street was quiet, and they were walking slowly. Palmer was hoping for someone to appear, or even better, a passing police cruiser, but there was no one in sight and, for now, they looked like three chums taking a slow walk along 64th Street toward Park Avenue.

"Marvin Taub," Palmer said.

"Very good."

"Edward Franco."

To that, neither man responded.

"Peter Frost."

That name got a rise out of the man to his left, who spun Palmer to face him, apparently ready to hit him again. Instead, the man said, "We're playing nice now, just take it easy."

Christina had provided only a vague description of the gray-haired man who had been following her, but now that Palmer had a good look at this second goon, he was certain this was the guy. "Do I know you?"

"I wouldn't think so," the gray-haired man replied.

"You going to rough me up some more, or is there some message you want to deliver? Either way, I've already had a long day so let's get on with it."

The gray-haired man appeared ready to throw the punch he had wanted to throw a moment before, but this time Palmer acted first. One of the unforeseen benefits of having been bullied in his youth was a talent for surviving a beatdown.

Using his legs to create momentum, he sprung forward and drove the palms of his hands into the man's shoulders, knocking him off-balance. Then Palmer charged at him, nailing him under the chin with the crown of his head, sending him sprawling backward onto the pavement. Before the baboon behind him could react, Palmer opted for the adage about living to fight another day. Relying on speed rather than strength, he took off, sprinting back towards Lexington Avenue, where there was more pedestrian traffic and a number of taxis heading south.

Hailing a cab, he jumped in, slammed the door shut, and told the driver, "Just head south a few blocks, fast as you can."

In typical New York City cab driver fashion, the man asked dully as he pulled away, "What is this, we in some sort of action flick?"

"Exactly," Palmer said, "and if you can get me to the King Cole Bar without being stopped there's a fifty in it for you."

As they sped south, the driver looked in his rear-view mirror, then reached to his right, grabbed a paper napkin and handed it to Palmer in the back seat. "You better wipe your nose before we get there."

Palmer craned his neck to get a look in the mirror and saw his nose had been bloodied when he drove his head into the gray-haired man's chin. Even worse for Palmer, some of the blood had dripped onto his white shirt.

"Damn," he said aloud.

Doing his best to clean his face, he wondered what would be coming at him next.

He would find out a few hours later.

CHAPTER THIRTY-ONE

After making his hasty escape, Palmer took his time with a Woodford Manhattan at the King Cole Bar, then headed home without further incident. The next morning, after his workout, he was not completely surprised to receive a phone call from Peter Frost. The man's name seemed to be coming up everywhere recently, and Palmer was certain it was Frost who had set the two hoodlums to ambush him.

Now Frost was asking him to lunch.

He could have declined the offer and, given what he knew about the man, that might have been the sensible response. But Palmer had things to ask Frost, and not just about Christina or the assault last night. There was Joey D'Angelo's murder. The effort to frame Taub for it. The attack on Sammy Burdick. RDMO. And the most obvious question of all…

Why does Frost want to see me?

So, he decided not to tell Whyte about the invitation, knowing his friend would say he was crazy to go without him. But Palmer figured the meeting was worth the risk—if Frost meant to do any serious damage, his two henchmen would have thrown more at him than a couple of body shots. He hoped the meeting would help to bring a murky picture into focus.

Live in hope, he told himself, *die in despair*.

There are areas in the Bronx where you wouldn't park a twenty-year-old pickup truck with bald tires for more than fifteen minutes without expecting everything but the chassis to be gone when you returned.

Then, there are other, select enclaves, where you can park a Rolls Royce with the doors unlocked and the motor running, knowing that when you get back, it's more likely the car will have been washed and waxed than stolen. These are neighborhoods populated by groups that provide their own vigilante brand of justice, guaranteeing security in the city's northern borough, where the police can be counted on to look the other way.

Joe Erico's is a restaurant in one of those safe havens, and that afternoon Palmer felt comfortable driving his Porsche SUV up there rather than taking a cab. He wanted freedom of movement, especially in case he needed to leave in a hurry.

Palmer pulled up and double-parked directly in front of the restaurant. Not only was this neighborhood safe, it was also a place where the owners of expensive cars didn't worry about minor details like parking tickets. He stepped onto the sidewalk and had a casual look up and down the avenue. Dressed in a dark gray suit, white shirt, and yellow silk tie with small lavender squares, Palmer felt good about himself—which was vital when meeting a man like Peter Frost.

When he walked into the restaurant, Palmer noticed that all discussion seemed to come to an abrupt halt. The place was patronized by an insular crowd that shared a collective suspicion of strangers. It was a garish place, decorated in an extremely Italianate manner. *Beyond rococo beach*, Palmer thought. But neither the customers nor the décor was going to tolerate any sort of ridicule. The food was excellent, the prices high, and many of the denizens were drawn from the part of New York City life affectionately known as the underworld.

Palmer spotted Frost seated at a table in the far corner of the dining area. When he gave Palmer a slight wave, it was not only a greeting. It was a signal to others that he was Frost's guest, and conversation around the room resumed almost at once.

The head waiter hurried over to Palmer and said, "Right this way."

When Palmer reached the table, Frost motioned for him to take the seat across from him. He made no effort to get up or offer to shake hands, which was fine with Palmer. He avoided physical contact whenever he could—except, of course, with women.

"Well," Palmer said as he sat, "it's been a while."

Frost's muscular build and stiff posture gave him a military bearing, while his close-cropped, preternaturally white hair and icy blue eyes provided an unmistakable indication of menace. Even when he managed one of his rare smiles, as he did now, Palmer could feel the chill.

"How have you been?" he asked.

"I'm all right," Palmer said.

Frost nodded. "Say hello to my associates," he told him, gesturing at the other two men at the table.

The tall, heavy-set man on Palmer's left looked to be in his fifties, with thick arms and hands the size of two small pot roasts. He was introduced as Ronny. The shorter man to Palmer's right appeared to be around the same vintage. He was bald and wore wire-rimmed glasses, looking more like a bookkeeper than a thug. Frost identified him as Leo. No last names were offered.

Palmer nodded to each of them in turn, struck by the fact that all three men were dressed in suits and ties, looking like respectable executives rather than the criminals he knew them to be. He took the empty seat, turned to his host, and said, "I can't wait for you to tell me why you've invited me here."

Frost stared at him for a few seconds, causing Palmer to wonder if the man ever blinked. "You always come right to the point. Not polite, but I have to admit it saves time."

Since he had no idea what *polite* had to do with this meeting, Palmer said, "I don't think you asked me here to socialize."

Before Frost could reply, the man called Leo said, "How do we know he's not wired?"

Not taking his eyes off Palmer, Frost said, "Not the way he plays the game. He believes in fairness, always on the up and up." Then, to Palmer, he said, "You're not wired, are you?"

"No, I'm not," Palmer said.

Frost ended their brief staring contest, turning to Leo as he said, "That's good enough for me."

"I appreciate that," Palmer told him. "So, what's the occasion?"

Frost tilted his head slightly to the side as he said, "The food is very good here. You ever been to Joe's place before?"

"Sure. And I agree, the food is good."

"So, what's your rush?"

Palmer knew he was speaking with a dangerous man, but he had battled Frost before, and he came here today determined not to be intimidated. "You're the one who seems to be in a rush. You said you needed to see me right away, and that you didn't want to talk on the phone."

"Maybe I just wanted to reminisce about Paul and Artie. Sometimes a man likes to look back."

Paul and Artie had retained Palmer some years ago, when they had problems with the fancy restaurant they owned on the Upper East Side. They had borrowed money from Frost and, after they fell behind on the usurious interest payments he charged, the pressure began—financial and otherwise. Palmer stepped in and, every time Frost pushed, Palmer pushed back. When matters became violent, Palmer and Whyte saw to it that the henchman who had taken a baseball bat to Artie's legs ended up in jail. That led to a sit-down with Frost, where Palmer worked things out.

At the time, Frost said he didn't know whether Palmer was stupid or crazy. As far as Palmer knew, the man was still not sure.

"Haven't seen either of them in a while," Palmer said.

"I have," Frost told him. "Still in the business, still hanging on by a thread."

Palmer waited.

"Haven't seen you for a while though," Frost said.

"As I mentioned."

"Not since you caused those problems for my friend Ralph."

Palmer could not stifle a laugh. "You think I caused his problem? Maybe he should have left his baseball bat at home that night."

Frost stared at him.

"He out of prison yet?"

"No thanks to you," Frost said, "but yes, he's out. Ralphie is a good boy."

"Not an opinion shared by everyone," Palmer said. "Particularly not by Artie, who still walks with a limp."

Frost shook his head. "I'll tell him you said hello anyway."

Palmer leaned back and folded his arms across his chest. "Please don't bother."

Frost turned to the man on his right, the large one he called Ronny. "See what I mean? It's like I told you before he got here. Palmer's tougher than either of you two."

Palmer was not sure what to do with that endorsement, so he said, "If we're done reminiscing, how about we discuss something more current?"

"For instance?"

"For instance, maybe you'll explain what's going on with our friend Marvin Taub."

Frost looked around the table, then began to laugh. Unlike Palmer, his was a brittle, cheerless sound. "You really are a piece of work, you know that?" He signaled for a waiter. "Have a drink, will you?"

"Sure. Bourbon and ice," Palmer told the man who had hurried over. "Blanton's, if you have it."

"And another round for us," Frost said, then watched as the waiter rushed off before turning back to Palmer. "First you tell *me* about Taub, then I'll see if I have anything to add."

"Is that how this works?"

"That's how this works," Frost said.

"What would you like to know?"

"Why don't you start by telling me what he has to say about killing Joey D?"

Palmer smiled. "You know I can't reveal anything he told me."

"Tell you the truth, I don't really give a fuck what he told you. I want to know what *you* have to say."

"I'm flattered."

"And?"

"And I know Marvin did *not* murder D'Angelo."

"Good, because I like a man who can tell me straight what he thinks."

"Good," Palmer repeated, "because I like a man who keeps his bargain." The bald-headed man called Leo flinched, but Palmer ignored him. "It's my turn to ask questions, and I've got a few."

"Wait a while, we're still on Taub. I want to know how you think you're going to win the case with his gun at the murder scene."

"Once again, I'd have an ethical issue revealing anything about my defense."

Frost frowned. "I don't consider that a straight answer."

The drinks were served before Palmer could respond. After he took a swallow of the whiskey, he said, "I may be able to share some general ideas, but that'll depend if you'll tell me who planted the gun. And who told D'Angelo to stage the argument with Taub? And who called the police to tip them off about that whole phony scene? And for that matter, who roughed up Sammy Burdick after Whyte left his place the other day? All of which leads to bigger questions, like why you're so interested in Taub, and the D'Angelo murder, and me." He had another taste of his drink as Frost stared at him. "Jump in any time you like."

There was a quiet pause until Leo began to say something, but Frost held up his hand, his gaze on Palmer. "You know who you're dealing with here, right?" He kept his voice level and quiet. "You think you're going to come in here with your fast mouth and outtalk me like I'm some asshole DA on Centre Street?"

"You invited *me*, remember?"

"Shut up for a change and take some advice. You don't know what you're into, and you're already way over your head."

Palmer didn't respond. He just stared back at Frost, amazed at how rapidly the man's chatty demeanor had morphed into the ominous tone of a killer.

"You hear me?" Frost repeated.

"I hear you. What I don't hear are answers to my questions."

Frost looked around the table as if he were about to poll the issue of Palmer's sanity. "You want answers? For instance, about Sammy

Burdick? Why not?" He lifted his glass, but did not drink. "Burdick is a two-bit faggot with a big mouth. Someone probably figured he needed a lesson in manners. And Taub, he's nothing to me. We have a bad past. I never liked him, never will. If he goes down for Joey's murder, then he goes down. That's all there is to it."

Palmer put his glass on the table and leaned forward. "You know me better than that. If you called me here—"

"I'll tell you why I called you here. I don't want you in my way, that's why. I've had enough of your bullshit. You fucked me on the restaurant on 57th Street, and you put Ralphie in jail. That's enough interference for a lifetime. I know you're a bit of a loose cannon, and I make allowances for that, because I know you're an honorable guy, which means something in my world. But you get in my way again, and I'll step on you like a bug."

Palmer threw his napkin on the table. "Your boys paid me a visit last night, as you obviously know. I'm guessing you wanted to have me smacked around like Sammy. That's what guys like you do, right? Have someone else run your errands for you?"

Frost surprised him by managing an authentic smile. "You really are something. You think I sent some guys to rough you up last night, but you have the balls to come up here today and meet with me?" Frost looked at the other two men, then returned his attention to Palmer. "What am I going to do with you, young Palmer?"

"You're going to do whatever you want, but don't tell me my job. You and I both know Taub is innocent, and I'm going to get him acquitted."

Frost reverted to his default expression, which was cold as steel on a wintry day. "You think so, eh?"

"I do, and it's too goddamned bad if that doesn't fit with your plans." Palmer stood and looked down at Frost. "I don't know what you're up to, but I also intend to find that out," he told him, disappointed to notice how fast his heart was racing now. "Anyway, thanks for the drink," he said, then turned and walked out of the restaurant, keeping his gait slow and not looking back.

The three men silently watched until Palmer exited through the front door. Then Frost said, "I hate to admit it, but I like that fucking guy. He really is one crazy sonofabitch."

Ronny nodded. "You don't think our friend has anything to worry about?"

"Not a thing," Frost said with a cold smile. "Not a thing."

Neither of his companions had to ask what he meant.

CHAPTER THIRTY-TWO

An hour later, Palmer was sitting in his office listening to Whyte shout at him.

"You were crazy to go up there without me."

Palmer had expected Whyte's reaction, the response of a protective older brother, which he appreciated more than he was willing to admit. He said, "If he really wanted me out of the picture, his boys could have taken care of that last night. There's something else going on here."

"Like what?" Whyte demanded, his voice still loud.

"Not sure. Whatever he's up to may be a key to this whole mess."

Whyte frowned. "Maybe so, but walking into the lion's den, right after you were roughed up by—"

"I know, I know, maybe not my best idea. But if there was any chance of learning something, I had to go alone. He sees you as an ex-cop."

"I *am* an ex-cop."

Palmer nodded. "I realize this will sound a little strange, but Frost and I have a sort of, uh, rapport."

"A rapport you'll live longer without." Whyte shook his head, finally calming down. "All right, you went there. Was it worth it?"

"Maybe. For one thing, it's clear he's the one framing Taub."

"He admitted that?"

"Of course not, it was the way he reacted when I brought it up. And he didn't bother to deny it. For the life of me, though, I can't figure out why he'd go to all this trouble, although I do think he's trying to scare me off Taub's case."

Whyte gave that a moment. "But not the Franco case?"

"Never really came up. He alluded to his issues with Taub back when. Could be as simple as that."

"But why would he care if you defend him?"

"Not sure."

"Okay, then toss one of your legendary theories at me."

"Wish I had good one," Palmer told him. "But I know this much for sure—if Frost framed Taub, it means he was likely the one behind Joey D's murder."

"That would make sense," Whyte conceded.

Palmer thought it over. "Which leaves us with one more leap of faith. Frost seems to be in league with Edward Franco. If he had D'Angelo killed, could that mean Joey D had something to do with Platt's death?"

"Possible."

"Joey might have even been the guy who shoved Platt off the balcony, although it's not the sort of thing Joey was into." Palmer shook his head. "But even if all that's true, I still don't see why Frost would complicate things by trying to implicate Taub. And forcing him to get another attorney."

"By shoving you around and throwing a smoke bomb into the backyard?"

"For instance."

"If Frost has the police going after Taub for D'Angelo's death, no one has a reason to link Joey to Platt. Keeps the Platt headline about suicide rather than a possible murder."

Palmer nodded. "That's not bad. Now we just need some facts to back that up."

"I may have something on that. Got a call from Hugh Lawson, said he wants to talk. All right if I tell him about your chat with Frost?"

"Why not? Just remember, when you lay all this out for him, Frost hasn't admitted anything."

"As if he ever would," Whyte said.

Palmer shook his head. "If they really want to frame Taub, why do such a lousy job? Like planting the gun after Joey was found."

"Another good question," Whyte said, then picked up the phone and dialed Lawson. "Hugh, it's Robbie."

"You have some time?" the lieutenant asked. "I think you're going to want to hear what I have to say."

"Of course. I'm in the office with Palmer, want to stop by?"

Palmer could hear the policeman laugh in response. "You kidding?" Lawson asked. "Visit a lawyer's office? I have a reputation to protect. How about meeting at the corner of Sixty-Sixth and Third?"

"When?"

"I can be there in ten."

"I'm on my way," Whyte said.

Whyte took the short walk to meet Lawson, then climbed into the passenger seat of his sedan.

"I've got some news on Platt," Lawson told him. "Forensics is finally backing me up." He began by describing Vernon Platt's apartment and what he initially found in the course of the investigation. As Whyte well knew, Lawson was a detail man, and he provided them all. Lawson was convinced the place had been scrubbed, particularly the bathroom, which, as he pointed out, is a place where porcelain sinks and marble counters lend themselves to recognizable fingerprints. But none were found. "How is that possible?" Lawson asked rhetorically. "Platt must have used his bathroom at some point, right? The sink? The tub? The shower?"

Whyte offered no argument.

Then Lawson told him about the easy chair in the bedroom and the book on the table beside it—something that had fascinated Lawson from the beginning. He shared his idea, of how Platt must have been sitting in the chair reading until, as he described it, "Whatever happened, happened." Then he went on. "I had the book tested and found Platt's fingerprints on several pages ahead of where it had been left open and placed face down on the table."

Whyte stared at him. "What did that tell you?"

Lawson smiled. "Come on, Robbie."

"He'd already been past the page it was opened to?"

"That's the obvious conclusion."

"A bit of a stretch, no?"

Lawson shook his head. "The book is some boring history about Russia. Not even a guy like Platt was likely to go back to re-read entire sections. Which leaves only one reasonable explanation."

"The book was knocked off the table and someone, who was not Platt, put it back. But he wasn't sure what page he was up to, so it was face down but opened to the wrong page."

"You get a gold star."

"It's an interesting premise," Whyte said, "but not much to go on."

This time, when Lawson smiled, he had that knowing look Whyte recognized. "Not much until we brought forensics back to have another look around. And guess what they found?

"You're killing me, Hugh."

"I noticed traces of blood on the balcony railing the first day I was there."

"The killer's?"

"Platt's."

"Not as good, but I think I see where you're going."

"Have a try."

Whyte nodded. "Someone roughs up Platt, probably knocks him unconscious. Then this hitter goes around wiping the place down, including the bathroom, puts the book back on the table, cleans up after himself. Then he gives Platt the heave ho off the terrace and runs out, not realizing there was blood on the railing."

"Right. It was dark. Never saw it."

"Where's the rag he used to do all this housework?"

"That's easy. Kept it with him, dumped it someplace."

Whyte took a moment to think it over. "I'll argue the other side," he said. "What if Platt somehow cut himself before or during his jump off the balcony? Left his own blood behind?"

Lawson was shaking his head before Whyte was done. "The blood was found on a lower part of the railing. Assuming I'm right and someone sat him there, the traces of blood were around head-high, if you can get a mental picture of this."

"I do. No way Platt cut himself there."

"Agreed."

"Which means the killer dragged Platt out there, propped him against the rail, and then did his housework."

"Makes more sense, don't you think? You wouldn't want Platt bleeding all over the apartment, making a mess you couldn't hide. And you wouldn't send him over the side before you got done wiping the place down and were ready to run out of there."

Whyte thought it over. "But still no trace of anything from the killer? DNA, fingerprints?"

"Nothing," Lawson said, his disappointment evident. "I have circumstantial evidence proving Vernon Platt's death was murder and not suicide. The identity of the murderer is yet to be determined."

Whyte hesitated. "What about Joey D'Angelo? The night after Platt died, Joey shows up at Taub's place and picks a fight for no apparent reason, according to Taub and his people. I say someone put him up to that scene, probably without knowing why."

"Then he gets smoked himself."

"Right," Whyte agreed.

"Bit of a stretch, though, connecting that to Platt's murder."

"Not if you factor in the rumors that Joey and Platt knew each other."

"There is that," Lawson agreed. "Whoever was pulling the strings must have convinced D'Angelo it was all part of some cockeyed scheme to frame Taub, although for the life of me I can't see how that part makes any sense."

Whyte did not disagree. "D'Angelo was not a deep thinker, but if someone got him to murder Platt and help frame Taub, he must've thought he was going after a big payday."

Lawson allowed himself a short laugh. "And they have the nerve to say Black people are stupid."

Whyte smiled. "You know I've never said that. Seen you solve too many tough cases."

Lawson paused for a moment. "You realize all this speculation could be a lot of bullshit. These two murders could be unrelated."

"Of course," Whyte said. "So, what's next?"

"I reported our findings to the powers that be. Media will have it soon, then all hell will break loose in Washington."

"Their star witness isn't just dead, he was murdered."

"You got it," Lawson said.

"What's next?" Whyte repeated.

"I'm going back to look for any security video in the area around Platt's building. Maybe there's a CCTV setup nearby."

"Well, I appreciate the heads up. Might be helpful in the Taub case."

"That was my thought. Share and share alike, right?"

Whyte nodded. "On that score, let me tell you what happened to Palmer last night, and about his visit with Peter Frost today."

"Palmer met with Frost?"

"As you pointed out last time, my partner is a strange bird."

"That he is. And I'm always interested to hear about Frost," Lawson said. "Then I might have something to tell *you* about him."

CHAPTER THIRTY-THREE

Later that evening, Palmer was sitting on the leather sectional in his second floor living room, watching cable news, when he received a call from Sloane Taylor.

"To what do I owe the honor?" he asked.

"I find myself in your neighborhood, thought you might want to buy me a drink."

Palmer uttered a soft laugh. "Reporters never just find themselves in a neighborhood, Sloane. Where are you?"

"Around the corner."

"I see. Well, I was settling in for the night, going to read some Proust, have a madeleine, and nod off."

"Come on, Palmer, it's only eight o'clock."

"Oh, all right. You're definitely more interesting than Proust, and you undoubtedly have something up your sleeve."

"Up my sleeve? You can do better."

He let that go. "Where did you say you were?"

"I told you, around the corner."

"Doesn't give me much time to freshen up. Where would you like to meet?"

"How about I come to you?"

It was only a couple of minutes later when the doorbell rang. Palmer was already waiting in the downstairs foyer, and let her in.

"Thanks for the invitation," she said. "It was only a little easier than pulling teeth." She was dressed in a fitted navy-blue skirt, white silk blouse, and dark stiletto heels.

"You look great," he said.

She smiled. "And you didn't need to get all dressed up for me."

Palmer was in gray sweatpants, a black t-shirt, and sneakers. "I told you, I didn't have time to change. But I did brush my teeth." Spreading his arms he said, "Welcome to my humble dwelling."

"Not so humble. You going to show me around?"

"The full tour?"

"Why not?"

"Let's get a drink first," he said, then pointed her up the stairs, following close behind.

"You getting a good view?" she asked without turning around.

Palmer laughed. "Not at all. I tend to be clumsy, so I'm looking straight down, counting the steps."

On the second floor, he showed her into his living room. "I was going to abstain this evening, but since you've graced me with this visit, I'll celebrate with a bourbon with a big cube. I also have wine, red or white, and almost anything else you can name."

"Bourbon sounds good," she said.

He nodded his approval, went to the bar in the corner of the room, placed a large ice cube in each crystal tumbler, and poured their drinks. Handing Sloane her cocktail, he said, "Here's to pleasant surprises."

She touched her glass to his and, looking into his eyes, said, "That's something worth drinking to."

After having a taste of the whiskey, Palmer asked, "Where do you want to start?"

"Meaning what?"

"You said you wanted a tour of the place?"

"I do."

"Well, we could take it from bottom to top, if you really want to see everything."

"I'm game."

"All right, but be warned," he said as he had a look at her shoes, "there are a lot of stairs."

"I've worn high heels before."

Palmer took her back down to the main floor, then through a door that led to the basement. It was divided into two main areas: One for utilities and storage, the other his high-tech gym that included an elliptical, a Peloton, a Hydrow rowing machine, various other exercise equipment, free weights, and a steam shower.

"Very nice," she said. "Use it much?"

"Almost every day."

"Not inclined to join a health club, mingle with other work-out addicts?"

"Don't believe in group sweating. I have a trainer come by every couple of weeks. I'm more the one-on-one type. In almost everything."

She smiled, then followed him back to the main floor.

"You don't need to see the office, but I have a great garden and patio out back."

The night air was dry and warm and they sat with their drinks in hand.

"So tell me," he said, "what brings you by, other than an assignment from *Architectural Digest*?"

"I have to have an agenda?"

"Most people do, especially when they already have as many things in common as we do."

"Do we?"

He smiled without responding.

"All right, you choose a category."

"Let's start with the Franco divorce."

Sloane nodded. "From what I hear, it's going to be a mess. Word has it that the dragon lady of New York City matrimonial law has entered the scene."

"You're referring to my adversary, Lillian Bartz?"

"I am indeed."

"You've had experience with her?"

"I've covered a couple of the bold-type breakups Lillian's handled. She can be a nasty one, you better be prepared."

"I appreciate the warning."

"Then there's another of your clients, Marvin Taub. His gun was found at the murder scene. Not good news for the home team."

Palmer shrugged. "No prints on the gun. No witnesses. No real motive."

"What about the rumors of his argument with the victim. In Taub's flesh palace? In front of all sorts of witnesses?"

"Come on, Sloane, nobody bothers to kill a low-life hustler like Joey D'Angelo for acting up with a snoot full of coke and a bad attitude."

"I don't disagree," she said. "But that raises the question, why would anyone go to the trouble of framing Taub?"

"That's an excellent question. If you have any ideas, I'd be happy to hear them."

When she shook her head, her carefully groomed dirty blonde hair danced across her shoulders. "Theories are way above my pay grade, I only deal in facts. Remember, I'm just a lowly television reporter."

"Uh-huh. And that's why you're here? You have facts you want to share?"

"That depends. Are you going to be a good sharer too?"

"You know there are legal limits to what I can say."

"You hide behind the attorney-client privilege quite a bit, Palmer."

"When it's convenient."

"I'm not asking you to divulge any confidences. I just want to hear your theories. You do have something of a reputation for solving legal riddles."

"I have a reputation?"

"Several, in fact."

"You must enlighten me some time."

"We'll see about that."

"You'll keep everything off the record?"

"Until you tell me I can run with a story, any little gems you impart are as good as in a vault."

He smiled again. "You want me to take the word of a reporter for that? Especially one who deals in gossip."

"You certainly know how to romance a girl."

"Is that what I'm supposed to be doing?"

This time, when she picked up her glass, she had a full taste of the Blanton's. "I called you. I asked you to buy me a drink. I came to your place. The least you could do is show some enthusiasm for the opportunity."

"Opportunity," he repeated, as if thinking it over. "I didn't think you needed any more encouragement than the way I've been staring at you."

She smiled, her eyes seeming to light up even in the dark. "See, that wasn't so difficult, was it? Now how about the rest of the tour?"

Back on the second floor, they moved through the living room and then headed up another flight. He showed her a bedroom that he had converted into a study, and the master suite.

Standing near the doorway of the latter, she asked, "Where were we?"

"You wanted to know if I'm a good sharer, and I would say yes, I am."

"You want to show me?"

Palmer finished his drink in one long swallow and placed the glass on a table. Then he stepped towards her and held out his hand. Sloane reached for it, and he led her into his bedroom.

Later, after they made love and engaged in some pillow talk, she climbed out of bed and disappeared into the bathroom, leaving him to wonder what was missing. They had shared as much of each other as they could, until their desire shuddered to its sudden, grateful conclusion. But he believed making love, like love itself, must be a bit reckless for it to be wonderful. And yet he sensed a measure of restraint behind her actions. The bedroom should be a place where self-control is all but abandoned.

Was that not the essence of true intimacy? Palmer asked himself.

He was willing to forsake caution at the right time, under the right circumstances. Maybe that was why he felt deceived so often. Sloane was withholding some part of herself, even in the throes of passion. Not that the experience wasn't great, because on a strictly physical level it was. But she was emotionally distant, as if part of her remained beyond reach.

Now, as he lay there waiting for her to return to the bedroom, he realized how casual that made this encounter feel and how it was likely to mean very little to either of them later. With a touch of sadness, he returned his thoughts to something she said in those moments after the lovemaking was done.

She had asked questions about the Francos and Taub, which he ascribed to her natural curiosity as a reporter. But then, she casually mentioned a name that surprised him. *Henry Carrigan.* She apparently wanted to see how he would react, but he said nothing, just letting it pass. Now he wondered, *How did she come up with Henry Carrigan? What did she know about the man's relationship with Edward? Or Christina?*

A part of him said, *That's why she's here, to find out what I knew about the man.*

But why?

As he considered that question, she returned, wrapped in a towel and, seeing the look on his face, she smiled. "I'm catching you in mid-thought," she said. "Something good?"

"Very good," he lied.

She leaned down to kiss him on the mouth, her breasts brushing against his chest. Then she said, "I have to go."

"What, no more tête-à-tête?"

"Another time. And soon," she added.

Palmer nodded, then watched as she gathered up her clothing and went back to the bathroom to dress, letting the towel down to provide him a full view of her naked ass as the door closed behind her, leaving him with the suspicion it would be his last.

CHAPTER THIRTY-FOUR

The next morning, Palmer was back at his desk, trying to focus on the papers before him, with Whyte seated across from him.

"What were *you* up to last night?" Whyte asked.

"What do you mean?"

Whyte shook his head. "After all these years you're not that hard for me to read, although the cat and canary image doesn't fit this morning. Almost looks like the cat is choking on the canary bones."

"Remind me not to play poker with you anymore."

"Why would I do that? I count on that income."

Palmer looked away before saying, "Sloane Taylor stopped by last night."

"Stopped by? As in, delivered a package, waved at you through the window—"

"We had drinks. One thing led to another."

Whyte responded with a brief nod. "But you don't have that look you normally have when you think you're falling in love for the umpteenth time."

"No, I don't. The whole thing was odd. A bit stilted, to tell the truth."

"That's too literary for me. Give it to me in English."

Palmer bit at his lower lip, then said, "I don't know, it was just a little too, how should I say, rehearsed?"

"Selling yourself short, aren't you Casanova?"

"Maybe."

"I assume there was some conversation as part of this fandango."

"The usual things lovers discuss in bed. Murder. Congressional hearings. Celebrity divorces."

"Please tell me you didn't share anything Lawson gave us."

Palmer held up his hand. "It was just a few moments of lust, Robbie. I didn't have a psychotic episode."

"Sometimes those two events are the same for you."

Palmer frowned.

Whyte studied him for a moment. "If you had fun, as the bartender said to the horse when he walked into the saloon, why the long face?"

"I told you, I can't exactly say."

"You didn't ring her bell?"

"Thought I did. We were noisy enough."

Whyte drew back and folded his hands in front of him. "Could it be that you feel used, RP?"

Palmer reacted with a theatrical roll of his eyes.

"All right, just watch yourself with this woman. You know who she is and what she does."

"And she does it well, I'll admit that."

"TMI," Whyte said as he shook his head. "Now, how about you tell me what exactly you discussed with her? About our clients, I mean."

"Nothing you can't find in the tabloids, but when we got to Taub, she had me thinking about something. Been wondering about it all night and called him this morning." He looked at his Rolex. "He should have been here by now."

"Oh, for joy."

Palmer ignored the crack. "I want to take him through what we discussed yesterday."

Just then, Maureen's voice came over the intercom telling them that Marvin Taub had arrived. Palmer asked her to show him in.

"I don't get up this early for anyone," Taub announced as he strode into the office. He was unshaved and haggard looking, the weariness in his eyes visible even behind his tinted glasses. He dropped into the seat beside Whyte without acknowledging him and, looking straight at

Palmer, said, "I worked till four in the morning and didn't get to bed 'til six, so this had better be good."

Palmer never failed to be amazed by clients who believed their problems became his. "You're the one being charged with murder, Marvin. If you prefer to get some beauty sleep, we can have this discussion while you're serving twenty-five to life in Attica."

"All right, all right, what's up?"

"Your gun, that's what."

"Come on, you know I—"

"Where did you keep it?"

"We've been through this."

"Indulge me. Robbie wasn't there when we spoke, and I want him to ask you a few questions."

Finally looking in Whyte's general direction, Taub said, "It's licensed, I have a carry permit, and I almost always keep it in the desk drawer in my office."

"Your office in the back of your club," Palmer clarified.

"Only office I have," Taub said.

"Does the drawer have a lock on it?" Whyte asked.

"It does, but I don't usually bother with that."

"That's a little careless," Whyte said, "since you're talking about a licensed gun. You keep it loaded?"

"I do."

"Was it in any sort of case? You use a trigger lock?"

"No to both," Taub said, then turned back to Palmer. "What's this about?"

Palmer nodded at Whyte, who continued.

"How about your office door? You keep that locked?"

"Unless I'm in there. I have a safe back there. Sometimes there's a fair amount of cash on hand."

"But you don't keep your gun in the safe?"

"If I was getting robbed, it'd take a little too much time to get to it, if you see my point."

"I do," Whyte said. "Who else has the key to your office?"

"No one."

"Combination to the safe?"

"Same. Only me."

"Interesting," said Whyte, sitting back as he thought it over. Looking at Palmer, he said, "I think I see where you're going with this."

"Damn, am I easy to read this morning or what," Palmer grumbled.

Whyte smiled, while the look on Taub's face made it plain he had no idea what they were talking about.

Palmer said, "Our defense is based on the claim that someone took your revolver from the desk in your office."

"Not a claim, it's the truth," Taub reminded him. "I've been wracking my brain, trying to figure out who."

"That's why you're here, so we can help you figure that out. You say you keep the door to your office locked, and you have the only key. That means there are only a few possible ways the gun was lifted. Just to be clear, there's been no recent sign of a break-in at your place, someone in there after hours, nothing like that, correct?"

"No chance. We have a top-notch security system."

Whyte responded with a look of disgust. "Which means you're more concerned about protecting your liquor and your dancers' greasy poles than a loaded firearm."

Taub glared at the detective, about to say something, but Palmer cut in.

"Who has the security code for access to your place?"

"Only me."

"And the security company who set it up, right?"

Taub shifted in his seat. "It's a reputable company; I don't believe they sold the code to anyone."

"And you're certain no one else has it?"

Taub took off his glasses and rubbed his eyes with the palms of his hands as he thought it over. After a moment he looked at Palmer. "Actually, Richie has it, in case I'm not available when it's time to open."

"Richie Phelps, your major domo?"

"That's right."

"No one else?"

"No one."

Palmer knew that Taub was no fool, and the implications of what he had just realized hung over them as they fell silent for a moment.

Then Palmer said, "Okay, here's what I've got so far. If the pistol was taken during business hours, it might've been at a time you left the place and didn't bother to lock the office door."

Taub shook his head. "Whyte is correct, I may be a little careless about locking the desk, but I never leave the office door open."

"Then it could've happened right under your nose, although I know the layout of your bar, and if you were there, it would be hard for someone to get in and out of the office without you noticing."

"Impossible," Taub said, sitting forward in the chair. "The door to my office is always in my line of sight. Like you say, that's the way the place is laid out."

"All right, what if someone stole your key to the office, went in and got the gun when you were out, then somehow replaced the key?"

"Also impossible. The key is on a chain in my pocket. They'd have to knock me out to get it."

"That's what I figured," Palmer said. "Which means we're down to two viable possibilities. You were in your place, the office door was open, and you never saw who went in and snatched the weapon. Maybe you were in the men's room at the time."

"I don't ever take a whizz without locking that door."

"Then the other possibility is that—"

"Your manager Phelps went in after hours and grabbed it," Whyte finished the thought.

Taub twisted to his right, staring directly at Whyte for the first time. "I don't believe it," he said, but the lack of conviction in his voice was evident.

"You have another idea?" Palmer asked.

Taub, who by now had inched all the way to the edge of his seat, sat back and took time to consider the question. While he did, Whyte asked another.

"Who knew you had the gun in your desk?"

Palmer could see Taub's anxiety grow. "Not many people," Taub told them. "Let's face it, I'm running a topless joint, not a tea parlor. All kinds of people move in and out of there. I wasn't about to advertise that a Smith & Wesson was sitting in the drawer."

"But Phelps knew," Palmer said.

"True," Taub acknowledged as he nodded slowly. "But even if he went in after hours, he didn't have the key to the office."

"Come on, Marvin, how tough would it be to pick that lock? He would have had all the time he needed and no one around, maybe even got coached on how to get in. I've seen the door, not exactly Fort Knox. Then there's the possibility he made a copy of the key somewhere along the line. Maybe he borrowed it from you at some point?"

"No way," Taub said, although he was becoming less convinced himself.

"I know you trust him," Palmer said, "and I'm hoping we end up back at option one, but we've got to cover all the bases. You recall the last time you saw the pistol?"

"Last week, maybe? Not something I focus on much."

"Was it there the night you had the argument with Joey?"

Taub was shaking his head before Palmer finished the question. "Never looked. After my bouncer threw the little creep out, it wasn't like I ran into my office for a gun so I could shoot him."

"Maybe not," Whyte said, "but somebody shot him, and the gun they used was yours."

"Richie Phelps." Taub intoned the name, sounding more betrayed than angry. "Why would he—"

"Money," Whyte suggested. "He gets a stack of cash, you go to jail, maybe he ends up with your bar. Keep in mind, he might not even have been the one who pulled the trigger."

"You're saying he gave the gun to someone else?"

Palmer nodded. "Not a unique scenario."

"Let's say you're right," Taub responded. "Let's say Richie screwed me. Then you have to answer the next question."

"Who would frame you for Joey's murder?"

"Right. I have plenty of enemies, believe me. But someone went to a lot of trouble to set me up. And how stupid was D'Angelo? Whoever is behind this obviously had him come to my place that night to pick a fight with me. Which obviously was intended to set up a half-assed motive for me to go after him. But what did *Joey* think he was doing?"

"My guess is he never knew and never asked," Palmer said. "Once again, it was probably about money. He didn't see the real finish coming."

"Finish is right," Taub groaned. "Now what?"

"Precisely what I've been thinking about since last night," Palmer said, "and I have an idea."

CHAPTER THIRTY-FIVE

Edward Franco walked down the corridor of his company's large suite, entered Henry Carrigan's post-modern office, and closed the door behind him.

Carrigan looked up from his desk and blinked once, but said nothing.

"What's the word from DC?" Franco asked.

"On which front?"

"Either or both," Franco said as he lowered himself into one of the chrome and black leather Barcelona chairs.

Carrigan was a plain-looking man, clean-shaven with a square Irish jawline, even nose, dull brown eyes, and light brown hair he kept neatly parted and in place. He looked especially commonplace when compared with his tanned, handsome boss. "I'll start with the FDA," he suggested.

"Fine," Franco agreed, "Just give me the headlines."

Carrigan nodded. "The approval process has slowed to a crawl. Between the congressional investigation and people starting to poke around our applications, the agency is moving at a glacial pace."

"What people are poking around?"

"The media for starters."

"Who else?"

"My source tells me some enforcement officer here in New York has started asking questions. Vera Alexander. Been with the FDA a long time, has a tough rep."

"How did she get involved?"

"No clue," Carrigan said.

"Clueless is not what I need from you, Henry."

"We've been trying to piece it together. Best guess so far is that someone lit a fire under her."

"Any guess on who the arsonist might be?"

"Your wife's lawyer works with a former cop who's been asking around."

Franco took a moment before saying, "Find out if he's the problem and how high he's turned up the flame." Without waiting for a response, Franco asked, "What about the congressional hearings?"

Carrigan's fair complexion seemed to become a shade paler. "Indictments are inevitable, as you've heard."

"How soon?"

"Soon." When Franco started to say something, Carrigan added, "A matter of days."

"Any word on who's going down?"

Carrigan shook his head. "But we have to assume—"

"Spare me," Franco snapped. Then, as if speaking to himself, he said, "We waited too long."

"No one expected them to act this quickly. Especially after Platt—"

"How the hell can they get indictments without his testimony? You don't indict people without evidence. They have nothing concrete, not unless someone else flipped." He was staring intently at Carrigan now. "Your *source*," he said with unmistakable disdain. "He have anything to say about that?"

"Not a word."

"Could it be he got scared off? Is it possible he's the weak link?"

"No way," Carrigan said. "He's in too deep."

"In too deep?" Franco shook his head. "They don't want *him*, you jackass. They want me, my father-in-law, names they can broadcast all over the evening news."

"He would never give us up." After a brief pause, he said, "He knows better."

"Maybe so, but it's time to see who's in and who's out. I'm calling my white-haired friend, just to be sure he's ready."

CHAPTER THIRTY-SIX

That afternoon, Palmer saw Jeanette Scott again, this time in her Manhattan apartment. Various news agencies were reporting that the RDMO investigation was heating up, Palmer's office received several predictable calls, including a request from Jeanette that they meet.

He walked to her place, one of the grand old buildings on Park Avenue, just a few blocks from his brownstone. After passing through lobby security, an elderly gentleman took Palmer up in the elevator to the full-floor residence, where the butler showed him into a richly appointed living room. As Palmer expected after visiting her home in Bedford, this was another showcase of classic opulence, complete with beautifully upholstered furniture, tapestry drapes, mahogany tables, and walls covered with exquisitely framed oil paintings.

Taking a seat in a plush club chair facing her, Palmer asked, "How are you doing? With this news on RDMO, I mean."

Her face instantly clouded over, and the uneasy way she made that quick transformation led him to wonder if she had already begun hitting the bottle, even though it was not yet eleven in the morning. "It's difficult," she admitted. "There are things not being reported by the media. Not yet."

"Such as?"

"The principals in the company are not the only ones being investigated."

He waited.

"Gene is also part of this probe, or whatever they call it."

"I see. What about you?"

She attempted a smile, although it ended up one of her sad looks. "They don't care about me. I've told you before, this is all about politics."

"It could become a lot more than that if he was part of an illegal conspiracy."

Jeanette frowned.

"You want honesty, right?"

"It's about Edward and Henry," she replied, as if mentioning Franco and Carrigan explained everything.

Palmer felt himself wanting to believe her but knew there was so much more. "You want me to get you answers, Jeanette, but you may not like them when I do."

"Gene was trying to help Edward. It's only natural to try and help your daughter and son-in-law."

"But you also invested in the company."

"Yes, there is that."

"It's time for you to tell me what Platt would have said to Congress that would be damaging to your husband. Or the rest of you."

She turned away from him, staring out the window at her generous view of the iconic New York skyline. "I don't know."

Palmer gave her a moment, then said, "You asked to see me. I assume there's something you want to tell me."

"It's Edward," she said. "There *were* conversations I overheard. About RDMO and the FDA applications. About money and forcing people to move the process forward. Things like that."

"Who had these discussions? Edward and your husband?"

"Yes, and Henry."

"On the phone or in person?"

"In person. Here, in Gene's office down the hall."

"Anyone else present for those conversations?"

She hesitated, then said, "Vernon was also here once or twice."

"Can you recall anything specific that was said?"

Jeanette shook her head. "I remember Edward raising his voice, arguing with Vernon. I could hear that."

"Go on."

"Vernon said something about making a mistake, about the trouble they were creating, things like that. Edward was angry about something."

Palmer nodded. "Did you hear any other names, people they might be pressuring about the application?"

"No, I never did."

"Was Platt telling them they were wrong to be doing what they were doing, is that basically what you heard?"

She took a long time before saying, "Yes, that's what I heard him telling Edward."

Palmer drew a deep breath and sat back, staring at Jeanette as if he were seeing her for the first time. "You're saying that your husband, your son-in-law, and one of his associates were being warned by Vernon Platt that their actions were improper."

"Yes."

He sat forward again, not removing his gaze from hers. "You realize the implications."

"I do."

"Why are you telling me this, and why now?"

"Because I asked you to find out what happened to Vernon, and because I'm convinced it's why he was murdered."

She was not talking about "if" this time, Palmer noted, *but "why"*—which left him to wonder, *when the hell was someone in this case going to tell him the entire truth about anything?*

CHAPTER THIRTY-SEVEN

That morning, Senator Detweiler was again hosting Eugene Scott in his private office. The senator had settled his rotund frame into the oversized leather seat reserved for his use, Scott facing him in an upholstered club chair.

Scott had begun the discussion with a catalogue of his concerns.

When he was done, Detweiler advised Scott in his measured drawl "Don't be gettin' yourself all worked up. I'm not the hunter here, Gene. I'm your scout."

Congressman Scott nodded vigorously. "Of course, of course. I apologize, Harlan. It's just the uncertainty, that's all."

"Understood."

"You getting any feedback?"

"In fact, I am," Detweiler said. "That's why I called you. Want some coffee? Somethin' stronger?"

Scott shook his head. "Had my coffee, and it's little early for anything else. What have you heard?"

"It may not be much, but you'll find it particularly interesting." Detweiler could make a word like "particularly" sound as if it was a melody.

"I'm all ears," Scott urged him.

"This is all hearsay, you realize, and I don't raise this issue to cause you undo concern."

"All right," Scott replied anxiously.

"What we have here is the old good news, bad news situation. The good news, if you could call it that, is, despite their best efforts, the prosecutors in the RDMO matter seem to be sufferin' from a terminal lack of key evidence against you. This is due primarily to the untimely demise of our friend Vernon Platt." Detweiler paused to measure his friend's reaction, but Scott offered nothing more than a slight pursing of the lips. "The bad news has to do with the circumstances of his death."

Scott shifted slightly in his seat, waiting for the senator to go on.

Detweiler folded his hands across his generous girth, his attention keenly focused on his guest. "Appears there's some officer in New York in charge of the case who's got himself convinced this was no suicide. Says Vernon was pushed off that balcony. Not clear yet what proof he might have, but as I understand it, they're lookin' into it, and they're lookin' *deep*."

An uncomfortable silence descended until Scott said, "It would obviously be terrible to think Vernon was murdered, but why is that bad news for me?"

Detweiler's laugh began in the depths of his large belly, making its way up through his throat until it emerged a full-blown guffaw. "Jesus, Gene, don't go gettin' all disingenuous on me. After all, that's been *my* act for decades. That ain't never gonna work for a Yankee from New York."

Scott was clearly embarrassed, and did not want to make matters worse by persisting in his feigned ignorance. "All right. They're claiming Platt would have been a crucial witness against me, and now they think his death was a murder. But it's still just speculation, correct?"

"Don't know," Detweiler admitted. "They say this police detective is a sharp cookie. A Black gentleman who appears to know his business." He uttered a throaty cough. "Whatever he's got, he's keeping it close to the vest, but according to my sources he has somethin' he believes to be proof of a homicide. As far as how this might affect you, there's another link in the chain that you need to know about."

Detweiler was working his slow-paced country bumpkin act, forcing Scott to ask, "Such as?"

"First off, this officer seems to have an old friend who was with the NYPD himself, now one of those so-called private eyes. Turns out he's a fairly clever guy in his own right who's been workin' on his own to put some pieces together on Platt's death."

"How would you know that?"

Detweiler responded by narrowing his eyes but offered no answer. "Second, this shamus just happens to work for a lawyer by the name of Russell Palmer. That ring any bells?"

Scott's shoulders slumped as he exhaled a lung full of stale air. "Yes, it does."

"Seems Mr. Palmer has an unusual law practice that finds him involved in all kinds of interestin' cases."

"Including my daughter's."

"That's what I'm given to understand." Detweiler paused. "Are you aware he's also been meeting with your wife?"

"Jeanette?"

Detweiler chuckled. "I know somethin' about your lady friends, but I don't think you've got another wife."

Scott replied with a disapproving look.

"All right, you didn't know your wife called this Palmer character, but now you do and that leaves us to try and find out why."

"She might be asking about Christina's divorce."

"Could be, but the fact that this private investigator works for him and is lookin' into Platt? Well, that makes me wonder."

"Vernon was Jeanette's best friend, all the way back to their childhood."

"That's my point, Gene. All roads seem to be leadin' us back to him."

Scott shook his head. "I don't care what anyone else says, it's impossible for me to believe Vernon was going to give any testimony that would be damaging to me or my family."

"That may well be your belief, but that doesn't mean it's true. Or, maybe more important, that anyone else is going to buy that story. You see where I'm goin' here?"

"You're saying the prosecutors and these detectives may think I'm involved in Vernon's death?" He could not bring himself to use the word murder.

"And perhaps this lawyer Palmer, he may think the same thing."

"I can't even imagine such a thing."

Detweiler held up one of his pudgy hands. "We're speculatin', as you say, but if things keep movin' in that direction, this inquiry could go south in a hurry. You understand?"

"No, I don't," Scott protested without much enthusiasm. "I'm not the only target of this investigation. There are all sorts of people Vernon could have testified against without hurting me."

Detweiler slowly raised his eyebrows.

"You don't agree?"

Detweiler sat back in his large, comfortable chair. "None of them, whoever they might be, is a United States congressman. I told you last time we met, this isn't about truth or even results. This is about innuendo, accusation, and rumor. And politics."

Scott looked as if he'd just been kicked in the gut.

"For you, it's the appearance of things that matters, not the reality. You're a politician. You're the man with exposure." As Detweiler drew closer to the point, his drawl became even more sluggish. "Congressman Gene Scott is the man they want. If they can make it seem like their principal witness was murdered—and he had evidence against you—they'll dirty you up so bad you'll never be able to wash it off."

Scott shook his head. "You believe I've already lost."

"Not necessarily," Detweiler said, his voice an octave higher. "I hear that there's some fair-sized pressure on the prosecutor's office to wrap this up. And you've still got some friends in high places. If there's proof Vernon was murdered, they're gonna have to start showin' their cards soon. And my guess is, if they have anything linkin' you to such a deed, I would've heard about it already." He paused before adding. "Or you would have."

"There's nothing to that," Scott insisted.

"All right, we leave it there."

"But what should I be doing in the meantime? The media is ramping up as if indictments are coming."

"As I recall, you have a connection to that young reporter, Sloane something-or-other, might want to ring her up and see if you can buy yourself some help," Detweiler advised. "As far as the investigation, if you've got a finger on any of the strings that run the police department in New York, you might give one of them a little tug. Know what I'm sayin'?"

CHAPTER THIRTY-EIGHT

By the time Marvin Taub arrived at his bar, just after twelve-thirty, Richie Phelps had already opened for the lunch crowd. *Lunch* was something of a euphemism, since the menu in this squalid place was limited to overpriced pretzels, chips, and peanuts, accompanied by an assortment of beers and liquor.

The two men exchanged a brief greeting, and Taub headed to his office, unlocking the door and settling inside to wait. At exactly one o'clock, as Palmer had instructed, he got up and called Phelps to come inside.

"What's up," the burly manager asked as he sat in the only other chair in the small room.

"Why don't you tell me," Taub replied.

"What's that supposed to mean?"

Before Taub could answer, Palmer and Whyte entered, closing the door behind them.

"Hello Richie," Palmer said.

Phelps stared up at them, and said, "What the f—" but Palmer stopped him.

"This is only going one of two ways, the easy way or the hard way. The choice is yours."

Phelps was still gaping at them. "I have no idea what you're talking about."

"Sure you do," Palmer said with as unfriendly a smile as he could manage. "I'm talking about Marvin's gun."

Phelps made a move to get out of the chair, but Whyte took a step forward, grabbed him by the shoulder, and shoved him back into the seat. Phelps was a lot taller and heavier than Whyte, but the detective was standing over him and had the leverage. Now, in this cramped space, there was nowhere for Phelps to go without slugging his way past all three of them.

He remained seated.

"You were smart," Palmer went on, "but not smart enough. You knew the interior CCTV cameras were easy to bypass, so coming in and grabbing the revolver early in the morning was easy. You just didn't think it through."

"I told you, I have no idea what you're talking about," Phelps repeated.

If Palmer had any doubts about his theory, the lack of conviction in Phelps' second denial made it clear he was correct. He let a few, slow seconds go by as he watched Phelps' jaw tighten and the tension in his eyes increase. Then Palmer said, "You didn't think about all the cameras up and down this street, which *do* show you coming and going. You also made a mistake when you wiped down the gun—not just to clean Marvin's prints off, but your own as well. Problem is, DNA can be stubborn. In the movies, they just swipe the thing with a handkerchief, as if that's all it takes. Wrong." Turning to Whyte, Palmer asked, "Was he wrong?"

"Totally," the detective said.

"Now then, here's how this is going to work," Palmer continued. "You're an accessory to murder, and you're going to serve some hard time, especially with your priors."

Palmer saw Phelps' eyes widen.

"Oh yeah," Taub chimed in. "You think I didn't have you checked out before you came to work for me all those years ago, you rotten, two-faced bastard." Taub suddenly followed that with an effort to launch his oversized frame across the desk at Phelps, but Whyte stepped between them, this time forcing Taub back into his seat.

"Easy, big guy," Palmer said. "Whyte's not here to be a referee."

Taub resigned himself to sitting back in his chair, at least for now.

"Where was I?" Palmer asked, looking up at the ceiling. "Oh, right, the charges. Accessory before the fact, conspiracy to commit murder, illegal possession of a weapon, and so on and so forth." Looking down at Phelps, he said, "In case I haven't been clear, that's the tough way out of this."

Phelps gritted his teeth but said nothing. The room fell into total silence.

"I'll bet you want to hear the easy way, am I right?" Palmer asked, but Phelps stayed quiet. "You'll admit to taking the gun, tell us who you sold it to, and we'll try to get you a deal with the DA. Maybe keep you out of jail altogether, if you help them crack the D'Angelo murder case." Smiling again, Palmer added, "Assuming you weren't the shooter."

"I didn't shoot nobody."

"Anybody," Palmer corrected him, then asked, "What's it going to be, the tough stretch or a deal?"

"I know all about those *deals*," Phelps said, Palmer pleased that the man was already abandoning his declaration of ignorance. "They sound great until crunch time. Then bam, you're screwed. Anyway, how the hell can you make me an offer? You're not cops."

Without turning around, Whyte reached behind him and opened the door.

"No," Palmer admitted, "but he is."

And in walked Lt. Hugh Lawson.

"Welcome to the party, Lieutenant," Palmer said. "I would offer you a seat, but that would be Marvin's lap."

"I'll take a pass. How goes it, Counselor?"

"I think Mr. Phelps wants a deal."

"I never said—" Phelps began, but Palmer cut him off again.

"I forgot to tell him, Lieutenant, the offer only lasts for as long as it takes you to read him his rights and for us to have this conversation. After that, you can cuff him and take him downtown, book him on every charge you can think of."

"Seems fair to me," Lawson said. Taking his time, he made a show of pulling out a small card, then slowly recited the Miranda warnings.

After that was done, Palmer said, "What'll it be, Mr. Phelps, door number one or door number two?"

Phelps took a moment to look at each of the four men in turn, ending with Lawson. "No jail time."

"I honestly can't promise that," the lieutenant said, "but the value of the information you provide will have a serious impact on what the prosecutor decides. Off the record, are you ready to tell us who ended up with the gun?"

"Off the record?" Phelps repeated, making it sound like he had just eaten a bad oyster.

"On my honor," Lawson said.

"Which is worth more than you can know," Whyte said.

"Was it Peter Frost?" Palmer asked, trying to move this along.

Phelps forced a harsh, one-syllable laugh. "Frost? Get his manicured hands dirty? Are you kidding?"

Palmer suggested, "One of his men, then?" and the look in Phelps' eyes told him he had hit paydirt.

"You know his name?" Lawson asked.

"You want me to sign my own death warrant? You think I'm a fucking idiot?"

"All I asked was whether you know his name."

"I know who he is, or what they call him anyway."

"Okay, when?"

"Huh?"

"When did you give him the weapon?"

Phelps paused before admitted, "That morning, before the night Joey showed up here."

Taub had kept his mouth shut since that first outburst, but his face was turning crimson as he finally hollered, "What did they give you to set me up? Money? Was that it?"

Phelps couldn't even look at him. "They said after they put you away for the murder I'd own the place. They would see to it."

This time, when Taub sprang out of the chair, Whyte did not move fast enough to stop him. Taub ended up on top of Phelps, the two of them rolling around on the floor of the crowded room until the other three men pulled them apart.

"Enough!" Lawson hollered as Whyte wrangled Taub under control.

Looking down at Phelps, who had gotten back into his seat, Palmer asked, "You've admitted you took the gun and gave it to one of Frost's men. They tell you why they wanted the gun?"

"You kidding?"

"That's not an answer."

"They didn't say, and I didn't ask."

Lawson had heard enough. "You ready to go downtown and make a statement?"

"No jail time," Phelps said. "And keep Taub away from me."

"You miserable fuck," Taub said, making every word count.

"Get up," the lieutenant told Phelps, then cuffed his hands behind his back and led him out of the office.

Before any of the remaining three could say anything, Lawson came back in and shut the door behind him. "I hooked him up to one of your dancer poles," he responded to their look of surprise. "Seemed appropriate, and your patrons are amused."

"I love a happy ending," Palmer said.

"I need to know what you told him," Lawson asked.

When Palmer did not respond, Whyte said, "You don't want to know."

"Look, you had me wait outside until you opened the door. I respect the fact that you kept me out of it until he was ready to make a deal. But just among the four of us, I want to know what you said to get him to talk."

Palmer smiled. "I told him we had outside video of him entering the club that morning. I also said there were traces of his DNA on the gun."

Lawson's mouth broke into a wide grin, and Palmer figured he was stifling an outright laugh for fear Phelps would hear him. "He bought that bullshit?"

Now Taub stood up and gaped at Palmer. "That was bullshit? You made all that up?"

Palmer shrugged. "Here's the lesson, Marvin. There's a reason they read you your rights and explain that you're entitled to a lawyer before you speak with the police. For future reference, if you're ever in trouble again, wait for me to show up before you start talking."

"Won't he ask for a lawyer when he gets downtown?"

"We'll insist he get one," Lawson told him. "But we already have his confession, in front of three witnesses. Not even counting Taub here. It was freely made, after he was told his rights. Whatever was discussed and whatever he believed before I arrived, that's immaterial."

"He can't claim entrapment or some bullshit?"

"I'm not a policeman," Palmer said, "how can I entrap him?"

Lawson nodded. "I heard him admit that he took your revolver and gave it to a man who said he was working for Peter Frost. He said he did it to frame you for murder, in exchange for which he would end up owning this, uh, establishment. Anything that happened before, that's just his sad story."

"Amazing," Taub said.

"Betrayal is a bitch," Whyte said. Then, as he followed Lawson out of the office, he turned to Palmer and whispered, "Nice work, kiddo."

CHAPTER THIRTY-NINE

Lawson took Phelps to the local precinct, where he would obtain a full written statement and then book him. Meanwhile, Palmer and Whyte returned to their office, preparing to handle the next phase of Taub's case. The last thing they wanted to deal with was Christina Franco's divorce, but she was sitting in the waiting area when they arrived. Palmer brought her into his office and watched as she eased herself into an armchair.

"Where are we on my case?" she asked by way of greeting.

"I got word from your husband's attorney," he told her, "she's filing a motion for a protective order."

Christina responded with a bitter laugh. "He needs protection from *me*? What a pathetic joke."

Palmer took a moment to study her, which had become habitual since he realized her attire was such a large part of her persona. Today she was wearing a dark green dress, the color highlighting her eyes, while the silky fabric did a good job of flattering what it was supposed to—the designer price of which was likely enough to feed a family of four for a year. Her hair and makeup were flawless, as usual, and he could not resist wondering, *Is this how she puts herself together all the time, or is she dressing this way for our little visits?*

"You attacked him," he reminded her.

Her emerald gaze sparkled with anger. "Attacked him? It was just a slap across the face. And well deserved."

"Maybe so, but not the best move on your part, given the audience."

She sighed as if this was some annoying piece of business she wanted to be done with. "It means nothing in the big picture. Let's not forget, he threatened my life, now he's having me followed and he's a philandering scumbag."

Coming from the well-bred Mrs. Franco, that last word caught Palmer by surprise. "A protective order won't have much impact on the overall outcome of the case. I'm filing a cross-motion for temporary support. The question is whether you want me to ask for our own order of protection and introduce the evidence of him threatening you, including the use of Peter Frost's name."

She made a show of considering the idea, although Palmer was sure she had already thought through the consequences of releasing her video for public view. "Can we have the record sealed, or whatever you call it?"

"I can make the request, but even when it's granted there's always the likelihood someone is going to leak it."

She nodded, and he realized she had thought of that too. "What's the risk to me?"

"Maybe nothing, although Frost is unpredictable. Once you've outed him, he could back off. Or he might retaliate. No way to be sure."

"From what I've heard about the man, he doesn't back off easily."

Palmer could see that genuinely concerned her, and his protective instincts kicked in. "My sentiments exactly."

"What do you think I should do?"

"Nothing. We can work with his history of cheating, that should make it tough for them to convince the court you're the villain and he's a victim. We'll save your video for cross-examination. I'm a big fan of counterpunching."

She smiled for the first time since she sat down. "I like that."

"Good. I'll phone his lawyer, let her know we'll be filing a cross-motion for temporary support and access to a substantial portion of the marital assets. Let's see if they blink."

"You push them hard enough, she'll start talking settlement."

Palmer responded with a wrinkled brow. "That would be moving rather quickly. We still have to exchange financial information."

"I have my accountant working on mine. I'll have everything to you by the end of the day tomorrow."

"Impressive," Palmer said. "You really do want to get this done."

"More than you can imagine. Just be prepared when they stall on turning over his paperwork."

"I'm already serving a formal demand for his financial affidavit, bank records, stock statements, tax returns, all of it."

"Wonderful," she said. "I can't wait to pull his financial pants down for us to have a good look."

Palmer had a couple of clever answers for that image, but humor was not on his agenda at the moment. He said, "I have to say, I'm a bit confused."

"Why?"

"When you first came to see me, you said your husband would kill you if you tried to leave him."

"You heard it for yourself."

"I did. But you had me file papers anyway, which I considered very brave of you. Then you slapped him in public, refused to have me get you protection although it appears you're being followed, and now you want to reach a settlement as if this is some small claims case."

She sat back, a knowing smile crossing her lips. "Don't you get it?"

"I'm not sure I do."

"He tried to scare me, which was one of the main reasons I hired you instead of some empty suit who'd fold up at the first sign of trouble. You've taken a hard line with Bartz. You served him with the divorce. We've ignored whoever is following me. And you're not intimidated by this protective order, or whatever it is."

"You're saying—"

"I'm saying you've played them perfectly. You keep asking me what I know about Edward's business that frightens him, but it's not about that. It's all about the money, Palmer."

He sat back in his leather chair. "Go on."

"I've told you all I know about his finances, some things are complicated, some are not. We want to go after the uncomplicated assets.

Cash. Publicly traded stock. The house in Amagansett. Our apartment. You've got to maneuver them into a position where they'll agree to that, especially with the upcoming issues he has on that drug company."

Palmer gnawed at his lower lip, tempted to mention what her mother told him about all that, but said nothing.

"I want the things that are easy to take, which means they should be easy for him to give up. All of that will amount to much less than half of all the assets, which will appeal to him. And your idea about holding back the video is brilliant. Especially if you tell Bartz you have it."

He shook his head. "Once I tell her I have it, she'll demand a copy through the discovery process."

Christina nodded. "Maybe you just mention he's threatened me at different times and I'm trying to find proof. He doesn't know about the video or what other proof I might have, but he definitely will not want a claim of threats played for public consumption."

"And if we make a deal, even if it's substantially less than half—"

"Then he can have the video," she told him. "We can tell mother about it, which might convince her to cancel my trust fund, give me the money from that, and we're done."

Palmer took a moment to sort all of that out, still having difficulty reconciling the initial fear she claimed to have about her husband's threats with this rush toward the finish line. He felt it was time to tell her, "I saw your mother again."

"Really?"

"You haven't heard from her?"

Christina shook her head. "We haven't spoken for a couple of days. She's probably annoyed I slapped him." When Palmer did not respond, she added, "Mother is an intensely private person, as you've come to understand. She could never approve of that sort of public display."

"We didn't speak about you. We talked about RDMO."

"Oh. What did she have to say about that?"

"She's concerned about the investigation."

Christina nodded but said nothing.

"Are you concerned?"

"What do you mean?"

"I'm sure you've heard the rumors. They're not only going after your husband and his associates. They're also trying to implicate your father."

He watched as her enthusiasm over the prospect of finessing her husband in the divorce negotiation dimmed a few watts. "Hopefully they really are only rumors. I can't believe father was involved in anything improper."

"There are always people in Washington who want to politicize a matter like this, and things could get ugly fast. It could pit your father against your husband, as well as other players who might testify against him. Such as Henry Carrigan." He looked for a reaction from her to the mention of Carrigan, but she was a good card player.

"Yes," was all she said, infusing that single word with a touch of sadness. "I understand."

"Did you know your mother invested in the company?"

After a slight hesitation, she said, "No," and, once again, he did not believe her.

"What about Vernon Platt?"

"What about him?"

"Did you know he was invested in RDMO?"

"Not before, I mean before all this. Now I've seen it in the papers. Which is all the more reason to get my divorce done. I don't want to be mixed up in that legal tangle. I'll bet Edward doesn't want me involved either."

"If you know nothing about his business, why would he care if you were questioned, either before or after a divorce?"

She paused, then said, "I just think it gives us some leverage, the idea of getting me out now."

Palmer was not clear about what sort of leverage that might provide but decided to file the matter away for further discussion. "I'll call Bartz first thing tomorrow morning and let her know our position on the motions and the financials."

Christina's mood brightened again. She stood, thanked him, and went on her way.

After she was gone, Palmer sat there thinking about several things Christina had said, some of which did not make sense, others that caused him real concern.

As he hit the intercom to ask for Whyte, he realized once again there were more people lying to him than telling the truth.

All I have to do, he told himself, *is figure out if I can trust any of them.*

CHAPTER FORTY

The next morning, Palmer was in Part AP4 of the Manhattan criminal court building. Unlike some low-budget movie and television depictions of these courtrooms, 100 Centre Street was a worn, grimy old venue. Too many people passed through these chambers every day, and there was neither time nor the budget to clean it up.

Or, as Palmer thought, *It was time to tear the whole place down and start again.*

"All rise," the bailiff said.

Judge Cioffi came out, took his seat behind the bench, adjusted his rimless glasses, and told the courtroom full of lawyers, defendants, and spectators to be seated. After a brief discussion with the clerk, he directed that the first case be called.

"People against Marvin Taub."

Palmer strode through the short, swinging gate, his client right behind. They stepped up to the counsel table, Palmer standing to the left, Taub—who had managed bail—to his right, in front of the big yellow arrow pasted there bearing the word "Defendant."

"State your appearance for the record," the court officer said.

"Russell Palmer, One-Thirteen East Sixty-Fourth Street, New York City. Good morning, Judge."

Judge Cioffi nodded. "Good morning, Mr. Palmer. I see this matter is to schedule a motion to dismiss. Is that right, Mr. Frankel?"

The prosecutor was Mark Frankel, someone Palmer had dealt with before, and he knew he was no pushover. Frankel nodded. "That's correct, Your Honor."

"What have you got in store for us today, Mr. Palmer?"

"The underlying issue is suppression, Judge. I believe if you hear our motion, it will save the court a great deal of unnecessary time."

"I see. And what about your discovery rights?"

"I'd like to reserve those, your Honor, since I believe they will become moot."

"Well, that may be the opinion of defense counsel," Assistant District Attorney Frankel said sarcastically. "Unfortunately, if Mr. Palmer's confidence is misplaced, I don't see why we should have to repeat a hearing in this case. I would prefer that Mr. Palmer present all his arguments in omnibus fashion."

The judge had a look at Taub. "Well, Mr. Palmer?"

"Your Honor, as the prosecutor is well aware, the case against my client is based upon a suspicion of his involvement in a homicide."

"Charge, not suspicion," the ADA said.

"The *charge* is predicated solely upon the discovery of a weapon belonging to my client at the location where the victim's body was found. Found, I should add, the day *after* the body was located."

Judge Cioffi glanced down at the ADA, then turned to Palmer. "I've had a look at the file, Counselor."

"This gun is alleged to be the weapon used in the subject murder. Therefore, Judge, the issue of my client's connection to this weapon, if any, is central to this case."

"Connection?" Frankel repeated. "The weapon in question was registered to the defendant."

"Which we have not denied," Palmer said. "Yet I assure Your Honor, granting my request will prove judicially efficient."

Cioffi stared at Palmer. If this had been most other attorneys, he would have denied the request, but Palmer had appeared before him in other cases and always played it straight. "All right, I'll grant the request for a suppression hearing prior to additional discovery. I'm not convinced it will be as efficient as you claim, Mr. Palmer, but this is a serious matter. How long will you need to prepare?" The judge was looking at his calendar.

"I'm ready now, Judge."

"What?" Frankel blurted out. "Your Honor, this is highly irregular."

Palmer loved to hear opposing counsel utter those words.

Cioffi said, "I see nothing so extraordinary in Mr. Palmer's request, nor in his desire to move this matter forward." Turning back to Palmer, the judge added, "Unfortunately, the Court's schedule may not permit me to accommodate you. The soonest we could set this down for a hearing—"

"May we approach?" Palmer asked. He knew it was time to pull out his real surprise.

The judge agreed, and Palmer led the way toward the bench. Palmer handed both the judge and Frankel copies of two affidavits, one from Richie Phelps, the other from Lt. Hugh Lawson.

"What are these?" Cioffi asked.

"They are fairly self-explanatory, your Honor, but if you allow, I will summarize?"

"Please do, Counselor."

"As I've said, we do not dispute the fact that the gun found at the scene belonged to my client. However, we believe the weapon was intentionally placed there and had not been in the custody or control of my client for two days prior to the homicide."

"That's a serious assertion," the judge cautioned him. "Are you suggesting the police are engaged in a scheme to implicate your client in a murder?"

"No, Judge," Palmer was quick to reply. "To the contrary. As you will see from Lt. Lawson's affidavit, the police are helping me prove my claim."

"What is this?" ADA. Frankel demanded.

"You have the wrong man, Mark. As you can see, we have the sworn statement of an individual who admits to stealing Mr. Taub's weapon before the murder of Mr. D'Angelo occurred and selling it to a third party. Mr. Taub did not have control or possession of his weapon at the time of the homicide. Whoever used it to murder Mr. D'Angelo is yet to be identified, but my client is innocent."

The judge, who was reading through the affidavits, looked up. "Are you suggesting this Mr. Phelps is guilty of the homicide?"

"No, your Honor. Mr. Phelps is cooperating with the police. That's why I wanted to approach the bench, since we do not want to make his identity public, nor any of the statements in his affidavit. Mr. Frankel is free to discuss this with Lt. Lawson. We were hoping to avoid a full hearing where others would become privy to the information being provided here. This is still an active investigation."

Cioffi fixed Palmer with a skeptical look. "And to what do we owe Mr. Phelps' willingness to become such a cooperative citizen?" Then, becoming more serious, he added, "Stealing a gun that was subsequently used in a homicide is a serious crime."

"My firm uncovered facts pointing to Mr. Phelps' culpability. When we confronted him, he confessed in the hope that his cooperation would be viewed favorably by Lt. Lawson and Mr. Frankel."

The judge nodded but said nothing.

"The police expect that Mr. Phelps will ultimately lead them to the individual responsible for Mr. D'Angelo's death," Palmer told them.

Cioffi finished poring through the two affidavits, neither of which was lengthy and each of which came right to the point. "Well then," the judge said as he looked up at the prosecutor who had also gone through the two documents. "What do you have to say about this, Mr. Frankel?"

Palmer knew he had blindsided the ADA, who was not happy and not sure how to respond. "I would have given you advance notice, but these developments all occurred in the past twenty-four hours. I just received these written statements this morning."

"And they weren't delivered to the district attorney's office?"

"They were, Judge, also this morning. Probably when Mr. Frankel was already here in court."

Palmer and Cioffi waited as Frankel tried to gather his thoughts. "I will obviously have to speak with Lt. Lawson," he finally said, "and then interview Mr. Phelps."

"Of course," the judge said. "How long will you need?"

"Just a couple of days, Your Honor."

Judge Cioffi looked at his calendar and called his clerk over. After a brief discussion about dates, he said, "A week from Friday at ten, how would that be?"

"Works for me," Palmer said.

Frankel agreed.

"Very well. A week from Friday at ten for a hearing on the defendant's application for suppression. Which, at this point, sounds like a motion for dismissal of the charges."

"Yes, your Honor," Palmer said.

"In the meantime, we will keep this discussion and these affidavits confidential. Bail is continued." Cioffi shot Palmer a knowing grin, then rapped his gavel, saying, "Bailiff, call the next case."

Outside in the hallway, Taub asked Palmer to explain what just happened.

"What happened is that I'm trying to parlay your manager's mealy-mouthed confession into a dismissal."

"I want Phelps in prison," Taub told him.

"That's not our job."

Taub frowned.

"The key for us is to get Phelps to spill everything he knows to the ADA in exchange for a deal. They're not going to be interested in prosecuting a gun sale, they'll want to find D'Angelo's murderer." *Which could also lead them to solve the Platt case*, Palmer thought, but did not share that with his client. "Come on, Robbie is waiting."

They met Whyte in the lobby, the three of them stepping out into the blazing sun of the late June morning.

"How'd you make out?" Whyte asked

"The judge gets it. The ADA is in shock. We're coming back next week."

Whyte turned to Taub but said nothing.

"Look, I know you hate my guts," Taub said, "but you know I didn't kill that little creep."

Whyte nodded. “I know you didn’t. Just be glad you’ve got Palmer in your corner.”

Taub nodded, then Palmer and Whyte watched as he hailed a cab on Centre Street, climbed in, and rode away.

“I really don’t like that flesh peddler,” Whyte said.

Palmer nodded. “Let’s get uptown. I have some ideas I want to run by you.”

“Be still my heart,” Whyte responded with a smile.

CHAPTER FORTY-ONE

That evening, Whyte had arranged for them to meet for a drink with Hugh Lawson at P.J. Clarke's to thank him for his help. Maureen asked to come along, and the three of them were seated at a table in the back of the dining room when Lawson walked in and headed toward them.

The men stood and Palmer said, "Lieutenant, this is Maureen O'Brien. She runs our office."

"And our lives," Whyte said.

Lawson offered a polite smile. "Heard a lot of good things about you from Robbie," he said as the men took their seats. "The conscience of the firm, as I understand it."

"More like a den mother," she said. "And I hear nothing but positive things about you, which is rare for this team."

Lawson smiled. "Good to have you here, a definite upgrade."

"That she is," Whyte agreed.

"I'm also a fan of your son," Maureen said. Then she added with a smile, "My computers wouldn't run without his help."

"Caleb is a good man," he replied, then turned to Palmer. "I hear you've already laid the tracks for a dismissal on Taub."

"With your help," Palmer told him.

"You get the credit for that. I still can't believe the way you handled Phelps."

"He's a nitwit."

"Who thought he was being so clever."

"You were an ace," Whyte told Lawson. "Never would have worked if you hadn't been standing by."

The lieutenant uttered a soft chuckle. "Which means this is a celebration for helping Taub, a guy neither Robbie nor I like, and who doesn't deserve you as his lawyer."

Palmer nodded slowly. "He may be guilty of a lot of things, but he didn't murder D'Angelo. Which means justice was served."

"There is that," Lawson conceded.

After the lieutenant ordered a beer from their waitress, Palmer said, "Anything new on Vernon Platt's death? If you don't mind me asking."

"Who could stop you?"

"No one," Whyte said.

"Forensics is working on my theory," Lawson told them.

"What about D'Angelo's death?" Palmer asked.

"Not my case," Lawson reminded him.

"But, if Frost was pulling the strings on Joey, trying to frame Taub, it probably means he also controlled the guy who took Joey down," Palmer said. "Now that we know about Phelps and the gun, maybe people will begin to worry."

"Maybe," Lawson responded with a look that said he wasn't so sure. "You bluffed Phelps, but Frost is in a different league. And Phelps insists he doesn't have any direct information to incriminate him."

"He wouldn't risk giving up Frost if he did," Whyte said. "Even he's not that stupid."

Palmer was still looking at Lawson. "But you believe we're going in the right direction?"

The lieutenant turned to Whyte. "Your boy have any idea what he's doing, messing with these people?"

"My boy doesn't have the sense he was born with," Whyte said.

"Thanks, partner," Palmer said.

"But I didn't say you might not be on the right track," Lawson told him.

"I appreciate that."

Maureen had been watching the lieutenant. "You're careful about what you say, but you think this is dangerous enough for us to back off?"

Lawson took a moment. "You're going to get a dismissal on Taub," he told her. "Why not take a victory lap and let the rest of it go?" Turning back to Palmer, he said, "Go handle your celebrity divorce and leave the murder investigation to the experts."

"That sounds like a sensible approach," Maureen agreed.

"I believe Frost tried to frame my client," Palmer told them. "Even if we put that aside, he also had his thugs rough me up on the street."

"What?"

"Couple of hoods grabbed him the other night. I'll explain later," Whyte told Lawson. "He's on a roll, let him go."

Palmer nodded. "I'm convinced Platt's death, Joey's death, the divorce, and the RDMO investigation are all somehow connected, although I haven't put it together yet. And I made a promise to Jeanette Scott."

"Christina Franco's mother?" Lawson asked.

"To find out who murdered her best friend, Vernon Platt," Whyte explained.

Lawson looked at Maureen as she said, "You see what I'm up against?"

"I do," said Lawson. "And stubborn is putting it mildly."

"Tell me about it."

"Well, if you really are determined to get your ass in a sling," Lawson said to Palmer, "I have a bit more information for you to consider."

"We are a spellbound audience," Palmer said.

"Strictly on the down low, then," Lawson said. "Seems my commanding officer got word from above that someone believes I'm pushing the investigation into Platt's death a bit too hard."

It was Maureen who asked, "No kidding?"

"Not something I would joke about."

"When you say that word came from above—" Whyte began.

"You know how it works, Robbie. He didn't say who delivered the message, but he and I are close. It was more a polite heads up than a warning. I mean, he's like me, a big fan of hard evidence. But he told me it was definitely from the feds."

"As in the DOJ, FBI, what?" Whyte asked.

"Or the good Congressman Scott?" Palmer suggested.

Lawson nodded slowly. "All of which means, I'm now willing to look into your idea that D'Angelo might have murdered Platt. They knew each other, Joey could be bought, and he was taken out just a couple of days after Platt died. As for who took down Joey, *quien sabe*?"

None of the others responded.

Looking at Whyte, Lawson asked, "You think there's any chance Sammy Burdick knows something about that?"

"Not the impression I got when I met with him."

"Then why did they cave his head in just for speaking with you?" the lieutenant asked.

"We've been wrestling with that same question. Someone had already warned him off with that bullet in the envelope I told you about."

"Which means he had to know something important to earn him a stay in the hospital."

Whyte shook his head. "We're working on the assumption that Frost is somehow mixed up in all this, and Frost doesn't allow for loose ends. If Burdick could identify Joey's murderer, they would have killed him as easily as smack him around."

"True," Lawson agreed.

"Which leaves me with the same question. Why warn him off, then smack him around for talking with me?"

"What if he knew something about Joey visiting Taub's place that night and acting out?" Palmer asked. "What if he knew D'Angelo was there to set up Taub, but had no idea Joey was signing his own death warrant?"

"That's not bad," Lawson said. "If he knew about any part of the frame, that would certainly be something they wouldn't want him gabbing about."

Palmer sighed. "Too many things here don't make sense."

No one disagreed.

CHAPTER FORTY-TWO

After they left Clarke's, Whyte drove Maureen to her apartment building on 72nd Street and Second Avenue, Lawson headed home and Palmer walked back to the brownstone.

He needed some time to think and sitting in the warm night air seemed a good idea. After pouring himself a bourbon over a large ice cube, he went outside to the patio in the rear, not bothering to turn on any of the lights. He preferred the dark, especially after the other night. Sitting in one of the teak and blue mesh chairs, he stared up into the night.

When Palmer's instincts told him he was making a mistake, they did not necessarily cause him to reverse course. The prospect of trouble on the horizon did not stop him from charging ahead—in fact, it sometimes had the opposite effect, especially if there was some other influence that drove him forward.

Most prominent of which was his over-developed sense of right and wrong.

He knew that Whyte had a better ability to sense danger than he did, and the detective had warned Palmer against taking the Franco matter from the beginning. They did not handle much matrimonial litigation, which has a unique—if limited—array of legal procedures and problems. But that was a minor consideration compared to the collateral issues that had arisen since Christina Franco entered their lives. Peter Frost. The deaths of Platt and D'Angelo. The attempted frame of Marvin Taub. RDMO and the FDA scandal. Thugs accosting him on the street. Sammy Burdick ending up in the hospital for speaking with Whyte. And those anonymous phone calls.

There was no way to be sure all those events were connected, but together they certainly made it look like a train wreck waiting to happen. And Whyte thought they should send Mrs. Franco on her way so they could move on to worthier causes.

Maureen also had her doubts, which was another opinion he could not ignore. She teased him about Christina's money and sex appeal, but she knew Palmer did not engage in extra-curricular activities with clients. Her main concern was his reasoning for staying on the case. She thought his argument—that he was representing her because she deserved their help—was weak. Christina could well afford to find someone else, but Maureen understood the intangible factor was the involvement of Peter Frost. She told Palmer that getting into a clash with him again was the biggest mistake of all.

Palmer sat in the dark, wondering if he should take their advice.

But if Franco was really serious about his threat to his wife, and if Christina knew something about her husband that was potentially damaging enough to warrant the threat, and if Peter Frost was really prepared to do the bidding of Edward Franco.... Palmer stopped himself. That was a lot of *ifs*.

There were things about the Franco case that did not make sense, which also kept him thinking. For instance, Christina almost never mentioned her two children. He found that incredibly strange. What was her relationship with them? What was her husband's relationship with them? Would Edward really take the life of their mother? And what about how the kids were dealing with all this? In Palmer's experience, people with young children usually worry about how their divorce would affect them. They also discuss arrangements for visitation and so forth. His client had yet to mention any of that.

Was she that frightened for her own safety? If so, given her husband's threat, why did she want to move full steam ahead with the divorce?

Then there was Christina's mother. Jeanette's personal story was certainly a sad tale, but Palmer knew there were missing parts there as well.

In their few discussions, she never seemed particularly concerned about Christina's domestic woes. She always focused on what had happened to her old friend Vernon Platt, who was already gone. And speaking of Christina's children, Palmer wondered if Jeanette remembered she had grandchildren. She never spoke of them either. Did she have any worries about how they were doing?

Palmer shook his head. *What sort of people am I involved with?* Before addressing that concern, he went back to the global question—*How do all the pieces of this puzzle fit together?*

Palmer had a generous taste of his whiskey.

He had no doubt that Frost was behind the charge against Taub. Frost and Taub never liked each other, dating back years to The Honey Pot, when Frost and his crew tried to move in on the action. Palmer knew the story about the meeting that included various luminaries of the New York City underworld who exercised a measure of control over such enterprises. A deal was struck, but the bad blood between Frost and Taub lived on.

Yet the attempt to implicate Taub in D'Angelo's death was clumsily handled, and Frost was not a careless man. And Frost knew Taub would turn to Palmer to handle his case, which raised even more questions. *Was that why Taub had been chosen as the fall guy? Did Frost—or someone else—want Palmer in the middle of all this? And if so,* Palmer wondered, *how did that make sense if they tried to scare him off the case?*

That last question was left hanging when Palmer heard the alarm tone, telling him someone had just entered the front of the brownstone. A few moments later, Whyte stepped through the back door into the moonlit night.

"Any reason you're sitting here in the dark?"

"Easier for me to think. And less likely someone tosses another unwanted greeting over the wall."

Whyte nodded. "I'm going to grab something. You need any more of that?"

"I'm good."

Whyte came back with a Stella Artois and sat in the chair facing Palmer. Whyte clinked his bottle against Palmer's glass, then they both drank.

"I have an interesting update for you," Whyte said after settling back in the seat.

"I'm ready."

"After I dropped Maureen at her place, I got an off-the-record call from Vera."

Palmer grinned. He remembered Vera Alexander.

"She sends her best."

"Nice of her," Palmer said.

Whyte nodded. "She also told me that indictments are about to be issued in the RDMO matter."

"Without Platt's testimony?"

"That's what she heard."

Palmer shook his head. "Poor bastard may have been murdered for no reason."

"That depends on how good the prosecution's case is without him."

"Any word on who's being charged?"

"They say some big names may get caught in the net."

"Anyone we know?"

"She didn't have the headliners. Not yet."

"Didn't or wasn't sharing?"

"She would have told me if she knew."

"Just couldn't resist that ineffable Clarence Whyte charm."

"You're a funny man, but if you use my middle name again, I'm going to pull out my .38."

"I appreciate the warning."

"Vera did hear about some small fish that will be charged, including one close to the matters we're handling."

"Do tell."

"Henry Carrigan is the name I recognized. As we already know from our man in Washington, he's been spearheading the drive to get some RDMO drugs approved. Apparently crossed the line one too many times."

"Pushing for what you want is not a crime," Palmer said. "That's just good, old-fashioned capitalism."

"Depends on what line you cross and who you bump into when you get there."

"Any word on the timing for the charges being announced?"

"She hears it'll be soon."

"That's interesting intel. Could change the dynamics of our divorce case." Palmer tasted his bourbon as his cell phone rang. Seeing the number, he took the call. "Hey, Sloane."

She said, "I usually don't have to wait this long to get a call back after—well, you get the idea."

"Very ungentlemanly of me, I admit."

"And I won't argue. Just wanted to check-in."

"As in, how things are going with Francos?"

"That would be of some interest to me."

"All right," Palmer said. "Maybe we can get together in the next couple of days?"

"I'd love it," she told him.

After they said their goodbyes, Palmer put down his phone and turned back to Whyte. "What's with the look?" he asked.

After Whyte let a few moments pass, he said, "People can tell you to watch your back, but only a real friend can warn you about what's right in front of you."

CHAPTER FORTY-THREE

The next morning, Palmer received a call inviting him back to the Scotts' Park Avenue luxury high-rise.

But this time Jeanette was not the one asking. It was her husband's assistant.

Arriving at the building, he went through the same process, passing through security, then being escorted up in the elevator. When he got off in the foyer of the large apartment, he was met by a young woman he assumed to be the aide who had called.

"Mr. Palmer," she said, hand extended, "thank you for coming on short notice."

He took her hand and said, "Just happens my appointment with the president was postponed," but it was clear from her deadpan response that she was not going to be much of an audience.

"I'll bring you inside," the young woman said, and led him into the apartment.

This get-together was not taking place in the living room, where he and Jeanette had met. It was being held in the office off to the right of the long corridor. As Palmer was shown into the room, he found that he was not only meeting with Congressman Eugene Scott, but also with a large gentleman he recognized as Senator Harlan Detweiler.

He did his best not to betray any hint of surprise.

The way Palmer had it figured, if you're invited to meet with a United States congressman—no matter what the reason for the visit—the crucial thing was not to be intimidated by the event. Whether you were going to discuss campaign fundraising, the military budget, or the weather, it was critical to act as if you'd been there before. *Politicians are generally full of themselves—and other things. No need to feed the monkey,* he told himself. The key was to remember that you were their equal—maybe even their better—since you could vote these jokers into office.

Palmer had been coaching himself on this approach since he got the invitation. He changed from a causal look into a navy blue suit, white shirt, and dark red tie, then strolled crosstown, going over the obvious questions—*Why would Congressman Scott want to meet with me?* and *What's the rush?*

Various possibilities leapt to mind, but Palmer decided not to speculate. In his experience, it was best not to try and guess what sort of pitch you're about to see. Curveball? Fastball? Slider? Changeup? Unless you were clairvoyant, just let them toss the ball and rely on your instincts for the proper swing and accurate timing.

"Gentleman," Palmer said, and they got to their feet to shake his hand with the feigned enthusiasm they likely reserved for a serious campaign donor.

Each was also dressed in a dark suit and tie, probably their customary attire, but Palmer could not deny that it lent a measure of gravity to the meeting. This was no casual gathering.

Having a good look at each man, he thought that Scott had retained the fine posture and superior bearing of his youth, but his eyes lacked the intelligence that was evident behind the portly senator's sleepy gaze. Detweiler might be a physical wreck, but no one had to tell Palmer he was one of the most powerful men in the Senate, or that his presence this morning was no sort of accident.

After the introductions were done, they all took seats, Scott behind a small, carved wooden desk, Palmer and Detweiler in armchairs set side-by-side, facing their host. The aide had exited stage left, closing the door behind her.

"Thanks for coming by," Scott said with a smile Palmer had seen on television more than a few times. "Harlan and I are only in town for a few hours; we appreciate the chance to chat with you."

Palmer was tempted to get right to it by asking, "About what," but decided to stay with the spirit of forced bonhomie. "It's an honor to meet you both," he said, then wanted to kick himself for using *honor* instead of something like *pleasure* or—better yet—*burden.*

Detweiler turned to his left to face Palmer—the move requiring a real effort—regarding him with his wizened gaze as he said, "Bet you're wonderin' why we asked you here."

Palmer offered a smile in response. "The question had crossed my mind."

Detweiler uttered a hoarse laugh. "You have a reputation as a straight talker, young man, and I like that. Saves time and bullshit, don't you think?"

"Can't disagree, Senator, although I find it interesting that this is the third time in a week someone's told me I have a reputation."

"That so?" Detweiler looked ready to let out another chuckle, then appeared to think better of it, not sure if he was being sassed or not. "Well, better to have one than not," he said. "So let's get to it." Then he turned to Scott, passing an invisible baton.

"Seems you've become involved with my family," the congressman said. "Thought it might be helpful for us to meet."

"When you say involved—"

"You're representing my daughter in a divorce, and you've been speaking with my wife about the tragic death of our good friend Vernon Platt. Given that none of us knew you just a couple of weeks ago, I would call that involved."

Palmer smiled. "You know how it goes with lawyers. When you need one, they become the most important person in your life. Then, after the deal is done or the problem solved, they disappear." He paused before reminding them, "You also know I'm limited in what I can reveal about discussions with my clients."

"Is Jeanette a client?" Scott asked, appearing sincerely surprised.

"To the extent that she's shared confidences in reliance on my being an attorney, yes, she is."

Scott glanced at Detweiler, who was still watching Palmer but said nothing.

"Can I inquire as to the nature of the case you are working on for her?" Scott asked.

"She's apparently shared that with you already. She wants me to look into Platt's death."

"As an attorney or an investigator?"

"That depends on what I discover."

"We know that you have an unusual practice," Detweiler cut in. "That you work with a former police officer and that you are funded through some extraordinary arrangement."

Once again, Palmer was not pleased at the notion that anyone in the Scott family knew anything at all about his deal with Cameron Pinckney, but there was nothing to be done about it now. At the moment, he was marveling at how many beats the senator could wring from the word *extraordinary*. Since neither of them had asked a question, he decided to wait them out.

"I am going to tell you something," Scott said. "Something I hope you can hold in confidence. Not based on some legal obligation, but as a matter of your personal discretion."

Palmer remained silent.

"My wife is not a healthy person. To put it bluntly, she has some serious emotional issues that have plagued her for a long time. I have done my best to support her and minimize the impact of the pressures brought on by my career and the life I'm obliged to lead. Now, unfortunately, the upset over Vernon's death has become too much for her to bear. They had been the best of friends for many years."

Palmer nodded slowly but continued to remain quiet.

"We are at the point, I fear, where she will have to be hospitalized."

"Hospitalized?" Palmer asked.

Scott responded with a sad smile. "Her doctors feel Jeanette should be institutionalized."

Palmer looked to Detweiler, then back at Scott. "Since you are being blunt, I will concede Mrs. Scott's tendency to drink a bit too much is obvious. But I found nothing in her behavior to suggest that she's irrational or delusional."

"You will also doubtless concede," Detweiler said, "that you are not a mental health professional?"

"That's quite true."

"Or that when my wife sees you," Scott added, "she is determined to put her best foot forward."

"Also a valid point, though I've dealt with troubled people throughout my career and see nothing to suggest your wife needs to be locked up."

"That's a tough way to put it, young man," Detweiler said.

"Maybe so, but since we're opting for candor in this discussion, that would be the long and short of it, right? Which leads me to ask—"

"Why we have chosen to tell you," Scott said.

"Yes," Palmer agreed. "That would be my first question."

Scott paused for dramatic effect, or so Palmer read it. "It would be best if you do not pursue your relationship with Jeanette. You believe she is not delusional, but all evidence is to the contrary. She has convinced herself Vernon's suicide was a murder. Not only that, she believes it was a murder that is part of some imaginary conspiracy, the details of which are not even worth describing."

Palmer had been sitting back, doing his best to give the impression he was both relaxed and unperturbed by what was being discussed. Now he sat up a bit, ready to deliver the first blow. "As it happens, your wife is not wrong in her first belief, and may well be accurate with regard to the second."

"Beg pardon?" said Detweiler.

Turning to the senator, he said, "This has yet to be made public, but the police have discovered some convincing evidence that Mr. Platt's death was, in fact, a homicide."

The two men looked to each other, their expressions making it clear they knew Platt's death was no suicide, but wondered if this young man had better intelligence on the investigation than they did.

"Not only that," Palmer said, following up the right cross he had just thrown with a left hook, "they have some ideas about who shoved him off his balcony." He particularly enjoyed describing Platt's death with that last flourish.

Before he could suppress the urge, Scott uttered a hoarse, "What?"

"All true," Palmer said.

"Have you discussed any of this with Jeanette?" Scott asked.

"I have not. My sources are confidential, at least for now, but it will all come to light soon enough."

Looking at Scott, it appeared to Palmer that his two verbal punches had knocked all the air from his lungs.

"Let me be clear, gentlemen—and I say this respectfully—I realize that if you want to prevent me from communicating with Mrs. Scott, you can likely get that done. But if you asked me here in the hope that ending my contact with her is going to dissuade me from looking into Vernon Platt's death, that is not going to happen."

Detweiler abandoned his avuncular pose, leaning his large frame closer to Palmer as he said, "You know what Will Rogers advised when you find yourself in a hole?"

Palmer got to his feet. "Stop digging, as I recall. However, given how many of Rogers' witty criticisms were about the United States Congress, I would have thought he would be the last person you'd want to quote."

Neither man responded.

Palmer was tempted to mention what Lawson had told him last night, about someone in the feds trying to slow down his investigation. But he had promised to keep that confidential, so he took a different approach. "I appreciate you taking the time to inform me of this development in person. I will be guided accordingly." Walking toward the door, he turned back and said, "I have a feeling we'll be speaking again."

Detweiler fixed him with a stern look, as he said, "Yes, young man, I expect we will." Then he added, "Just be careful on whose toes you choose to tread."

Looking directly at him, Palmer said, "Thank you sir, but I've found that if you walk around looking down all the time, you never get where you need to go."

CHAPTER FORTY-FOUR

Two days later, the first court appearance in the Franco divorce case was held on the fifth floor of the New York State courthouse on Centre Street. A far more elegant structure than the Criminal Court building up the street, it housed many large courtrooms, judges' chambers, clerks' offices, and conference rooms. That afternoon, when Palmer arrived, he found his adversary there.

If Lillian Bartz was not the Dragon Lady of New York City's matrimonial bar—as Sloane Taylor had described her—Palmer wondered who else could possibly be worthy of the title. Having never seen her before, the first thing he noticed about the woman was the absence of a single curved line. She was short and slight, her body lacking any discernible shape, her face angular, her nose pointy, her lips thin, and even her blunt-cut auburn hair seemed designed to be intimidating. But her eyes told the real story. They were dark and angry, as if annoyance was her starting point, and things were only going to get worse from there.

As tough as she might turn out to be, for the moment Palmer was more interested in her client. This was also the first time he was meeting Edward Franco.

Bartz and Franco were standing near the railing, and as Palmer approached, he had to admit the man was as good looking in person as in his photos. He was about Palmer's height, tanned and fit, with full, masculine features, and a thick head of dark hair worn long and neatly styled. Palmer noted that his suit was clearly bespoke and his smile as genuine as pyrite.

Palmer held out his hand, and said, "Russell Palmer."

Bartz ignored the gesture. "You're late," she told him, "and your client isn't here."

Palmer grinned. "Good to meet you too. And I'm never late. You may have noticed the judge hasn't taken the bench yet." Not waiting for a clever riposte, he turned to Franco, who took his hand and gave it a firm shake. "You recover from that vicious slap yet?"

Before Franco could respond, Bartz was at it again. "You think this is a joke, Palmer? Your client assaulted Mr. Franco in front of thousands of witnesses, with millions watching it again and again on YouTube. You have any sense of the humiliation he suffered?"

"I'm often told I don't have *any* sense," Palmer replied, still studying Franco, "but it appears you've survived this horrific attack with great aplomb. Well done."

Franco could not help laughing, but his lawyer was not amused.

"Stop speaking to my client," she told him. "We'll see how funny you think this is once the judge is done with you."

Forcing himself to look at Bartz, Palmer said, "When the judge is done with *me*? What did I do?"

Before Bartz could snarl another reply, the clerk pounded on the door that led from chambers to the raised area at the front of the room and said, "All rise." The judge emerged and settled into his large chair behind the bench.

"Be seated," Judge Hellman told everyone.

The hearing was attended by newspaper and magazine reporters, television correspondents, and curious onlookers. As Palmer made his way to plaintiff's counsel table he turned around and spotted Sloane Taylor in the gallery. She greeted him with a warm smile.

After everyone found their proper places, Hellman appeared ready to inquire about the whereabouts of Mrs. Franco. That was the moment Christina made her grand entrance. She didn't exactly glide into the room, but Palmer thought her appearance was dramatic enough.

Hellman and his clerk had a brief, whispered conversation as Christina gracefully slid into the chair beside Palmer. Then the judge looked up. "I see the attorneys on the Franco matter are both here. With their clients," he added, as he peered over the top of his reading glasses at Christina. "Counsel, please approach."

Bartz rose as if propelled from her seat by a giant spring, virtually sprinting forward, while Palmer took his time, until they stood side by side, facing the judge as he leaned toward the side of the bench.

"So good to see you, Ms. Bartz," the judge said, his tone sounding to Palmer as if it were hovering somewhere between respect and irony. "And Mr. Palmer, we don't see much of you in these hallowed halls anymore."

"It isn't personal, your Honor."

Hellman smiled. "Neither of you has to tell me what this is about. I've read your papers, and I watch enough television to know what's going on. Your client," he said looking at Palmer, "has instituted a divorce action. Ms. Bartz," he continued, turning to face her, "has chosen as her first shot across the bow an application for a protective order based on the altercation between the parties at that charity event—"

Before the judge could finish, Bartz shifted directly from neutral straight into third gear. "Altercation? Your Honor, you make it sound like it was some sort of mutual clash, when it was an unprovoked and violent attack. That woman has—"

Hellman showed her the palm of his hand. "Counsel, you know me well enough to know that no one interrupts me in my courtroom. I get quite enough of that at home. And if you believe you're going to get any mileage by raising your voice so you can play to our audience in the back, that would also be a mistake." He paused, giving Bartz a chance to catch her breath. "Before I hear a word of argument or testimony, I want the two of you to go down the hall and use the conference room to work this out. If you need help from my clerk, or me, just let us know. But be assured, if you don't come back with an agreement, I'll figure out which side is being difficult and that lawyer's client will not be happy with the result in these proceedings. Am I clear?"

"As Baccarat," Palmer said.

Before Bartz could respond, the judge stood and said in a loud voice, "We will have a brief recess." When the audience uttered a collective groan of disappointment, he pounded his gavel and disappeared back into his chambers.

After telling Christina to sit tight and stay away from her husband, Palmer followed Bartz as she hurried down the wide, marble corridor to a small conference room at the end of the hall. As soon as they entered and Palmer shut the door behind them, his adversary's features seemed to magically soften.

She took a seat, smoothed out the skirt of her dark gray suit, and said, "When we were assigned Hellman, I knew he wasn't going to let us get into a public melodrama. Sort of a shame, don't you think?"

Palmer, who was still standing, looked down at her. "I'll admit, our clients seem to live for that sort of thing."

"Yes, they do," Bartz said, her manner having become downright friendly. "We should spend some time in here, make it seem like we slugged it out before we head back inside. We both know where this is going."

Palmer lowered himself into the wooden chair facing her. "Mutual protective and non-disparagement orders?"

"Makes sense, right? A win-win, it keeps the judge happy, and we move on."

"I guess so."

"You've also got a cross-motion for temporary alimony and child support. There's obviously plenty of money here, what did you have in mind?"

"My papers laid out—" Palmer started, but Bartz cut him off.

"I know, but you've got to give me a little victory on that."

"How little?"

"I know you asked for the moon in your cross-motion. Cut your numbers down by a third, and we have a deal."

Palmer stared at her. She had suddenly become so cordial he found himself wondering if she was schizophrenic. "That's it?"

"As I said, I'd love to argue this case, but Hellman isn't going to let us put on a show. This is the way to go."

"Seems very reasonable of you."

Bartz nodded. "What about your client's trust fund?"

"What about it?"

"How do we adjust for the income she gets from that?"

"It's discretionary, there are no guaranteed distributions, so it's not part of the marital estate."

"Thank you for that legal analysis."

Palmer smiled. "You don't agree?"

"Of course I do, but the trustee is her mother. Given the circumstances, don't you think Mrs. Scott is going to loosen the purse strings?"

"Not now, and not under the terms of the trust."

"Which doesn't end for seven years."

"Correct."

"Isn't mom inclined to be generous now that her daughter is getting divorced?"

"Not that I know of, but the possibility makes this a case we can probably settle."

"Meaning that your client will be asking for less than half of everything?"

"That's right."

She studied him for a moment. "I've checked you out. You don't do a lot of matrimonial work, but somehow you've managed to get involved in several high-profile cases. How do you manage that?"

"Just lucky."

"Come on, you can do better."

"Let's say I have an unusual skill set."

"I remember that case you handled, the billionaire and his showgirl wife. That was quite a coup."

Palmer resisted the temptation to describe exactly what kind of showgirl Charlotte the Harlot had been. "Robbie Whyte gets most of the credit for that one."

"Your in-house PI."

"Best in the business."

"Was that why Christina Franco came to you? Her family friendship with that older gentleman.... Pinckney, right?"

Palmer was not about to discuss Cameron Pinckney. "Tell you the truth, I'm still trying to figure out why Christina wanted me to handle her case."

Bartz responded with a thoughtful nod. "Neither of our clients is going to be nominated for sainthood any time soon. I'm guessing you've also reached that conclusion."

"I tend to be too judgmental, trying to break the habit."

She actually laughed. "I know what you mean. I do nothing but divorce work, and there's rarely anything noble involved. One side or both have done things to destroy what began as two people in love, which is sad when you think about it."

"With everything I've heard about your abilities in the courtroom, you could do something else if it bothers you that much."

"Like what? Criminal defense work, dealing with low-life scum? Corporate disputes, dealing with well-dressed scum? Or my personal favorite, chasing ambulances."

"Sorry to sound naïve, but do you ever think about the good you might do for the right clients?"

"I believe I do that now, in my own way. People want to end their marriages. I'm very good at getting them the best deal possible. They pay me a lot but, since I'm not the cause of their problem, I have no ethical issues accepting the money to help solve them."

And there in a nutshell, thought Palmer, *is everything that's wrong with the legal profession.*

They engaged in a detailed discussion about the case, the marital assets, and so forth—as Bartz had suggested, using the time to pretend they were slugging it out. After a while, she said, "That's enough, let's go see Hellman. And do us both a favor, make sure your client believes this was a struggle. If you say otherwise, I'll eat your lunch at our next hearing."

"I believe you will," he said. "First, I have a thought."

"Go ahead."

"Almost all of the marital assets are in your client's name. As I understand it, he has a range of corporate investments, which my client wants no part of. As I've already told you, she'll take less than half of everything to get this divorce done."

"Why would she agree to that?"

"Because she only wants the liquid assets. Cash, mutual funds, publicly traded stocks. The New York apartment and the house in the Hamptons."

"That's a lot, but it's certainly less than half of what shows up on his balance sheet."

"She doesn't want to be involved in any of his business ventures. For a variety of reasons." He had a good look at Bartz. "Speak with your client, see what he has to say. We wrap this up, and you'll come out with a bigger victory than you asked for."

She thought it over. "We're never going to get rich settling a case like this so quickly," Bartz said with a smile.

"Far as I can see, your client will owe you a large bonus."

"That could work," she said with another laugh. "First let's see if our clients agree to the concept."

"Right," Palmer agreed, then said, "one more thing."

"Don't push your luck, Counselor."

"I'm not asking for anything, just curious."

"Go ahead."

"When Christina came to me, she was convinced her husband would never agree to a divorce. In the past half hour, we may have worked out most of the terms for a full settlement. You think he's going to be all right with this?"

"He told me from the start he doesn't want a divorcc, but hc also said he would never block it, if that's what she wants."

"Interesting," Palmer said. "Suppose I told you he threatened her life if she filed for the divorce?"

"Why would he do that?"

"I don't know."

"Even if it were true, I have no idea why. Maybe she's just exaggerating something he said in the middle of an argument. No one denies they spend a lot of time arguing. People getting a divorce usually do."

He waited, but it seemed she was done. *Which means she probably knows nothing about the video. Does her client?* Palmer wondered.

Bartz stood and once again assumed her mask of arrogant outrage.

Palmer got to his feet but, before opening the door, he said, "You'd be one amazing actress."

She winked at him. "What makes you think I'm not?"

Returning to the courtroom, they had private discussions with their respective clients, each of whom seemed thrilled with the prospect of a global settlement. Once that was confirmed, Bartz told the clerk they wanted to see the judge in chambers. Seated before Hellman, it did not take long for her to describe their agreement for mutual protective and non-disparagement orders. Then she laid out some basic financial terms.

Palmer could see that Hellman was astounded that such a comprehensive arrangement might be reached so quickly.

"Impressive," he said.

Palmer smiled. "Seems there was enough to go around to make them both happy."

Since Bartz was a frequent visitor to Hellman's courtroom, she and the judge engaged in a discussion that rambled through other topics, and Palmer remained a polite observer for that interlude. Hellman, eventually having had enough of that banter himself, told them they should put the agreement on the record and led them back outside.

When Hellman announced that the parties had come to terms, the letdown among the spectators was audible once again. They had come there for a spectacle, not the dry recitation of some agreed-upon resolution. When some of them got up to leave, the judge pounded his large wooden gavel and called the room to order.

"No one enters or leaves this courtroom until we're done," he told the court officer. "Whatever those in the gallery thought they came to see, they'll remain in their seats, in silence, until this has been completed."

Since the original motion was brought by Bartz, she got to her feet and laid out the terms whereby neither party would attack, disparage, or otherwise trample on the rights of the other. It was a comprehensive statement, at the end of which the judge asked Palmer if he agreed with everything his adversary had said.

Rising from his chair, Palmer said, "That was very detailed and accurate. I just have one addition."

Bartz turned to him but said nothing.

"These restrictions should apply to any third parties acting on behalf of our clients."

"Third parties?" Bartz asked, not hiding her confusion.

"I don't want my client harassed, followed, or otherwise contacted by anyone acting on behalf of Mr. Franco."

Before Bartz could respond, Judge Hellman said, "I assume that will cut both ways, Mr. Palmer."

"Naturally, your Honor," he replied.

"Ms. Bartz?"

Bartz hesitated. Palmer knew he had taken her by surprise and guessed that she was weighing whether she should ask if an accusation was being made. In the end, she simply said, "Agreed."

"Good," the judge said. "The terms are so ordered. As to the financial terms we went over in chambers, they will remain confidential. I must congratulate both counsel on coming to terms so expeditiously. You have agreed that Ms. Bartz will reduce the entire agreement to writing, have it approved by Mr. Palmer, and deliver it to my clerk by next Wednesday. Meanwhile, the terms stated on the record are in immediate effect. The court is now in recess."

As the various players filed out of the courtroom, Bartz brushed up against Palmer, whispering, "Nicely played, Counselor. Some day you'll have to tell me what that last move was about."

"Yes," Palmer said. "Indeed, I will."

In the corridor, after Christina and Palmer moved away from the crowd, she said, "I can't believe it. You got me everything I wanted. Thank you."

"You're welcome."

"I really wasn't looking forward to taking the stand, about the assault claim I mean."

"The audience was not happy to miss the fun, but I'm glad you didn't have to go through it."

"I feel so relieved."

"Good."

"Was she tough to deal with?"

"Let's just say she was interesting."

"Now what?"

"We'll get the paperwork together and, once the agreement is in place, I can ask for the divorce to be granted."

"Amazing," she said.

"Yes," he agreed, "it is."

More amazing than you know, he thought, *but you're about to find out very soon.*

CHAPTER FORTY-FIVE

That evening, seated on the stone patio in back of the brownstone, Palmer was enjoying his customary bourbon. Whyte seemed to be taking forever mixing a whiskey sour at the outdoor bar, an unmistakable signal that he had something serious to discuss.

"You distilling that whiskey from scratch?" Palmer asked over his shoulder.

"Funny man."

"What's up, Robbie?"

"I have some things to discuss you're not going to be happy about."

"That's a lousy intro, since I've had a pretty good day so far."

Whyte finished his mixology and, drink in hand, made his way to the chair directly across from his young friend.

"Fire away," Palmer said.

"I'll start with our client Christina Franco and the men she thinks are following her."

"Great. If we can prove her husband sent them, we can bring a contempt motion for violating the agreement. Might change the calculus on the deal I cut for her."

"Assuming they admit they're working for Franco."

Palmer smiled. "That's your area of expertise."

Whyte was not smiling. "Point is, I've had a couple of the guys I use keeping an eye on her the past several days. They don't see any signs of her being tracked."

"That's all right."

"Not if she's been lying to us, which is possible after what they did see last night. When she stopped for a drink at the rooftop bar at the Gansevoort."

"I know the place. Very trendy."

"Yes, it is. Anyway, she sat in a corner, looking very casual, not wearing one of her usual million-dollar outfits. Almost incognito, if you catch my drift."

"Drift away."

"She was not there for the hip atmosphere."

"You're killing me, Robbie. Give me the punch line."

Whyte took a sip of his drink. "She met with Henry Carrigan."

Palmer sat back. "She went to a hotel bar to meet Henry Carrigan?"

"She did."

"We got some photos, and confirmed the ID. You ought to have a look. And it's clear she wasn't there to tell him he's the rat she described to us."

"You're saying they were, uh, friendly?"

"Very. Which also doesn't square with the things Carrigan had to say to you on the phone about the fair Christina."

Palmer realized that nothing about Christina Franco would surprise him anymore, but he was clearly disappointed. "It seems our girl has been playing us, and I admit I've wanted to believe her."

"I know you have," Whyte said as kindly as he could manage. "I've told you before, you tend to see the best in people, which is not such a bad thing."

"Except when it clouds my judgment."

Whyte did not disagree. "She pretended to be followed. Had her boyfriend call to say she can't be trusted. Who knows what else she lied about?"

"You're right," Palmer admitted. "I had hoped for better, even when you suspected the worst."

Whyte nodded.

"Now we have to figure out how it all makes sense."

"You're the brains around here," the detective said.

"Not so much on this case, apparently. And what does that make you, the muscle?"

The detective smiled. Then he said, "There's more."

"I can hardly wait."

"I've had another of my freelance guys keep an eye on your friend Sloane Taylor."

"What for?"

"Call it professional curiosity. Or looking out for my best friend, if you prefer." He had another taste of his tart cocktail. "Guess who she met with?"

"Don't tell me Edward Franco."

"See what I mean, kiddo, you really are the brains."

Palmer shook his head. "Seems this group is turning out to be more and more incestuous. What next, Jeanette Scott sleeping with Senator Detweiler?"

"That's an image I can do without."

"How friendly did Sloane and Franco look to be?" Palmer asked.

"Let's say they looked quite familiar."

"Familiar, as in they already knew each other?"

"Oh yes."

Palmer thought it over. "She reports on celebrities, maybe she was looking for information about their divorce."

"Maybe, but it didn't look like any sort of an interview to my man. And even then you'd have to explain why he would bother meeting with her to talk about his split."

Palmer shrugged. "The Francos are publicity hounds. Maybe he was hoping she'd put a good spin on his side of the story. Worth treating her to a cocktail."

"More than one cocktail, and more than a few laughs. Then they left together."

"Where did they go?"

"Take a guess."

"No thanks."

"Back to her place, which means we're being played by her too," Whyte said.

"What do you mean *we*? I'm the one she snuggled up to, trying to get information."

"Of which you gave her very little."

"About the Francos? Zero. I did spend that evening with her and Benny Parsons. All she got there was some background on Joey D."

"And a name."

"Sammy Burdick," Palmer said, none too happy at the next thought.

"That's right. Which might solve the mystery of how Mr. Burdick just happened to end up having his face rearranged right after I met with him."

Palmer bit at his lower lip. It was painful to think that Sloane would have told Franco what she learned from their night with Parsons. Best case was that she might not have realized what the consequences would be to Sammy Burdick. *Still,* Palmer reminded himself, *when no other solution fits, you're stuck with the one that does.*

"I know what you're thinking," Whyte interrupted his musings. "Someone was following me that day, possibly to see what I was investigating, including background on RDMO. But it doesn't explain what happened to Burdick after I left his place."

"Unless Frost was the one having you tailed."

"That's where it falls apart for me," Whyte said, then took a sip of his drink. "Why the hell would Frost bother to have me followed at that point? We were only in the early stages of sorting out this puzzle and the players involved."

"You're right," Palmer admitted.

"Sorry, kiddo, but it looks like your girlfriend might have been the tipster. Whether the result was due to evil intentions or merely accidental remains to be discovered."

"That's one I did not see coming," Palmer conceded with a sigh. "And you might spare me the girlfriend bit, even if I can't argue the rest of it."

"I told you none of this was going to make you happy."

"No, it doesn't. But it keeps bringing us back to the big question behind all of it. *Why?*"

"I've had more time to think about this than you have. Mind if I take a crack at it?"

"Please do."

"Christina Franco convinced you to take her case by showing us the tape of her husband saying he would have her killed if she tried to leave him. And the mention of Peter Frost really grabbed your interest. Fair?"

"Go on."

"Despite her husband's threat if she tried to leave him, she's been pushing you to get her divorce done as quickly as possible."

"I've noticed."

"Which doesn't square with her claim that she's afraid of him."

"I've said as much to her."

"Next, she claimed she was being followed, which only increased your protective instincts. Just to be clear, I've had her under surveillance for five days, and we've seen no sign of anyone tracking her."

"You sneaky devil."

"It seemed the thing to do."

"Glad you did."

"Meanwhile, she had Carrigan call you, warning that she can't be trusted, another angle to keep you worried about her. You still with me?"

"Like a rash."

"Then there was the night she and her husband just happened to arrive at that charity ball at the same moment, giving her the opportunity to serve up a fresh one to the side of his head with the whole world watching."

"I think I need some Pepto-Bismol."

"Have a swig of your bourbon instead."

Palmer polished off his whiskey. "I thought I was supposed to be the brains of the outfit."

"I was just a bit ahead of you on this new information."

"So it seems. Please keep going, you're doing fine."

"All right, let's get to Frost. We have no idea how he fits in this cast of characters, whether he's acting as a principal or on behalf of someone else."

"Such as Edward Franco."

"Such as." Whyte paused. "That's as far as I got, now it's your turn. Tell me what your keen, analytical mind makes of all this?"

Palmer took some time before saying, "First we need to identify a few other pieces to the puzzle, some of which were supplied in my get together with Scott and Detweiler."

"It didn't sound to me like you learned much there, except their intention to have Mrs. Scott locked up. Presumably so she stays away from you."

"On the surface, that's correct, which now makes even more sense," Palmer said. "They were concerned about my discussions with Jeanette, but what do you think they fear she might tell me?"

"Something about the family's dealings with RDMO."

"Precisely. Which means I should find out what Jeanette Scott really knows, assuming they haven't cut off my access to her yet."

"Things Christina Franco continues to deny she knows anything about."

Palmer nodded. "That's something else I haven't mentioned to you." He sat up a bit straighter. "It may not be much, but in my latest conversation with Jeanette, she made a point of telling me her daughter never discusses business with her, but that Christina and Edward were as thick as thieves when it comes to his investments."

"That so?"

"The way she tossed out that little tidbit," Palmer said, "at the time I wasn't sure whether it was a casual observation or a pointed bit of intel she wanted me to have."

"What's your best guess now?"

"She's a bright woman, despite the booze. When we spoke it didn't seem like she was sending up any flares but, as we're going through all of this, it helps to make a number of things clearer."

CHAPTER FORTY-SIX

Just before noon the next day, Maureen walked into Palmer's office and said, "Peter Frost is on the phone."

It was Whyte who responded. "Frost?"

Tilting her head slightly to the side, Maureen told him, "He asked to speak with Mr. Palmer."

Palmer and Whyte stared at each other, then Palmer hit the speaker button. "Palmer here."

Frost uttered a brief laugh. "Wasn't sure you'd take the call."

"It's always a thrill to hear from you. Never know what's coming next."

"I'll take that as a compliment."

"Take it any way you please, as long as you're in front of me and not coming up from behind."

Whyte shook his head, to which Palmer responded with a look assuring him he should not worry.

"We need to meet," Frost said.

"Again? You just can't get enough of me lately."

"I said we need to meet," Frost repeated, any trace of warmth in his tone having vanished.

"I can't imagine why."

"We may have some interests that are beginning to align."

"Now there's something I *really* can't imagine."

There was silence until Frost said, "I put up with your attitude for reasons I've explained, but don't push it. You're on speaker, so may I assume the loyal Detective Whyte is with you?"

"He is."

"You've got enough experience," Frost said, "to tell your young friend he should mind his manners."

"As I do, quite frequently," Whyte said.

"All right. Let's do this soon," Frost said.

Looking across the desk, Palmer watched Whyte nod, then said, "Want to come to my office?"

"That would not be sensible for either of us at the moment, but I understand you're a big fan of P.J. Clarke's. How about a quiet table there, say an hour from now?"

"Good."

"You should come along, Detective, you're going to want to hear what I have to say."

An hour later, Palmer and Whyte were seated in the back of Clarke's dining room when Frost walked in. He was wearing a dove gray suit that fit perfectly and looked as if it had never been worn before, a white shirt that appeared to have been pressed twenty minutes ago, and a smile that said he knew something they did not. At least not yet.

None of that was unusual for Frost, except the fact that he seemed to be alone.

Neither man got up as he approached but, when Frost extended his hand, Palmer rose to his feet. *Never shake hands while you're sitting down*, he told himself. And, despite how much he disliked sharing another man's germs, he was not going to begin the meeting by insulting Frost.

Whyte could not suppress a smile, knowing what his germophobic friend was going through.

After the brief greeting was done, they all took their chairs, Frost with his back to the wall.

"Saved that seat for you," Palmer said.

Frost nodded his appreciation. "Can't be too careful, gentlemen, not in my line of work."

"One of these days you'll have to explain exactly what line of work you're in."

Frost's gaze narrowed, but he did not respond. Looking to Whyte, he said, "It's been a while, Detective."

When Whyte merely nodded, Palmer fought the urge to point out that all lucky streaks come to an end. As a better option, he said, "No henchmen in tow? Is that wise for a careful man?"

"I didn't think I'd have anything to worry about, having a drink with you two. Was I wrong?"

"I think you'll be fine," Palmer told him.

Frost nodded again. "I have a driver outside, if you care, but this discussion needs to be confidential."

"Fair enough," Palmer said.

"To that end, I would ask that neither of you record our conversation."

"We have no such intention."

Frost appeared to be considering that. "As I mentioned when we met the other day, there are very few people I would take at their word about such a thing. Why is it that I feel I can believe you?"

"Maybe because we're not like anyone else you deal with," Palmer suggested.

"You may be right," Frost said, "or maybe it's because you're a couple of cards short of a full deck." Then he paused again.

"You're looking very prosperous," Palmer told him. "Whatever your business is, it must be doing well."

"I manage to keep busy," Frost said. "You boys have also been busy. Dealing with some of the same people I've been working with."

"Such as?" Palmer asked.

"The Scott family, the Francos, executives at RDMO. Do I need to go on, or should we get down to business?"

"You left out a few other things we've been working on," Palmer reminded him. "Such as the murders of Vernon Platt and Joey D'Angelo, the attempted frame someone tried to hang around Marvin Taub's neck—"

"And the beating of Sammy Burdick," Whyte added.

Frost sat back, crossed his legs, and wiped away an imaginary piece of lint from his expertly creased trousers. "That's all history."

"Is it?" Whyte asked. "The police think Platt was murdered, but they don't have a suspect. For that matter, they don't have a suspect in the D'Angelo case either."

"Except Taub," Frost reminded him.

"Which is about to go away, as you undoubtedly know," Palmer said.

"I've heard," Frost admitted. "Which begs the question, why should those other things matter to you now? Taub is your client, I understand that, but he's going to walk. And, I might add, I expected nothing less from you."

Palmer resisted the urge to say something about what Frost knew about that but let him go on.

"The two victims you mentioned are not going to be raised from the dead, are they?" Frost asked rhetorically. "And Burdick is a little man with a big mouth, as I told you the last time we met. Nothing more than collateral damage. History. Take it from me, you should never waste time on things that cannot be undone. Your involvement with the other people I mentioned, however, is current. Some might even say urgent."

Palmer gazed at Frost, marveling at the detached manner with which he discussed murders and assaults. *That he is likely responsible for*, Palmer noted. "I take it that urgency is what motivated you to meet with us today."

"Our interests, quite unexpectedly, are becoming aligned."

"So you said on the phone."

"And I meant it. I think we can help each other."

Palmer laughed. Sometimes he simply couldn't help but see the humor in situations, even when staring at a ruthless killer. "You may recall that I've had experience seeing what happens to people you help."

Frost shrugged. "More spilt milk."

Before Palmer could respond, the waitress arrived and placed their drinks on the table. "Would you like to order anything to eat?"

"Not yet, thanks," Palmer told her.

After the young woman walked away, Frost lifted his glass and said, "Cheers," then had a taste of his gin.

Palmer and Whyte had a go at their cocktails, then waited.

"You represent Christina Franco in her divorce case," Frost said.

"And you work with her husband," Palmer said.

Frost slowly shook his head. "Things are not always what they seem and, as I've said, my interests have changed."

"You willing to provide any details?" Palmer asked.

"Let's just say Edward Franco and I were on the same path, but our roads have diverged."

"Very *Robert* Frost," Palmer said. "He any relation of yours?"

Frost responded with a frown.

"I believe you were about to discuss RDMO," Whyte said.

Frost lifted his glass again. "I've always said you were a fine detective. A loss for the NYPD became young Palmer's gain."

"Maybe I should order something to eat," Whyte said. "I'm starting to feel nauseous."

Both he and Palmer were more than a little surprised when Frost broke into a hearty laugh. "You two don't like me," he said to Whyte, "and given our past dealings, I fully understand that. But you should realize it's a mistake. Fact is, I like both of you, even with all of Palmer's peculiarities. Maybe *because* of them. I think we could do some interesting things together."

"Why not begin with your involvement in RDMO?" Palmer asked.

"You see," Frost replied, still looking at Whyte, "your impetuous partner insists on getting right to the main topic. No polite exchanges, no effort to build fellowship, just a demand to know whodunnit without reading the book."

"But you *are* here because you're willing to discuss RDMO, correct?" Whyte asked.

"I am."

"And what it has to do with us."

"Come now, Detective, we all know what it has to do with you. You think I'm not aware of the visit you made to your old paramour at the FDA and your subsequent trip to Washington? Or the link between the pending congressional investigation, Platt's death, and the request by Jeanette Scott that Palmer determine who murdered her dear old friend?

And yet I admit, all that takes a back seat to the real issue, which is the involvement of Edward Franco and Congressman Scott in the company, and how that might affect your client's divorce."

Palmer remained silent as he glanced at Whyte, his look asking, *How the hell does he know all this?*

Frost reacted to their silence with a confident grin. "Just like you, I have sources everywhere, gentlemen," he said, responding to the unasked question. "For instance, I know that your client, Mrs. Franco, is not what she appears to be."

"We finally agree on something," Whyte muttered, but before Frost could ask him what he meant, Palmer broke in.

"People have been telling me that since I took her case. You have something concrete you can share?"

Frost uncrossed his legs and leaned toward Palmer. "She told you her husband threatened her life if she tried to divorce him."

It wasn't a question, and since Frost was referring to a statement made to him by a client in confidence, Palmer said nothing.

"She also suggested that I would be the instrument of that vengeance." Holding up his hand, Frost added, "You don't have to reply, I understand your ethical obligations. But I know all about the cell phone video."

"What do you know?" Whyte asked.

Without moving his gaze from Palmer, Frost said, "It's all bullshit. The threat, the argument, all of it."

"Why would I believe that, coming from you?" Palmer asked, then quickly added, "no offense."

Frost smiled at the apology. Then, sounding as casual as he ever did, he said, "Because I have no reason to lie."

When Palmer reacted with a frown, Frost went on.

"Think about it. Your client filed for divorce despite the alleged threat. Have I done anything to harm her? Have I even contacted the woman?"

"She told me you called her at home," Palmer said, "pretending to be looking for her husband."

Frost offered one of his mirthless smiles. "You believe her?"

"We know you had her followed," Palmer said, trying that out for size. But Peter Frost was not Richie Phelps, and Palmer realized the man was not going to be so easily conned.

Frost shook his head, looking a bit disappointed at the effort. "You really believe that? Even if she was being followed, why would I be behind it? And if I were, it doesn't prove I meant to hurt her. Because she obviously has not been hurt, as I've said. Correct?" When neither of them answered, he sat back again and looked at Whyte. "What you may find interesting, however, is that I am aware others have followed Christina Franco, which should have yielded some useful data. Am I right, Detective?"

Whyte did not answer.

"I repeat, I have done nothing to harm your client since the divorce was filed, and you gentlemen know me well enough to know that if I mean to do something, it gets done."

"Usually by someone else," Palmer said.

Palmer saw the look of danger as it flashed in the man's eyes, then passed just as quickly.

Frost said to Whyte, "I have to make allowances for your partner's impulsive tendencies, but let's not split hairs, since there is a second point to be made. Ask yourselves, how would I even know about the video if it wasn't a setup?"

Again, neither Whyte nor Palmer replied.

"The facts are these," Frost continued. "Christina Franco persuaded you to handle her divorce by convincing you she was in mortal danger. You don't normally take divorce cases, another fact about which there is no dispute. That indicates she did a very compelling sales job." He took a moment to pick up his glass. "Since you two and I have history, the idea that I was the ultimate cause of her fear added an irresistible dimension to her case. We all know your desire to right every wrong."

Whyte grunted but said nothing.

"Then the alluring Mrs. Franco even pushed you to move the divorce along quickly, providing a focal point for the dispute when she assaulted her husband in front of countless witnesses. I'm not asking you to reveal confidences, but can you disagree with any of this?"

Neither man responded.

"I will accept your silence as tacit acknowledgment of the truth." He had a taste of his martini. "Since you are both highly intelligent, you must have asked yourselves, *Why?* Why did she come to Palmer and Whyte in the first place? Why not get some high-powered matrimonial attorney? Why rush a divorce of this magnitude, as if it was some inconsequential matter? Why did her mother ask you to investigate the death of Vernon Platt? Why has Henry Carrigan called you? That question—*Why?*—goes on and on, for even the simplest items, such as, why did she and Edward arrive at that gala at precisely the same moment, both of them on the staircase, in full view of the world?"

Palmer saw the look on Whyte's face, as if he were ready to shout *I told you so*, then storm out of the restaurant. Fortunately, the detective sat there and said nothing.

Without admitting he had been wrestling with the same question for all of those events, Palmer said, "I suppose you have answers."

This time, Frost's smile was one of his genuine efforts. "What do you lawyers say? Never ask a witness a question if you don't already know the answer, am I right?"

"It's been said."

"There you have it. But the real point from my perspective is not about Christina, it's about her husband. Mr. Franco has let me and my associates down. He behaved badly, and we are therefore no longer allies. That is all you need to know about that, but it should explain why I now see my interests in lockstep with yours. Up to a point, of course."

Palmer thought it over. "Since you're disappointed in Franco, you have no further motivation to protect him or his family. Putting aside what motivation you may have to exact a measure of revenge from him, you want to put an end to our investigations into the murders of Platt and D'Angelo while we wrap up the Marvin Taub case."

"Well done, Palmer."

"And you're about to dazzle us on that score, I take it?"

"Yes I am."

"And provide answers to some or all of those questions?"

Frost reached inside his suit jacket and, using his handkerchief, pulled out an envelope. "You're intent on finding Vernon Platt's murderer. That's the centerpiece to this entire affair, is it not?"

"It may be," Palmer admitted.

"I can simplify that for you," he said, placing the envelope on the table. "The parties we've mentioned could not afford to have Platt testify before Congress. That much should be clear. Everything else flows from that fact."

"A fascinating approach," Whyte agreed.

Frost pointed to the envelope that he had placed on the table. "You'll find the video on the enclosed thumb drive rather informative. My two conditions for providing it are simple. First, you must never ask me who took the footage. In the final analysis, I would never tell you, and the answer would be meaningless anyway. Second, you may do with this as you please, other than reveal that you received it from me."

Palmer looked from Whyte back to Frost. "Doesn't that depend on what the video shows?"

"Not good enough," Frost said, then made a move to take the envelope back.

Whyte said, "It's obvious there's nothing on there that's going to incriminate you." With a slight smile, he added, "Not even your fingerprints on the envelope."

Frost finished his gin. "Do we have a deal? Your word will be good enough for me."

Palmer took a deep breath, then said, "Yes," and watched as Whyte took the small package, using one of the napkins on the table, and placed it inside his coat.

"The second murder you want to solve is Joey D'Angelo's," Frost said. "I cannot provide the answer there, but I can provide some advice."

Palmer and Whyte waited.

"You managed to dupe that moron who works for Taub into a confession."

"Richie Phelps," Whyte said.

"Yes, a two-digit IQ on his best day, but I applaud your work in getting him to talk. He admitted he took Taub's revolver and sold it, which is true. He gave a description of the buyer, which was false. You will never learn the identity of that buyer, I can promise you that. Mr. Phelps will do a short stretch for his crime, since there is no way to directly connect him to D'Angelo's death, nor can anyone prove he knew the intended use for that gun. He will come out of prison, I will see that he is given a job appropriate to his limited intelligence, and he will be permitted to live out his years. On the other hand, should he breathe another word to anyone concerning that transaction, he will not survive his jail term. Am I clear?"

"We understand what you're saying," Palmer told him. "I just don't see why you make it sound like a threat against us."

"It's not. It's merely advice, since you now hold the fate of various individuals in your hands. Including your own," he added.

"That certainly sounds like a threat to me," Whyte said.

"It's not, since I am not the one who might mean you harm. I'm actually warning you against the dangers others might pose, if you don't heed my advice."

"What do you expect us to do?" Palmer asked.

"Your job," Frost replied. "The recording in that envelope will answer your questions about the Platt murder. The D'Angelo murder will go unsolved, but who really cares? As for the Scotts, the Francos, and the rest of this crowd, I am convinced your continued efforts will ultimately resolve those matters, now that you have gained supplementary information. Once you now identify the roles each of these various people have really played, you will have a complete understanding of what has occurred here. Perhaps not the way you expected to gather that intelligence, but there will be no harm to you or to me."

"I appreciate your faith in us," Palmer said, "but I'm not worried about harm to me. My clients are my concern. I'll take care of them and then myself."

Frost smiled at Whyte again. "Do you see why I put up with him, Detective? Why any of us do? I wish he would represent me." Turning back to Palmer, he said, "Even in the face of all the duplicity involved, I believe you, I honestly do. But sometimes you need to have a clearer look at the big picture."

"Meaning what?" Palmer asked.

"Meaning," Whyte interrupted, "whether we like it or not, he's already ensured that our interests really are aligned."

"You see," Frost said, turning to Palmer, "not only are you an extraordinary attorney, but your partner really is a wonderful detective."

CHAPTER FORTY-SEVEN

Back in his office, handling the envelope with care, Palmer removed Frost's thumb drive, inserted it into the port of his computer, and Maureen opened the only file it contained. Turning the monitor so all three of them could watch together, they waited until an image came onto the screen.

As Frost said, it was a video, obviously taken at night, and at first, it was hard to make out anything at all. There was no ambient light except for some muted illumination coming from behind the area being recorded.

"My guess is that it's a shot of the balcony to Platt's apartment," Whyte said after a few moments. "Taken from across the way. The curtains behind the door are blocking any view inside."

Palmer nodded. "From the angle, it looks like whoever took this must have been on a higher floor in the building on the other side of the street."

"Or on the roof," Whyte said.

It was late, dark, and the balcony filled the screen. No windows of Platt's apartment or anything else were visible. After a couple of minutes, the lighting inside the apartment that one could see from behind the drapes suddenly went out, and the video was even darker. Moments later, the doors leading out to the terrace were flung open, and there, in the center of the shot, a man stood in full view.

"Joey D," Palmer said.

"Certainly is," Whyte agreed.

They watched in silence as D'Angelo hurried back inside the darkened apartment, reappearing seconds later, this time dragging the inert form of a man and placing the body with its back resting against the balcony railing.

"Can't see the face," Palmer said.

"Doesn't matter," Whyte told him. "We know who it is."

D'Angelo rushed back inside, and they waited nearly three minutes before he returned, obviously after cleaning up whatever had occurred in the apartment. This time, D'Angelo stood at the edge of the terrace and had a furtive look, first at the street below, then to his left and right and even up—clearly unaware that his actions were being taped. Apparently convinced there was no one in sight, he bent down and began lifting the body—and for one instant, the dead man's face was turned to the screen.

"Vernon Platt," Palmer said simply.

Then they watched as D'Angelo hoisted Platt over the railing and sent him plummeting toward the street, twenty-two stories below.

"Oh my God," Maureen said.

They stared at the screen as D'Angelo raced back into the apartment and shut the doors behind him. For a few seconds, there was no movement, then the picture finally shifted, as the camera slowly panned to the dark street below, where a blurry image of Platt's body lie motionless on the sidewalk. Then the screen went black.

For a while, the three of them were quiet, until Whyte said, "That confirms why Lawson found Platt's blood on the wrought iron."

"What's that?" Maureen asked.

"That's how he became convinced Platt was murdered. They found residue of his blood halfway up the railing. Tried to figure out how it would be there if he jumped."

Palmer nodded. "Lawson's a smart guy, that certainly wasn't much for him to go on. Platt could have scraped an ankle when he went over."

"We discussed that. If it happened that way, if he caught a foot or something, the blood would have been at the top of the railing, not the bottom. We can run this again; it was tough to make out, but there was probably some bleeding from the back of Platt's head. When Joey propped him up, it must've run onto the post. D'Angelo wouldn't have seen it in the dark."

"But dead is dead," Maureen said, startling both men. "Platt and D'Angelo are both gone, and Frost is never going to tell you who took the video."

"He made that clear," Whyte said.

"He'll even deny he gave it to us," Palmer added.

"But the man who took this video—" Maureen said

"Might even be the same man who shot Joey," Whyte finished the thought.

"It's all so creepy," she said, "I'm going to have nightmares."

"Maybe you shouldn't have watched it," Palmer told her.

"It's all right," she said. "But why did Frost give it to you? And what does he think it means to your case?"

"He gave it to us to stop us from looking into Platt's death," Palmer told them as he returned to the chair behind his desk. "It's irrefutable evidence of what happened, which means we don't have to search any further for an answer about the murder."

"As well as any related issues," Whyte added.

"Precisely. He wants us to stop looking into RDMO."

Maureen shook her head. "That still doesn't make sense."

"Think about it," Palmer said. "Why did we become interested in RDMO in the first place? Platt was subpoenaed before Congress to testify about the company, but turned up dead. That had nothing to do with us at the time. Not until Jeanette Scott tapped me on the shoulder and asked me to look into it, convinced it wasn't a suicide."

"She turned out to be right," Maureen said.

"True. And so was Lawson," Whyte said.

Maureen ran her fingers across her lips. "But Jeanette might have just wanted to know what happened to her friend," she suggested. "She might not have been involved in the rest of this…this—"

"Mess," Palmer said.

"Then we got the crank call from this Henry Carrigan, bad-mouthing Christina Franco," Whyte reminded them. "Just happens to turn out that he works for Edward Franco at RDMO and just happens to be his point man in dealing with the FDA."

"And has a relationship with Christina, of some kind or another," Maureen pointed out.

"Yes," Whyte said. "Then Mrs. Scott told you that she also owns a piece of the company."

"A tangled web," Maureen said.

"It certainly is," Palmer agreed. "Especially when they had us running down the side roads, chasing the Taub case, and Burdick, and all of that."

Maureen thought it over. "You're saying we've been misled from the beginning?"

Palmer uttered a long sigh. "Looks that way."

"But why?"

"Not sure," Palmer admitted, "but I have some theories."

Maureen smiled. "The legendary Palmer theories. Maybe we really are getting someplace."

"Finding the right one is the point," Palmer said, "which is why we have to figure out why Frost keeps saying our interests have become aligned." Turning to Whyte, he said, "You seemed to have an idea about that when we left him."

"I did, and I do," Whyte said. "I think Mr. Frost is about to hang Mr. Franco out to dry."

Palmer nodded. "Makes sense. Frost may have some serious money of his own in RDMO."

"Or money from his partners."

"Or both," Palmer said. "With Franco becoming toxic, it may be time for Frost to cut him loose."

"Right. Which makes him an adversary for Frost as well as our client."

"All right," Palmer said, "you should get a copy of this video to Lt. Lawson. Tell him we found it in a plain envelope at our front door."

"I don't like lying to Hugh."

"We don't have much choice," Palmer said. "You mention Frost, and Lawson will be knocking on his door, which means—"

"Frost will deny knowing anything about it," Maureen said, "and then he'll send someone to knock on *our* door."

"Precisely," Palmer told them. "He gave it to us based on our agreement to keep the source secret. That protects him *and* us."

"Okay," Whyte said. "Let's get back to your assumptions."

"Frost says we have common interests and, as you say, they begin with Edward Franco as our common enemy. But I believe there's more to it."

"Let's play it out," Whyte said. "He says that our client, the lovely Mrs. Franco, is a liar and a manipulator. Which is consistent with everything you and I talked about last night, and everything my men have observed. The question is, to what end?"

Palmer smiled. "I definitely have a good theory on that one."

CHAPTER FORTY-EIGHT

The next morning, back in the office, Palmer and Whyte discovered that the timing of Frost's request for a meeting was no accident. The indictments in the RDMO scandal were being announced, the most prominent among those accused—with crimes ranging from stock fraud to unduly influencing the FDA—were Edward Franco and Henry Carrigan. Missing from the list of defendants thus far was Congressman Scott, which Palmer assumed was due to the considerable reach and influence of Senator Detweiler. He also wondered if Frost was somehow involved in that.

Despite Scott's ability to dodge criminal charges, the media was still bashing him, reporting on his involvement in the company and the close business ties he had to his son-in-law. Time and politics would tell if he would be swept up in the net being cast by the Department of Justice.

One of the first calls Palmer received was from Lillian Bartz. "I assume you've heard," she began, not bothering with any sort of preamble.

"It's all I'm hearing."

"We need to discuss where this leaves us."

"I had the same thought," Palmer agreed. "According to the talking heads, they've only seized your client's assets relating to RDMO, that true?"

"Off the record, it appears so. Without divulging too much, I can tell you my client saw this coming and had his financial ducks in a row. He'd already lawyered up with a big firm downtown for the criminal charges. In fact, I'm told it's where you used to work." She recited the name, and Palmer laughed.

"That's the place," he said.

"Quite a coincidence."

Maybe so, maybe not, he thought. "They've already been watching his back?"

"That's what I understand," Bartz told him, "and you know the drill. They're white-collar defense counsel, and now that he's been charged, I just became a lowly divorce attorney on a need-to-know basis."

"Maybe, but I have some ideas we should discuss. What's your schedule tomorrow afternoon?"

"I have a hearing in the morning, should be available after lunch."

"Great," he said, "I'll get back to you."

The next call he took was from Sloane Taylor. "Haven't heard from you in a few days. Something I said?" she asked with a slight laugh.

"Maybe it's the company you keep," Palmer told her, which clearly threw her since it took a few seconds before she reacted.

"I'm sorry, did I miss something?"

"Just an old joke," Palmer lied. "You calling to flirt or to check in on the Francos?"

"Flirting doesn't seem to be on the menu today," she replied, her tone several degrees cooler than it had been a moment ago. "You're obviously aware they're on the front page again."

"But not for fighting one another."

"You're right about that," she agreed. "Their current brawl is with Uncle Sam."

"Uncle Sam? How prosaic of you."

"You think? Then I won't use it when I run the story. How about you give me a quote on behalf of Mrs. Franco? Something sensational, like maybe she hopes he rots in jail for the rest of his life?"

"I'll have to pass that by my client first, but I'm guessing it'll get a thumbs down. I'm also guessing they'll be circling the wagons."

"That so?"

"Not for publication yet, but if you're free tomorrow afternoon, I should have a very juicy exclusive for you."

"Really?"

"Stay tuned," Palmer said. "I'll be back to you later."

One person who did not bother to use the telephone was Christina Franco. She burst into the waiting area like a small hurricane and demanded to see, "My lawyer!"

Palmer did not have to wait for Maureen to announce her, he could hear the commotion from his desk. Hanging up with Sloane, he came to the door of his office and said, "What a nice surprise. Come in."

Christina stormed past him and took a seat as he closed the door and went back to his chair. "This is just what I've been warning you about," she said before he could sit down.

"Could you be a little more specific?"

"I kept telling you that we had to move this case along. Now Edward's been indicted, which means the government is going to tie up all of our assets."

"I've already spoken with his divorce attorney. All they've seized so far is his interest in RDMO."

"You got that from Bartz, did you? What the hell does she know about a federal criminal prosecution? The authorities have been at Edward's office since dawn, taking his files, his computers, his *checkbooks*," she hollered. "I'll be lucky if I don't end up in a homeless shelter."

Palmer was not surprised the feds were stripping Franco's office. "I'm told your husband retained the firm where I used to work to handle the indictment. They're very good, and I still have friends there. I'll find out what's up."

"That might be helpful," she told him. "Maybe you'll get me ten minutes' warning before they come and take my clothing and jewelry."

"Christina, you haven't been charged with anything. Under the agreement we reached, we'll start moving certain marital assets into your name, which the government should not be able to touch."

"That *pittance*," she shrieked again. "I thought you'd be different, not some matrimonial hack just milking the file for a large fee. I thought you would get this *done!*"

Palmer resisted the urge to unload with everything he knew about her, her husband, and her father, but he kept his cool. He had a better plan. "I've done everything I can to move your case along," he replied as calmly as he could manage.

Slumping in the chair, she asked, "Now what?"

"As I said, I've already spoken with Bartz, and we've agreed to meet tomorrow afternoon. I have some ideas and, by that time, we'll have a lot more information. You should be here too."

"When?"

"I'll call and let you know. Meanwhile, stay away from the media. There's nothing you can say that's going to help."

They went back and forth a bit longer until Palmer placated her with assurances that tomorrow he would have a plan in place, and she finally went on her way. Whyte, who arrived during her rant, had decided to remain in his office and out of sight until she was gone. He now appeared at Palmer's desk.

"Where have you been while I was blocking her lefts and rights?"

"Hiding," Whyte admitted. "I don't see any marks on your face. Were they all body blows?"

"And a couple of kicks in the groin."

"The wages of war. What's happening with our plan for tomorrow?"

"Things are shaping up. Bartz is available. Christina will be here. Sloane Taylor will stand by for the scoop. Now I've got to call my old firm and get them to bring Franco."

"That's who he hired?"

"Small world, huh?"

"No coincidences?"

"No coincidences," Palmer agreed.

"You going to be ready for this?"

"Every angle. And you said you have me covered, right?"

"Always."

"Then now is the time—let's do it."

CHAPTER FORTY-NINE

The following day, just after noon, Palmer and Whyte were waiting in the conference room when Christina Franco arrived. Maureen showed her in, and the two men got to their feet.

"I didn't understand your last message," she began, but Palmer held up his hand.

"There are some details we need to clean up," he told her. "Have a seat."

Christina took the chair Palmer pointed to between him and Whyte.

"Is the divorce done?" she said.

Palmer ignored her, turning to Maureen. "You can bring them in now," he told her.

Christina responded with a puzzled look as Maureen left, returning moments later with Edward Franco and Lillian Bartz, who had been waiting in Whyte's office. They were accompanied by Martin Egli, a criminal defense attorney from Palmer's old Wall Street firm, who was now lead counsel for Edward Franco in the RDMO case.

There was no mistaking the look of anger on Christina's face. The question for Palmer was, *To whom is it directed?*

Palmer greeted each of his guests in turn, then gestured to the seats across the table from him. He waited for everyone to sit, then said, "I appreciate you all coming."

Bartz, wearing her game face, said, "This better be good." Palmer already understood that confrontation was her launch mode.

"It will be," Palmer said as he took a seat.

"Then get on with it," Bartz demanded.

Palmer sat back, had a glance to his left, at his client's ferocious gaze, then returned his attention to the threesome across the table. "It's become evident that our clients want their divorce finalized as soon as possible. Given the issues and assets involved, I would say Attorney Bartz and I have worked hard to accomplish that for them."

Everyone waited.

"Do any of you find it curious that two people who claim to despise each other so thoroughly have been willing to reach an agreement this quickly?"

"Not at all," Bartz piped up. "They've made it clear they want to be done with each other."

"Come on, Lillian. When my client came to me, she wanted out of this marriage as soon as I could get it done. But she claimed her husband opposed the divorce. Somewhere along the way his objections evaporated. You have no thoughts about that, no curiosity?"

"It's not my job to judge my client's motives, Mr. Palmer. My role is to represent him in a manner that achieves the result he seeks."

"Would that be true if his motives were improper? Even illegal?"

Egli jumped in, saying, "Hold on there, Palmer. You're not going to sit there and accuse my client—"

"Oh, but I am Martin, make no mistake about it. And my client as well," he added with another brief look at Christina.

"May I remind you," Bartz said, "your license to slander my client without consequences ends at the courtroom door."

"I appreciate that. And may I remind you that factual statements are not slanderous."

Edward Franco finally spoke up. "I don't know what games you lawyers are playing, but I have no obligation to sit here and listen to this."

He began to get up, but Palmer said, "I think you should hear what I have to say before you engage in histrionics, Mr. Franco. I promise, your future is going to depend on it." Franco lowered himself back into the chair as Palmer turned back to Bartz. "We're all familiar with the fact that there's been an investigation into RDMO, that there have been allegations of various offenses, and that your client has just been indicted."

Bartz did not bother to reply.

"You're also aware that the death of Vernon Platt impacted that investigation."

"I represent Mr. Franco in his divorce, nothing else."

Palmer smiled for the first time. "Maybe you should have been a bit more interested in your client's various business dealings since they affect his finances and the terms of the divorce settlement we reached."

"How dare you presume to tell me my responsibilities?"

"No insult was intended, Lillian. I admit I had more motivation than you did to investigate Mr. Franco's holdings."

"How's that?"

"I have a client charged with a murder of which he is innocent. I have another client asking me to discover what I can about the circumstances of Mr. Platt's death. And then there was the ongoing issue of Mrs. Franco's safety." The looks coming at him from across the table ranged from confusion to impatience. "I know, these things may sound unrelated, but I assure you they're not."

"Please enlighten us," Bartz said, "or I'm taking my client and leaving."

Palmer shook his head. "Everyone seems so anxious to go, while I find all of this so fascinating. All right, for this to make sense, we have to go back to our day in court last week. As you'll recall, I gave you a wish list of the assets my client wanted for settlement. They included cash, stocks, and real estate."

"Yes," Bartz said. "That was the basis of the settlement we made."

"Which you recommended to your client, and he accepted," Palmer said. "Apparently on the belief that my client was taking far less than half of the marital assets. Fair statement?"

Bartz nodded, impatience morphing into curiosity.

"Since then, my associate, Mr. Whyte, and I have spent a great deal of time looking into those business interests your client would be retaining. We all believed them to amount to more than two-thirds of their property, which was confirmed by both Mr. and Mrs. Franco. But what do you think we discovered?" When Franco and his two attorneys remained silent, Palmer asked, "Come on guys, doesn't anyone want to know?"

"Get on with it," Bartz told him again.

"First, we discovered that several of those holdings are shell corporations that have become worthless. Second, there were some that still have value but are laden with debt. Do you want to know why? Because they've been stripped of their cash by Mr. Franco's firm, Breakfinch Capital. They did it through huge loans, the proceeds of which were used by Mr. Franco and his colleagues to fund their lavish lifestyles. Sadly, those companies currently have little or no ability to pay off their debt, and most of the cash is gone." Smiling, he added, "Except, of course, the personal holdings Mr. Franco accumulated and was allowing Christina to take in the divorce settlement. Then there's RDMO, a company that had been doing good work until Breakfinch came along. After their initial investment, Franco and his associates were so desperate for cash flow that they changed the focus of the company's research, pressuring the FDA for approvals on anything that would drive the stock price up so they could sell. When that strategy failed, they decided to take short positions and then intentionally drove the stock price down by damaging the company. The illegality of those actions, on numerous levels, is what led to the indictments. As a result, if RDMO still has any value, none of that will belong to Mr. Franco or his Breakfinch partners. Have I lost anyone here?"

No one responded.

"The Francos both knew RDMO was in trouble, despite my client's repeated insistence that she knew nothing about her husband's business. The two of them realized they needed a way to preserve their personal property since it appeared Edward might be indicted and his assets seized. We'll put aside the death of Vernon Platt, and the insulation the Francos thought that might provide against criminal charges. The important thing for this discussion is the scheme they came up with to be divorced."

The room was dead silent as Palmer went on.

"The plan was for Christina to claim she was in fear of her life, provide evidence to back that up, create stories about being followed, have Henry Carrigan call me to confirm her role as victim, and then offer to get out of the marriage on the cheap. Not a bad scheme when you consider all the moving parts. Christina and her husband would agree that she take all the personal assets, claiming they represented far less than half of what they owned. She would get all those in her name so they would be out of the reach of the government and other creditors when the authorities came for Mr. Franco. Then, sometime down the line, she and Edward would have a miraculous reconciliation and live happily ever after."

Bartz was speechless.

"Then, there's the matter of my client's trust fund."

"Which we discussed," Bartz said.

"Yes, we did, but let me simplify this for the others," Palmer suggested. "As I say, our clients' decision to divorce came after they learned that RDMO was under investigation. That news was followed by the untimely death of Vernon Platt, which was staged to appear as a suicide but was, in fact, a murder. Please stop feigning surprise. I have incontrovertible evidence of the homicide, but for now you'll just have to take my word for it. The point here is that Mrs. Franco used Platt's death as another way to support her continuing claim that she was in some sort of peril. She did that by giving me the name of an extremely dangerous man, someone I know to be as ruthless as she said, someone identified by Mr. Franco as the man who would carry out his threats against her. Am I losing anyone here?"

"I'll sue you for malpractice," Christina hissed, baring her teeth like an animal about to attack. "You have no—"

"Can't wait for that trial," Palmer told her, glad to have the opportunity to interrupt *her* for a change. "Now where was I? Oh yes, we have the claims of infidelity made by both parties, not unusual in a contested divorce, the details of which are not important. The twist came when my client repeatedly expressed her concern that her husband's philandering would somehow leave her destitute. That never made a lot of sense to me, but it led to her suggestion that her mother invade her trust fund and turn the principal over to her as soon as the divorce was finalized." Palmer again turned to Christina, who was now glaring at him with undisguised hatred. "You want to jump in, add anything here?"

"You betray my confidences," Christina said, "and I'll take you for all you're worth."

"I'll keep that in mind," Palmer told her as he nodded thoughtfully. "But so far, I haven't revealed anything you haven't told anyone who would listen." Palmer nodded to Whyte, who slid a file folder toward him. Palmer left it unopened.

"Do you have a conclusion to all of this?" Bartz asked. "If not, I see no reason—"

"Let's say I have a theory I'd like to share."

"A theory?"

"Yes. I am obviously convinced this entire divorce is a sham. I think the parties conspired to protect their assets from the various civil lawsuits and criminal charges about to be filed against Mr. Franco and his company. Once the authorities begin looking into Breakfinch, the entire Jenga tower will crumble." He glanced at Whyte and smiled. "They also tried to take advantage of Christina's mother by pressuring her to break the family trust."

The room fell silent, and before anyone could respond, Palmer added, "That's when everything went wrong." Then he opened the file folder Whyte had passed to him and spread a series of photos across the table.

"These are all date stamped from just a few days ago," Palmer told them. "They're pictures of two meetings between Mr. and Mrs. Franco at the Hudson Hotel. As you can see, from these fairly romantic moments, they clearly believed their rendezvous was being held in private." As the others stared at the photos, he said, "The black wig was a nice touch Christina, although not your best look. And it certainly didn't fool Robbie's men."

She continued to glare at him without speaking.

"Big deal," Edward said with a dismissive wave of his hand. "What do they prove? You have no idea what we discussed."

"No, but we do have proof that both meetings ended with the two of you in a hotel room together. Not exactly the conduct of an angry couple in the middle of a nasty divorce."

"Why does any of this matter?" Christina said as she got to her feet, staring down at Palmer, her arrogance having returned. "When we spoke yesterday, you said the papers were being filed and we'd be divorced. You did a wonderful job, thank you very much, since the assets you talk about now belong to me. And soon I'll also have the principal of the trust fund," she added with a triumphant smile. "How long was I supposed to let my alcoholic mother control me, as if I'm some idiot child?"

"Your alcoholic mother?" Palmer repeated. "That's not nice."

"Don't pretend you're not aware that she's a doddering old drunk."

Palmer and Whyte shared a knowing look. "You'd better sit back down," Palmer told her, "I have some other information to share."

She remained standing as Whyte handed him a second file folder which Palmer opened, spreading out another group of photographs. "On days when you were *not* meeting your husband for those private interludes, he was a busy man."

Christina stared down at the images of Edward with Sloane Taylor in a series of what appeared to be intimate discussions over cocktails.

"As you can see," Palmer told her, "these are also stamped with dates and times, and some of these shots were taken at the same hotel you and your husband used."

Christina now fixed her angry gaze on Edward. "You son of a bitch," she snarled. "You promised this was over."

"Sweetheart—"

"Don't sweetheart me—"

"I'm sorry to get in the middle of a family squabble," Palmer cut in, "but did I forget these?" He fanned out another series of photos, this time of Christina Franco and Henry Carrigan at the rooftop bar of the Gansevoort Hotel.

"You rotten bastard," Christina hollered at Palmer.

"You two really are quite the post-modern couple," he responded with a smile.

Christina turned to her husband. "Well, *sweetheart*, I have all the *real* money now. You can deal with those worthless assets the government is going to take. What do you think about *that*?"

"Christina—" Edward Franco began, but Palmer stopped him.

"I am compelled to once again interrupt this tender exchange," he said as he looked up at his client. "Fact is, I wouldn't count on any of that money, not yet."

Egli, who had been reduced to silence throughout all of this, now asked, "What is that supposed to mean?"

"Simply stated," Palmer said, "our clients are not divorced."

"*What?*" Christina demanded.

"After Mr. Whyte developed the information you see before you, I contacted the judge's clerk and told him not to proceed with the paperwork." With a slight smile, Palmer said, "I felt obligated, as an officer of the court, to alert them to the likelihood this divorce action is a sham. A sham, in fact, intended to circumvent the rights of our government to reach the subject assets."

Christina erupted in a fit of profane fury. Edward was not certain whether to be relieved that he still shared ownership of their liquid assets or worried over what was to come. Bartz sat back, a look of confusion on her face.

Just then, the door to the conference room opened and Jeanette Scott walked in, accompanied by her personal attorney, a tall, aristocratic looking gentleman a few years her junior. The room fell silent as Christina and her mother stared at each other.

When Jeanette finally spoke, her voice was quiet but firm. Looking directly at her daughter, she said, "When Mr. Palmer told me what you were up to, I did not believe him. I could not believe him. My own daughter engaged in this cheap fraud. It was unthinkable. And then, the way you spoke of me just now. I would never have believed it, but I heard everything in the other room." She pointed to the phone in the middle of the conference table. "Mr. Palmer invited me to listen in on the intercom."

"I didn't mean any of it," was all Christina could manage. "I swear Mother—"

"You mean, 'alcoholic mother,' don't you, dear?" When Christina did not respond, Jeanette said, "Fortunately, I accepted Mr. Palmer's advice and did not sign the final documents that would have invaded the trust. I remain the trustee, and any distributions remain in my sole discretion. You can be assured there are a number of charities that will be pleased to hear they will be benefitting from my largesse before you see another dollar."

Palmer got to his feet. "I'm really sorry, Jeanette."

"Never apologize for being honest, young man," she told him, "no matter how painful the consequences." Turning back to Christina, Jeanette said, "I lost my best friend when Vernon died, which seems to have been a consequence of all of these sordid business dealings in which you and your husband were involved. That's a sadness I will have to deal with. But the real tragedy is that I've also lost my daughter." With that, she looked down at Edward. "I have seen visual proof, beyond any doubt, that Vernon was murdered. The only logical motive for such a despicable act would have been to prevent him from giving testimony to Congress about you and your godforsaken RDMO. Which means you, or someone working for you, is responsible for his death. You can believe me, Edward, when I say, I will not rest until you are punished for your actions." With that, Jeanette Scott and her counsel turned and left.

With the room now silent, Lillian Bartz stood and looked down at Palmer. Without so much as a glance at her client, she said, "I'm going back to my office to prepare a motion to withdraw from this case."

The others watched as she gathered her things and followed Jeanette Scott's path out the door.

After another brief silence, Edward Franco got to his feet. "Well, I guess that's that," he said.

"The best-laid plans," Palmer replied.

"I suppose so," Franco replied, then turned to leave.

Whyte, speaking for the first time, said, "There is another matter to be resolved."

Franco stopped and turned to face him. "And that is?"

It was Palmer who answered. "As Mrs. Scott mentioned, responsibility for the murder of Vernon Platt."

"You don't really believe I had anything to do with that," Franco said.

"We have no reason to believe otherwise," Palmer told him.

"Well, as they say in the legal business, I'll leave you to your proof," Franco replied.

"Yes indeed. And you can count on the fact we're going to help the police put that together," Palmer told him. "As well as your illegal activities involving RDMO."

When Franco offered no reply, it was as if everything came to a stop, no one moved and all was still—until Franco lunged across the width of the conference table, like a linebacker launching himself in the air to take down the opposing quarterback. His arms were outstretched, his eyes on fire, and, before anyone could react, he grabbed Palmer's throat, toppling his chair backward against the wall and began choking him.

Palmer was doubled over with Franco's weight atop him, but he managed to drive both of his forearms up, which momentarily loosened Franco's grip on his neck. In the end, however, it was the barrel of Whyte's S &W .38, shoved hard into Franco's right ear, that brought the proceedings to an abrupt halt.

"I don't want to have to blow your puny brain across the room," the former NYPD detective growled, "but if you don't get your friggen hands off my partner right now, I can promise you I will."

Franco froze, then began to move slowly, careful not to do anything that might cause the gun to fire—accidentally or otherwise. As he got to his feet, with the revolver still pressed against his head, Whyte quickly patted him down with his free hand. Satisfied Franco was neither armed nor wired, Whyte took hold of his right wrist and twisted his arm hard behind his back.

"Easy," Franco squealed, "you're going to break the damn thing."

"If I do, it'll be your fault," Whyte said.

By now, Palmer was also standing. He righted his chair and stepped forward, eye to eye with Franco. "You're a bigger asshole than I thought. With all your other troubles, I can have you arrested for assault and battery."

Franco let out a long, uneven breath. "Like you say, Counselor, I have so many other troubles, that would be like a drowning man worrying about a headache."

Franco's other attorney, Martin Egli, appeared to be in a state of shock, having also gotten to his feet and moved off to the side. Not knowing what else to say, he told Palmer, "I'll be in touch." Then he followed Whyte as the detective provided a rough escort to the front door of the brownstone where, gun still in hand, he shoved Franco out onto the street in front of a few startled pedestrians.

When he returned to the conference room, Whyte found Palmer there with Christina. "You okay?"

"Never better," Palmer told him as he waited for his client to say something.

Christina remained standing throughout the scuffle. She was obviously struggling with her own range of emotions, which Palmer figured must run the gamut from rage and loathing to the realization her plan had failed and her life was in now in shambles.

When he tired of waiting her out, Palmer said, "This could have gone so many other ways. All you had to do was trust me."

"Trust you?" she repeated as if the idea were some unimaginable concept. "I don't trust anyone."

"Why did you come to me, then?"

She offered no response.

"I'll tell you why," he said, looking into her angry, emerald eyes. "You knew I wouldn't treat this like an average divorce lawyer, wasting months on paperwork when you claimed to be in fear for your life. You kept harping on the need to be free of your husband and his dangerous friends, and how you wanted me to rescue you. You had me convinced, I admit that. And it wasn't a bad ploy, just poorly played."

"Smart man. Maybe I *should* have trusted you," Christina said. "Now what happens? What should I do?"

"You're asking me?" Palmer shook his head. "I would say you better start by lawyering up. And I mean a good criminal defense attorney. Whatever your husband has done, when they start slinging accusations that he's a murderer and a fraud, be careful none of that mud splashes onto you. Conspiracies involve more than one person."

She stood there transfixed, as if searching for the next thing to say. But she finally turned away and also left, slamming the conference room door behind her.

Palmer turned to Whyte. "I think that went well."

"Who could disagree?"

"I believe Cameron Pinckney would approve."

"So do I," Whyte agreed. "I actually felt the entire thing was very Nick and Nora Charles, wouldn't you say?"

"Who?" Maureen asked as she walked in.

"Before your time," Whyte told her.

She nodded without comment, then said, "Well, I would say you've found a unique way to prune our client list."

"I would say so," Palmer said.

"That just leaves one thing left for us to do," Whyte told him.

"I know, you need to remind me that the next time you tell me not to take a case, I should listen?"

"Also true, but that's not what I meant," Whyte said.

"How about, I should listen when you warn me about choosing the wrong women?"

"Can't argue that either, but what I was actually going to say is, I think the three of us could use a drink."

"Before we go," Maureen reminded Palmer, "you had me get Sloane Taylor on the line for the big scoop you promised."

"You ready to give her the message?"

"I wanted to be sure."

"Just tell her, 'Palmer said it's been real, but this time I'm afraid you may become the headline.' That is all."

Maureen smiled. "I'll use those very words."

"Good," Palmer said, "then we'll go to Clarke's."

THE END